Coming soon by the same a  KW-221-475

Six aging men sit, the worse for wear, outside a Hertfordshire pub. They have given grave offence. One hundred yards up the slope an equivalent number of young men are arming themselves from the arsenal in a builders' van.

How I Envy the Young almost certainly won't get mainstream published either.

Paul W
Jan 2011

NOSTALGIA FOR THE FUTURE

By

Paul Lefley

Published in 2010 by YouWriteOn.com
Copyright © Paul Lefley

First Edition

The author asserts the moral right under the Copyright, Designs and Patents Act 1988 to be identified as the author of this work.

British Library C.I.P.
A CIP catalogue record for this title is available from the British Library.

Cover design by Isil Onol
Cover photo © Paul Castro

Dedicated to my parents: a mother who fought hard against dementia, and a father who remained the toughest of men when terminally ill.

Also to celebrate the wonderful victory of the people of Skye in winning a toll-free bridge.

My thanks to my wife, Diane, and my children, Jack, Kate and Laura for their active support, and to Alex Wright for her enthusiasm. My especial thanks to Isil Onol for her patience, perseverance, tolerance and above all her creativity with the cover graphics
Thanks also to yourpcuk.com and Oliver for technical help

"...we condemned them, our children, for seeking a different future. We hated them for their flowers, for their love, and for their unmistakeable rejection of every hideous, mistaken compromise that we had made throughout our hollow, money-bitten, frightened, adult lives."
June Jordan

"If it takes a bloodbath, let's get it over with!"
Gov. Ronald Reagan (1970)

"Dejeme decirle, a riesgo de parecer ridiculo, que el revolucionario verdadero esta guiado por grandes sentimientos de amor."
Che Guevara

Donations can be sent to:
Alzheimer's Research Trust
The Stables
Station Rd
Great Shelford
Cambridge CB22 5LR

I

Taken your card from the cash machine, but left the money there? Keys anywhere other than they should be? The film you saw only days ago a blank? People's names gone with the gust passing between your ears? You have early onset; it's no way to live.

A full frontal lobotomy wouldn't do it, and brain implants are a long way off. Therefore you are deep in trouble. How deep exactly? Well, I am the last person who would know, but deep, or rather, bottomlessly deep, should cover it.

The horizon of a black hole looms and before long you will disappear from yourself.

****

What should have been the final day of my journey begins as most things affecting me do: with dependency.

'You're clear my way, Peter,' my passenger tells me. Then she adds, 'Oh, you're not up to this, are you? Put the brake on, make sure you're in neutral, and swap places with me.'

I don't like being ordered about, but I really shouldn't be left in charge of anything, so I do as I am told. My hand is squeezed and I squeeze back.

'Oh, too hard! Come on, if you're that strong you can handle anything. Remember we're in this together.' She's wrong and what's more I wouldn't wish that on anyone. It's a long time since we were truly together. I haven't even got my own company on this one. We're on our way to the Royal Free, where I'd like to be told I'm coming in for open head surgery. Hell, my mind has given me so much grief over the years I should be glad to see the back of it.

'Mo rang to wish you well.'

I reply, 'That simply does not impress me. What an unacceptable character he turned out to be, don't you think?'

'Eh, one problem at a time. Let's concentrate on the crisis in hand, shall we?'

Sweetly but firmly, that's her style. Still, she used the word crisis, so at least she's admitting the magnitude of what will be pronounced in the hospital. As we leave the Broadway, heading for Fortis Green, I know that I am more doomed than if I were already lying horizontal in a long black hatchback.

You're probably wondering how I got here. Well, I can still remember getting in the car, and being driven; as for the rest, you'll have to bear with me.

Through a mist I remember - it actually was a misty morning - I was late to a funeral. No, this isn't a happy tale. Somewhere, in an as yet unatrophied spongy fold in my skull, I was beginning to grasp that I was losing my grasp.

There is nowhere to park, so I store the car behind a run-down cemetery out-house.

'You can't stop there!' calls out a twat in uniform.

'Watch me.'

I've gone through red lights to get here, broken speed limits and, just now, screeched across gravel, sending a crowd of bereaved scattering. I did not know the person they are mourning, and I am genuinely sorry for them, but I'm running out of time.

You must be beginning to realise that I am not the sort of character you can identify with, not the type to make a tale compelling. Understand that I am not even half the man I used to be. When I was me I would never have behaved like this. What is left is hardly attractive. Someone agrees. I have gone up to the mourners and started to explain and apologise, but it's not working. A monster of a man has got me by the collar; he wants to belt me.

'I am sorry. Sorry,' I say, but I am not scared. He's welcome to knock my block off. 'I'm late and I'm stupid,' I explain, gesturing towards the chapel.

He wants, if not blows, then expletives to rain down on me. Instead, he shrugs, and snarls away elsewhere.

Blast, I can hear they've started. There's music coming from the chapel, and I think I can hear singing. Surely they can't start a funeral without the chief mourner anymore than they can start a wedding without the bride. Wrong, apparently.

I am in a panic and must have a pee. Thankfully, I remember where the Gents is located. I'm desperate, force open a creaking toilet door with rusty hinges, stand on concrete drenched in Jeyes fluid and do what I have to do. Then a petty panic seizes me. I've used the toilet bowl, but can't see a urinal anywhere. As I leave, two women are waiting to go in. They glare at me. A double take tells me I failed to see the Gents, and used the Ladies instead. It's a grown man's nightmare.

'I er… thought it was the gentleman's.' I am hot and flustered, and they are not convinced, but I'm in too much of a hurry for any more of this. One lunge and I am through the arched oak doors, trying to enter as quietly as I can. Just then the music pauses and the car keys fall from my pocket, crashing on the stone floor. Everyone glares at me, while I squint, trying to locate loved ones. My eldest daughter, Sylvia, grimaces. Her sister gives me a sympathetic wink and looks tellingly benign. She nods to the space next to her. Everyone else looks without any ill-judgement whatsoever in their eyes. They've seen me. They know there is something wrong, something I can't control.

I say, 'Hi,' to my youngest daughter and, 'Sylvia,'

to the other. She winces at the name. Once she used to like it with all its associations. I haven't spoken to Sylvia in a long while, which I know is my fault. My other daughter is Linda. Sylvia chides her as, 'Two Jobs', because she's a part-time unpaid volunteer in a nursery project and part-time in an office. Linda is softer on me than her elder sister, but for some reason she doesn't carry the same weight.

I don't understand how I got the time wrong. I was allowed to organize everything about the funeral, except the flowers. I knew when we had to be here; I just started mentally meandering and then got the hour all wrong. Funny, I am normally spot on for anything with figures, including times. They phoned my mobile, but I'd left it in a coffee bar and they had to go without me. I was later still, because I couldn't find my car keys. Eventually I found them in the cutlery drawer, which is not as unusual as it should be. I grabbed them and a knife with a serrated edge at the same time, nearly slashing the inside of my wrist. Now, here I am with a big Elastoplast on my thumb, still bleeding, undeserving of sympathy and getting little. I am embarrassed and flustered.

'You need some help, Dad?' It was Linda. She puts her arm around me. We're still on good terms.

'Sorry,' I excuse myself to her. 'I've got that ebbing away feeling. It feels like someone is blowing at a hole in the top of my head and my brains are slowly coming out through another hole at the bottom. It's hopeless, I'm hopeless.'
'Shh,' she whispers, because attention has shifted to me.

I am ashamed. I am here for someone special: my departed elderly aunt. She was the last but one of her generation. Linda passes me a fold of papers. It is the eulogy that I penned and she has remembered to bring for me. Her mother used to be like this.   10

My feet are cold. There are electric heaters high on the stone walls, but all they are doing is warming the dying voices as they reach the ceiling. A nice young vicar has managed to say some relevant words, eventually losing me in the usual nonsense about the Hereafter and some bizarre stuff about the Second Coming.

'Kingdom of Heaven, eh Daddy?' It's a wonder I hear it, Linda whispers it so quietly.

I try to be as discreet as her. 'Kingdom of Heaven? I don't think so. Now, if it was a republic I might be interested.'

Carol is missing but I daren't question that.

Something else is bothering me. It's the absence of my closest friend, who had faithfully promised to be here. He used to be Mr Reliable: dull but dependable.

'Where's Mo?' I ask Sylvia. She always seems to know what he's up to.

'Ask her,' she replies, indicating Linda.

For some reason Linda has moved round to the other side of her sister, so that makes no sense at all. I can't very well lean across and ask her at this moment because there is something else… Oh yes, I have to give this speech. I go ahead.

'She was truer and more generous than any.' I speak with feeling, but can't fully carry it off because I am shaking like a Parkinson's sufferer. I go for it again, but I am not making a good job of it. The priest rounds it off while music muffles the noise of the coffin's short, searing trip. Genuinely, this is the final curtain, or curtains, I think to myself as they close. The last music is from my own little player, which Linda has remembered to bring for me. It is the 'Hobo's Lullaby'. I was warned against this, but chose it anyway and now I can't handle it.

11

As I emerge through the crematorium doors into the true and sole Hereafter, my youngest daughter smiles and passes me a ten pound note.

'See, I can be of use at times,' she winks again.

She's always been tractable, but sometimes I just feel there isn't much to her.

'The money is to tip the undertakers,' she prompts me.

She knows I would want to do this and has even guessed that I've forgotten my wallet!

I take the tenner gratefully and am in the process of starting on one of my favourite subjects, when Sylvia cuts me short.

'There is more to life than death. You've got to move on. That's how aunt would have wanted it.'

That's the most words I've had from her since…since I can remember. She is right of course, but that doesn't stop me. As the funeral cars start up, so do I. 'It isn't that I am in thrall to death. It's what can happen alongside the physical decline that concerns me.'

'Get it off your chest now, please,' says Sylvia.

She never calls me Dad these days. I know I can't carry on like this once we get to aunt's place, where we're having everybody back, so this moment seems appropriate to give it an airing.

'The personality, the conscious being that is actually YOU can biodegrade long before any final breaths.'

Sylvia takes off her seat belt and leans round to stare at me. It's a silent tirade. She's not far from tears, so I am silent. Tears - there are too many of them. But thinking, while I remain capable, can't do any harm.

'Peter, you're one in a million,' is what my aunt said to me immediately before she died. She had not risen from her bed for two weeks, and hadn't recognised me for some time, but she found the wherewithal to

12

come round for a moment and make me feel good. Then she closed her eyes and never opened them again, and I lost the last remaining soul who gave me unconditional support. It broke my heart. I didn't weep, I didn't cry and nor did I sob. I wailed. The only thing that matched her generosity was her devotion. If I had told her I had bumped her neighbour off, she'd still have sent me Christmas cards. And now she was gone. I am at that stage in life where I can't seem to get away from the grim reaping. There are worse things, of course. Let me fall tomorrow, let me never wake up, but do not let me be one of the living dead.

'It feels like we ought to wash and remove our shoes before we go in. There should be water and flowers and a little lamp to light. If we could afford to keep this place exactly as it is… as a shrine,' says Linda.

She's not long back from Varanasi. Now she has friends there as well as all round the rest of the world. She got pregnant when she was younger and her mother dealt with it. She likes children and it wouldn't surprise me if she were to return from one of these jaunts expecting again. I understand how fond she and her sister were of my dear old aunt and her home. I will never forget her either, having spent so much of my childhood and youth here too.

'I tell you what. You and your sister could live here.'

'You could ask Sylvia,' she laughs, 'but that's a bit of a touchy subject, isn't it, Dad? Anyway, I've got plans. I might move in with someone who has a place of their own.' There is a surge in her voice as she says this.

'Really. I thought you were sharing with some work mates.'

'How did you get on at the doctor's yesterday? You were worried,' she changes the subject.

13

'Something and nothing really. I didn't bother in the end and cancelled the appointment.'

There is a lot to drink in my aunt's house and everyone is raising a glass to her in some way or other. Me? Well, I am the chief mourner, so I am getting utterly, maudlinly befuddled.

I tell my daughters, probably for the nth occasion, 'I spent almost as much time in her company as my own Mother's. The trouble was, she was literally demented at the end. Nothing could be worse for such an independent, pay-her-own-way sort of woman. We didn't want to lose her, but insofar as we felt we already had, it was best she went as quickly as possible.'

Not exactly a barrel of laughs, I know, and they'll only tolerate this sort of thing for a short while, and then move me along, but I am not being told off yet. Linda has a supporting arm around me and my eldest is being forbearing.

I'm loud and it is having an effect on an older cousin who is crying, so I tell them, 'Don't worry, I'll change tack. It makes you wonder why young priests, like this one, are so convinced. Doesn't it bother them that life's struggle is a round trip that brings you back to square one? Don't they ask themselves why God is so hard on those who have trodden the path the longest?'

My cousin is now wailing, so in for a penny... I resume, 'She was generous out of all proportion.'

There is a huge anguished sigh from somewhere in the room. In not so many words it means, shut up. Now my throat starts a rigid ache and I find fluid at the corner of my eyes. Another drink is called for. I repeat some of the speech I made at the crematorium, trying to deliver correctly what I got wrong earlier.

'Dad, all you're going to do is upset yourself and others. We all know this. We've heard it all before. We all agree,' says my youngest daughter.

'You are not the only one grieving,' her sister says glaring at me.

There is little that can stop me when I get like this, although a blow from a blunt instrument might do it.

'For the last two years…' I mis-time my breathing, swallow half a word and begin again. 'For the last two years the old girl was giving everything away. Old people do this.'

Sylvia tries one last time, 'You've got to give it a rest!'

But I am in motion now and without brakes. 'Is it because on their last journey they want to travel light?'

Sylvia takes my glass and says, 'That's enough.' I look at Linda and she agrees.

'No "Please, Dad?"' I say to Sylvia. She looks exasperated, but doesn't return fire. She's quelled me, but I don't like it, and I don't like her for it.

Linda then regales us with a tale. 'When she was young, aunt performed with a dance troupe at the Hackney Empire. She had to share costumes with other performers. Once, one of them must have been so nervous that she'd wet herself. Aunt had to put on her soaking tights and just get on with it.'

Everyone, including me, laughed, and that is where Linda kept it, with story after story. How like her mother she is. I understand why everybody loves tales like this. It is because when a personal history is compressed into a dozen anecdotes it all seems so colourful, so flamboyant. And it is true: the dead had a lot of life in them.

It wasn't solely my aunt who succumbed. Alzheimer's is a huge thing on my father's side of the family. He outlived himself to the extent that by his mid-eighties he was lost in that darkened space, half maze, half hall of mirrors. His father went the same way, and most of my uncles. It sounds like my great grandfather had it as well. Longevity and Alzheimer's are family

15

traits. Somewhere in that wonderful double helix that has determined my physical make-up, there's something out of place, and that speck of great ugliness will count for more than all the rest of my heredity put together. Four letters is all Nature has to play with; she makes this stupid spelling mistake and it causes tragedy. Sooner or later somebody will do something about Nature, they've got to.

I cross the room with a plate of finger food. A man helps himself then stubs out his fag in an ashtray which, contents and all, is then tucked away in his jacket pocket. He offers me a whisky.

'It's a good un,' he says. 'The old girl has got some terrific booze in that cabinet over there.'

'That's very generous of you,' I say. He is half a pint of whisky beyond sarcasm. I step back and look at him. I don't believe I have ever seen him before, which is unusual because for years now everybody has looked familiar to me. He is tall and thin, dressed in a black suit and has a long, drawn face with oversized features. He's got rings under his eyes as big and dark as a Panda's and his hair is slicked back with what smells like brilliantine. He is a natural-born ghoul, and I find myself agreeing with every word he says.

'Dementia, bloody dementia is the worst!' he confides. 'I've had to peel bodies from mattresses, but that's a pretty way to go, compared to that.'

He's more morbid than me!

'Believe me I've seen the perfect murder. Some old fellow had dementia bad and his relatives saw him off. They as much as told me so, told me how they'd done it. He'd made them promise to do it.'

He's an experienced drinker so, while obviously pissed, he is not slurring his words. On the other hand he doesn't catch my question. 'How? How'd they do it?'

He just carries on. 'But that's not the best of it. The old fellow was clever; he had done his homework and found something that was undetectable.'

'Now that is a good story!' I exclaim. Encouraged, he continues, 'One night, apparently, they gave him this special toxin and within days all that remained was a corpse. He'd gone. Free as a bird, and what's more he got his family a big insurance payout that way.'

This is ultimately impressive, exciting enough to raise anybody's morale. 'Was it painless as well?'

He evidently doesn't know and carries on. 'I tell you,' he tells me, 'this fellow must've seen inside some of those institutions.'

I know the sort too well, grisly places.

He adds, 'They swamp you with that stink of boiled urine and cabbage,' which isn't quite how he meant to put it.

'Yes, yes, but how, how did they do it?'

No answer.

'Tell me,' I shout at my drunken mate, 'was it painless?'

'That's the second time you've asked that. Well it's like this…'

Sylvia has sped over here for some reason. She takes the glass of whisky from my comrade and demands, 'How did you come to be here?' She's guessing I brought him in, and I'm guessing she's right. 'Time to go! There's nobody else from your firm here.'

Firm? Oh, the funeral directors.

'I'll take that,' she says, 'it's solid silver.' With that she removes the ashtray from his jacket pocket, takes him to the front door and pushes him out. He never stood a chance.

'Hold on, hold on,' I say because I want some answers from this man, but the door is shut. It's a wonder Sylvia didn't kick him as he went. She used to be good at that.

They say that one of the most distressing aspects of dementia is losing cherished memories. For the moment I retain one of being called to Sylvia's primary school by the head teacher, Miss O'Leary. Sylvia had been fighting various boys, kicking them and winning.

'Your daughter seems to think it's good to be strong,' Miss O'Leary said.

'Well it is, isn't it?' I responded.

Sylvia loved me for that for a long time.

I run outside and catch the thieving undertaker starting up the engine of a black Daimler.

'How was it done? How did they kill him? I'd give anything to know. Listen, there could be a drink in it for you. It'll be worth your while'

'Okay, okay. I'll see what I can do for you,' he says, passing me his card.

While I look at it he drives off. The card is for the funeral directors.

My daughters are now flanking me again.

'Most forms of dementia are not hereditary, Dad.' Linda tries to comfort me. 'You need something to take your mind off it, and I know just the thing. I want to talk to you about something very, very important. It's terrific, you'll love it, but this isn't the right moment, not here. I'm out of minutes on my phone. Will you ring me?'

'When?'

'The next few days; it's not that urgent.'

'Of course! I won't forget.'

There are still moments of clarity along the path to unenlightenment. I've encountered a sage whose counsel I may need. I am going to have to meet up with that miserable funeral directing bastard again. The business card is slotted securely into my back pocket.

Watching the vehicle driving off reminds me.

'My car! Damn, my car. My damn car and the funeral.'

One or two within hearing range stare at me.

'What are you talking about? That's the funeral car.' Sylvia is exasperated.

'No, no. I mean I have left mine at the cemetery.'

'Do you need a lift, Dad?' Linda offers.

Doesn't everyone?

II

There are four main stages to dementia. There is the Now where was I? stage, which is where I am currently. Then there is the Where am I? stage, which is followed by the Who am I? stage. Finally there is the fourth stage which I can never tell you about; nor can anyone else – not from the inside at least. It is the story that can never be told, and it could be the reason this tale finishes, but has no ending.

****

We're still in Fortis Green due to road works. My driver is struggling with the clutch on the old car. She is being unflustered and patient in a manner that is beyond me. I could never manage it. Having said that, I am in no hurry, because I would be content to sit here forever delaying my summit with misfortune, while being treated to a euphony of pneumatic drills. No I mean it: going nowhere and listening to them for an age would be fine by me. Damn, we can move on.

A few days after the funeral the hangover finally went and I determined on some action. I have a remaining uncle who has gone down with my family's own dedicated disease. He is in his eighties and a widower. He must have succumbed to it quickly, because the last time I met him he was jolly and fit for an octogenarian. I am going to visit him, but I can't face doing it on my own; I've seen it too often before. Thus I am going to call in on my mate Mo, and get him to take me. I can also put him on the spot about missing my aunt's funeral.

I don't like driving and never use buses, so a long walk towards a different life down by Turnpike Lane is called for. It is an old haunt and something down there warps the emotional space around it, drawing me in.

I leave the flower beds and delis behind, and head on down the steepness of Muswell Hill to a more colourful and riskier environment. Life is so tightly packed down there you'd hope at some point it would become volatile. It's a compelling hubbub, one I can observe, but not survive in these days. As I go I shame myself. Sitting on a wall at the top of the hill is an old alcoholic. Normally she is well dressed, and normally I talk to her. Today she has a carrier bag full of cans and has pissed herself. She gives me a broken-toothed smile of recognition as a puddle drains away from around her feet. I walk on by.

Mo lives in a third floor flat above a sari shop and a kebab take-away. It's Saturday, and he should be there. I press the bell, but there is no answer, so I ring him on his mobile.

'I can't answer the door, I'm in the bath,' he says, 'Give me ten minutes. Go round the corner to the coffee bar opposite the mosque. I'll meet you in there.'

'What bloody mosque?'

'Think about it. You know. As I say, I'll see you in there.'

I remember. The mosque used to be a synagogue, and before that it was a church. A Big Issue seller thanks me and calls me 'Boss' when I buy a copy. Wallet love, no doubt. I read it and have my coffee, and Mo's still not arrived.

I return to his flat, get someone else to let me in the communal entrance and then go up and bang on his door. He opens it, with a towel round him. Sighing heavily he lets me in. He looks different. Two decades ago his follicles spontaneously threw themselves off the top of his scalp, but he kept one of those ugly Friar Tuck rings of hair. Now he's shaved his head.

He returns the silent compliment. 'You've lost some muscle there,' he says poking my shoulder.

21

'No I haven't, thanks very much.' I am aware that the bulk from my shoulders has sought asylum around my waist in the last few years.

He ruffles my hair with his big mitt. 'You want to get that cut. Anyway what can I do you for, bro'?' he asks.

I tell him I want a lift to Ramsgate.

'No can do. I've got things I have to finish here first.' With that he closes his bedroom door. As if I'd want to look in there. Nevertheless I glance in that direction, but all I can see is a games console. 'One of the footie team lent me that,' he says, suddenly lurching over to his sofa and grabbing something. It is a pair of skimpy red briefs. They're bright with something close to a thong at the rear and are quite effeminate looking, but they go with the change of hairstyle, I suppose.

'Have you got something you can do for a couple of hours? Then I can give you a lift. On the way we can talk about a mate who needs some help. It's just up your street...'

He blethers on and I stop listening. 'It's a deal. Meet me at my aunt's in Tottenham.'

Off I go, but it's a mistake. Spurs are playing at home and crowds are condensing. I can't tell if there is a menacing air. I feel the apprehension of someone who has got it wrong and wandered somewhere that they knew well, but has become strange. I start as I pass a pub where supporters are riotously celebrating something that I can't quite get. I make an effort and now realise that they are celebrating being "the Yid Army". Before long I find myself outside the funeral directors. I decide to go in.

'Is...is...' I can't remember his name, if I ever knew it. 'Is the tall spooky-looking chap around?' I ask.

No, he's not around because he's out on a job. I don't know why I didn't ring him first. Yes I do: it's because I had no intention of calling by today.

Back out on the street there's a rock-fest of mobile phones going off, most of which are pretty familiar tunes. It is disconcerting because more than one of them sounds like my own. In fact my own phone is ringing. I check it and there is a text message that I swear has only just arrived, yet the message is a day old. Screwing up my eyes in good daylight I read that the doctor's surgery wants me to phone. It can't be urgent; they'd have rung if it was. I know I've got a slightly erratic heart, but according to what I've read, that's not unusual. If they want me for tests they can wait. One thing is for definite: this particular message, and maybe the crush of the crowd, has sent my pulse sprinting and leaping. I'm hot now and can feel a shortness of breath.

Past another pub, through a busy alleyway and round the corner I see the old house where my aunt lived. It's in a long terrace with the front door only feet from the road, but for me it stands out like the towering mansion above the Bates Motel. If I was struggling for breath before, it is worse now. My diaphragm plummets like a broken lift and every bit of air leaves me. I actually feel faint. It isn't nostalgia; I don't think I would ever want to go back. It is just the sure sense that when things have gone, they have gone irretrievably.

This is an area for those who can't afford to live elsewhere.

My aunt's house hasn't been decorated for years. I slump in a chair that hasn't changed position since before my daughters were born. The house was close to my secondary mod (in fact it was one of those infants-juniors-secondary-on-one-site schools. They'll re-discover they were a good idea one day). It was nearer than my own home, so this is where I came for my first sixteen years. I spot a photograph of my daughters twenty years or more ago, and I can't stop myself from looking at it. Both were smiling; being with

23

them was easy. They rarely argued, because they were of one mind then - mine.

That photo is on top of an old box that hasn't been touched for years. One picture in there in particular, of my father in his thirties, strikes me when I look at it. It is clear to see he was thriving, not just financially, but biologically as well. There is a full head of hair and a good suit gracing a body that is straight and true. The most striking thing is his eyes; they are the eyes of a man who can cope, and who envisages the life ahead as one in which he will triumph. Looking at that photograph you would be convinced too. Among the collection there is not a single image of any of the relatives once they had become deranged.

Memory is both a wave and a particle. Emotions rise like dust from the old box of photos and then repeatedly sweep over me. I jump when Sylvia walks in. Before my father became really ill she had already noticed a change in me. I remember she asked, 'Dad, you're not an apostate, are you?'

The change probably began when I moved house for the children's schooling, or maybe when I started white collar jobs. I suspect that I began to lose my way even before that. She wouldn't bother with such a question these days.

Sylvia demands, 'What are you doing here?'

'It was a spare moment so I came to get some papers. I can't stay away from the place. More to the point, what are you doing here?'

'I've a right.'

'Where did you get the key?'

'You gave it to me.'

'I'm finished,' I say and she looks at me as much to say she is well aware of that. She notices the photograph in my hand and I pass it to her to look. I know what it is with family photographs; they are meant to show people and life at their best. You know that for

24

the most part they got through it, and that life went on, but somehow what you actually feel is that they thrived.

'You can see they were settled,' I say.

Sylvia knows what I mean by settled. 'I don't need a man or a baby to make my life complete.'

'You love this place, why don't you move here?' I can't resist it. She eyeballs me. We don't quite throw handfuls of salt down and stamp each foot heavily on the mat, but I am sure she is ready for a contest.

'I have a place already, thank you very much,' she says, and then goes to the door and slams it behind her. I catch her shouting, 'You're supposed to ring Linda,' from down the street.

Sylvia lives on an estate with an unpopulated canal on one side and a road, hardly used by pedestrians of a night time, on the other. To me it doesn't seem safe for a young woman. On the other hand I've been stupid. Again.

I've begun to fear that there is a limit to the number of times you get the chance to make up. It could be like points on your licence: so many and you are disqualified. Reach a certain age and you'll never get the licence back.

The Spurs game is finished. I've got nothing better to do, so I pick up the things I came for and wander towards her estate. I walk through what used to be a Little Russia and is now a one way system with a retail park. Car lights flash as they stream by over the bridge. Large communal refuse bins are all out at the front of Sylvia's estate. The place looks ugly and god-forsaken. Several of the street lamps are not working. Some of the buildings are tall and most are packed tightly together with any number of dark recesses. It is a shadowy place, verging on the silent. Yet as I go forward I can hear whispering and see somebody, or bodies, slip behind one of the bins just ahead. There is an urgent secret discussion taking place. I catch the

25

sound of breathing, heavy breathing, and there is somebody hiding just there. I can hear someone distinctly and threateningly. There is a reference to getting good money for an expensive mobile. I hear a click, and I recognize the sound from a painful incident years ago when I'd tried to be a peace-maker. It is a blade being flicked open. At that moment a vehicle with no lights on and a broken exhaust comes roaring by me. My legs and heart are one as they both take a sideways leap. I look swiftly over my shoulder to see the car's tail lights come on. In the instant of turning back I see two shapes emerge from behind the bin. I make a fist with my aunt's sharp house-key pointing out of the knuckle. My lungs fill; slowly and deliberately I move in their direction. There would be no point in attempting to outrun them; showing weakness would merely encourage them. They aren't deterred and carry on towards me. As they are about to reach me, I realise there is a third character behind me. The two figures say, 'Ok, man?' and high-five a friend. Then they walk on by, carrying away a couple of flip top bins.

My heart is pounding. I feel faint and stupid. I believe the heavy breathing I heard may have been my own. From now on if I am going to get agitated it will have to concern something huge and real. Well, I've got that one covered.

The person behind me, the one they had greeted, turns out to be Sylvia.

'What are you doing here?' she asks.

'You keep asking me that,' I reply.

'You don't look good. You'd better come in.' Her flat is tastefully decked out with Japanese wood block prints of Mount Fuji, a pile of political and sociological books, and an unusual silk screen print of Camillo Cienfuegos entering Havana with his comrades. Sylvia makes jasmine tea and brings it to me on the balcony. Cup in hand I look out at lights from the newish private estate opposite reflecting off the river. There is a worn and frayed book on a small metal table. Its inside cover is inscribed, 'Go on change the world ' "Little Miss Pankhurst". Love Dad.' Next to this book is another on the techniques of kick boxing. I take it and chuckle, passing it from hand to hand. If there is a girl or a woman in the world who does not need coaching in this, it is Sylvia.

I do not know if I have already said about being called up to the school by Miss O'Leary, but it happened more than once. The second occasion was more serious.

Miss O'Leary was formerly a nun, which may be why she always wore sandals on her oversize feet. She was very gently spoken, but nevertheless a fix-you-in-the eye sort. She firmly fixed me in the eye.

'This will be embarrassing to hear Mr...'

She called me and everybody else by title and surname.

'...but I have to tell you, and there is no mild way of putting this, I have to tell you that your daughter has become quite expert in the art – and she is absolutely unerring in this – in the art of kicking boys directly in the bollocks. This very day she has pole-axed the biggest boy in the school: one who is also known to be the toughest.'

I have to admit the use of the word bollocks did rather throw me. I had focused on her hair which was the colour and texture of a discarded brillo pad, and resorted to the tactic of asking questions. 'Is there any reason why? Is he a bully?'

'He is alleged to have told her friend to shut-up. True or not, that is not sufficient reason. Her violence is totally disproportionate. What is more, this boy is in the early stages of puberty; he could have been done permanent harm.'

I really had no answer and promised to talk to

27

Sylvia about it.

She protested that the lad actually was a bully, but was concerned about the threat to his physical development. She used the word testicles and fully understood their place in puberty. We agreed she would tone things down and at the very least try to kick boys elsewhere, in the stomach for instance.

Sylvia interrupted my reverie by coming over, taking away the book and placing something else in my hands. 'It's your father's diary. I found it at your aunt's, and it's off the wall.'

She stopped calling my father Grandad at the same time she stopped referring to me as anything at all.

The last time I saw my father's diary it was by his death bed. Right there and then Sylvia had said, 'He didn't need to go this way.' What she didn't say, but I knew she thought, was that the responsibility was mine.

At that time I still had my aunt's unconditional allegiance. I wasn't alone until she went, but I suspect I have already said as much.

Where was I…? The diary Sylvia has handed me is a large, five year, leather bound one. The first thing I notice is that over a period my father wrote less and less and the hand writing became worse. The opening lines are:

Peace of mind. A pension.
That has to be a joke!

'I don't think it's off the wall. No, it sounds quite reasonable to me,' I say.

She doesn't respond because the house phone is ringing.

'His mobile? No, reception is bad around here… I'll get him for you.' She passes me the phone and says, 'It's Mo.'

'Well, where are you?' he asks.

It's always best to answer a question with a question, so I respond, 'Where are you?'
'In my car in Junction Road outside your aunt's, as arranged. You've left lights on here. I thought you were inside.'

He's been there for quite a while. The oldies in my uncle's nursing home will all be put to bed before long, so I decide it's best to go there tomorrow.

The road to Ramsgate and Sunshine Homes is pretty clear of traffic, which is a shame because I am not looking forward to this. I would rather look inside my own grave than have to see what will be waiting for us.

'Your cousin has told them you're coming,' Mo tells me. How does he know? Carol (I believe I've mentioned her) must have told him, they are always talking. He also rambles on about his troubled mate, while I feign interest with some automated responses.

Sunshine Homes is new and well built with good quality brick and stonework, and not at all what I am expecting. The gardens at the front are beautiful, and the foyer has the atmosphere of a hotel reception. The windows are large and everywhere is in comforting mellow colours. The chocolates I've bought are melting because it is a little too warm in here. Chocolate apart, the only thing I can smell is a slight whiff of air freshener, but then again it could be flowers.

We are met by an Anglo-Caribbean woman and a man with an American accent. In their own styles they are both smartly dressed and well groomed. They could be Jehovah's Witnesses, except they are slicker, more solicitous. We are given brochures of the place and a verbal update as we are shown to my uncle's room. We pass a TV lounge on the way; its occupants look far more like residents than inmates. There appears to be plenty of staff and they convey a sense of caring

29

efficiency.

As we enter my uncle's room he is pacing up and down, moving items and furniture around. He used to run his own furniture removals business. He shakes us both by the hand, and asks us what he can do for us. I tell him I'm his nephew, but receive not even a glimmer of recognition. I introduce Mo. My uncle is clearly quite content with his state. He excuses himself terribly politely and ducks into his toilet, which is en-suite. He comes out with a load of toilet paper and is trying to fold it. I remember he used to like origami, so I pass him my newspaper which he uses to make a hat and then a plane. I talk to him about his wife and he seems to be able to follow, and even laughs, albeit at nothing.

Then he says, 'Scissors, paper, stone.'

I am flummoxed, but Mo gets it and is still playing the game half an hour later, when I have to relieve him.

Eventually I tell my uncle, 'Time to go, uncle.'

He replies, 'Yes, yes. You must come again, Peter.'

I stare him in the face and place my arm around him. 'Uncle, uncle,' but the moment is gone. He follows us out and down the wide hall, straightening pictures and moving the odd chair. At the exit I turn to say goodbye, but he has slipped into the TV lounge. No doubt he is rearranging some furniture.

On the way home we stop for a drink. I have a beer and Mo has J2Os, whatever they are.

'That wasn't what I was expecting,' says Mo.

'Me neither. Perhaps he's the exception, or those places have changed.'

Then it hits me, and I get it, I get it. He had a woman in there. Not my uncle. Mo. Amazing! He has spent four decades plus perfecting being a virgin, and now I realize that he had a woman in his bedroom when I called by yesterday. That's why he wouldn't come to the door.

'You're unbelievable,' I tell him. 'I thought that was what's called a pouch, but those things you snatched up from your sofa were knickers, weren't they? You weren't at the funeral. (And now I remember to put him on the spot). Is that what you've been up to? Is that why you missed it?'

'You're off your trolley. You gave me the wrong date, mate. Check with Carol.'

On the last stage of the journey, Mo stops off at Junction Road so I can switch all but one of the lights off, something I failed to do the day before. The car moves up the road in the opposite direction to the one - way system, while I turn and look back. Necropolis or Shangri-La? For me they are converging.

Did I say I am married? It's a sort of closed marriage, closed most of all to us. When I get home, Carol, my wife, is out at some college or another. I believe, among other things, she's taking a drama class, but it's late, too late for any college course. I don't know where she gets the energy. I turn on a history channel and doze off until the door bell wakes me. I wait while I hear a fumbling with keys, but once I realise she needs help I jump up and open the door. Her hands are full of various materials. She glares, but at least it is simply a glare. On bad days she has that woeful look upon her face, and you think she has gone to war forever, so permanently that there can't be any way back. I am a little wary.

'Thank you,' she says.

I can't tell if there is some irony there. I know she's a victim, but it would almost be better if she stayed awful all the time. The way it is, it constantly catches me out, repeatedly wrong foots me.

'You were supposed to ring Linda. She wanted to talk to you.'

'Well I didn't know that.'

'Of course you did.'

'No I didn't.'

'You did, firstly because Linda said you agreed to at the funeral, secondly because I reminded you, thirdly because Sylvia texted me to say she'd told you only yesterday, and fourthly because it is in large red letters on the sheet pinned on the door where you went out earlier.'

I look, and it's there. The arithmetic is against me; all of them can't be wrong. To be fair to me, on the other hand, it can't be a broken promise if you have no recollection of making it.

'I'll ring her.'

'Too late, ring her tomorrow. What's that?'

'Oh, my father's diary.'

Carol goes for a shower. I sit back down and the diary falls open in my lap. Sylvia was partly right; there is a lot that seems incomprehensible, but only at first. What he is recording is genuine events chronologically, but they are primarily mental events. What he is trying to do is inherently impossible. He is trying to compile a list of all the things he has forgotten. Often sentences are unfinished, and every path he constructs is incomplete. It's as though each road he sets out on ends at the edge of cliffs that have collapsed. If he gets anywhere it ends prematurely and it frightens him. I read further.

She's kind but it's not my wife. My wife is not that hefty. I'd never have married someone that big. My wife is younger. She says she's my wife but…

My mother didn't deserve that, but then neither did my father. One thing in the diary that needs very little understanding is repeated every few pages. It comes across clearly. I read again and again:

What is happening to me?
What is happening to me?

What would finally happen, in a crucial sense, was my doing and an act of cowardice, one for which Sylvia has never forgiven me. At the time she implored me, 'We are fighters you and me, Dad. We stand shoulder to shoulder with people in trouble. If it's right, we do it, no matter. It's in our natures.'

When she talked about fighters, she meant for the rights of people like my father.

III

There is a danger my little car is going to overheat. We are still stuck in Fortis Green Road and are almost certainly going to be late for the hospital appointment. It is the next best thing to being late to your own funeral as far as I am concerned. Carol's body thermostat is often all over the place, jumping from cold to blistering in an instant and sticking there, but she's not overheating right now either. 'They'll wait for us,' she says.

I couldn't sleep thinking about problems Sylvia has been having with her bosses. Apparently they have threatened her with the sack. She can be such a stubborn hot head, so it's no good trying to speak to her. At least her sister talks to me.

Yesterday I went to the coffee bar across the way from where Linda works as a volunteer. I was sure this was the time she went in there, and had written it on my hand to remind me, but after an hour I realized I had got it wrong. Today I am going randomly back to the same place. If she turns up it will be a pleasant surprise for both of us.

I get to the coffee bar early and manage to get a seat by an open window. I am in my morning routine, sumptuously having coffee and cake while rubbing some sore lumps which formed in my hand a year or so ago. The doctor said they were nothing to worry me. I'm sure he says that to imminently terminal patients, too. Given time the lumps can turn the hand into a claw, although I'm not concerned about that far into the future. The enjoyment I usually get from reading a newspaper is interrupted today by a terrible noise. This time it isn't tinnitus, but it is almost as uncontrollable. It is the sound of the coffee house kindergarten: under-fives in a Wendy House riot. Accompanying it is something I find difficult to deal with: breast milk being delivered direct from the manufacturer. I know it's good and natural, it just doesn't feel safe. What is a man supposed to do with his eyes and where is he supposed to sit? Not opposite in direct line of sight, let alone at the same table. It is a fair guess that it wouldn't be appreciated if I disturbed a feeding mum by asking, 'Do you mind?' and sat next to her.

While I am waiting for Linda my heart beat becomes more even.

There she is, part of the rush. I wave whilst she flinches. 'Hello darling,' I say as she attempts to deliver a smile which is reluctant to come into this world. 'Let me get you something.'

I am a long while in the queue and keep looking back to her. Our eyes never meet because hers are fixed on the doorway. My order arrives and my hands are full as I assay a way back that has charm, but looks dangerous. Impact proof all-weather buggies are grouped in circles across the route like a wagon train under attack. Kiddies', whose faces are smeared with chocolate dust or the trails of lurid fruit smoothies, are on the move. I find it difficult to negotiate a path. Finally I am back at our table.

Linda abruptly finishes a phone call she has been attempting and smiles at me. She is struggling to look relaxed. 'I can't stay long. I'm running late, sorry. If I had known you were coming...'

'I thought you wanted to talk to me.'

She puts her hand on my upper arm and smiles and I can't resist it.

'I am glad to see you; I've something special to tell you.' She glances over to the door. I fear she's going to tell me she's on the verge of joining an obscure sect, or is going to emigrate. 'You are going to be a Grandad. I am two months pregnant. And yes, I have thought it all through. I know where I am going to live

35

and how the finances will be handled, and there will be support.'

There is nothing there I can challenge, or would want to. My chest cavity is full of victory rolls and my stomach joins in. This is life-affirming, literally. She is staying longer than she expected.

'Wonderful! Wonderful!' I say, but I have to ask, 'What about...' (I am not quite stupid enough to ask for an identity) '...the father?'

'That is for me alone at the moment. One step at a time.'

She's beginning to sound like her sister. I am not going to let it go there. I have to ask. 'Come on, I'm not looking for a shotgun wedding. The key thing is you are going to have a baby, but come on where is the harm in a name?'

'There may not be much purpose in it, Dad. I don't know if I am staying with the bloke, whereas I definitely know I'm staying with the baby.'

That is difficult to counter. 'I expect you've chosen well,' I lie.

'Look, you are going to be a Grandad. I know you'll be hands on. There will be plenty of time to get to know the details.'

I might yet get it out of her because she's a lot softer than her sister. The coffee and pastry are gulped down and the conversation is all celebratory. My phone bleeps. It is from the doctor's again. I text back, 'I'll make an appointment.' They can wait; I have to.

Suddenly it comes to an end. Linda gasps like she's having a contraction, and leaps up. I am still trying to put the key lock on my phone; I've wasted a fortune by forgetting to.

She has no problem getting through the moving obstacles as she rushes to the door. I glance up to see her hurriedly ushering someone out. 'Won't be a minute,' my daughter shouts to me over her shoulder. I see it, or her or them, and then I don't. They're gone. I've been led to a place of illumination, only to find it boarded up. She may have missed all the other obstacles, but she nearly tripped on the threshold as she went, pushing him before her. It was a him, I realise. All I got was half a glimpse, though I am sure he spotted me. I gauge that he was tall with big shoulders, and perhaps olive skin, although that could have been the shadow of the doorway. I think he had on a tan coloured woollen bonnet. Youths wear them pulled down over their ears. The rest was a blur. I know what has happened; he is the father and she doesn't want me to see him. Worse he doesn't want me to see him. What kind of a bloke does that make him, shunning and running? If he were decent he should have insisted on meeting the grandfather of his child-to-be. I have to wonder what sort of story Linda has told of me. It could be that I am appallingly forgetful and constantly verging on the inappropriate. That's the sort of relative you introduce when it's too late for the other party to back out. I hope I am not an embarrassment. I would have been polite and welcoming to him, she must know that.

My phone is ringing and I see it is the doctor's surgery again, but there are more important things to occupy me, so I re-send my text in response.

She must have given him a dire report of me. It is a lousy start to the relationship I surely will have with him. I'll make certain we have a relationship, whether he wants it or not. I'll give him no choice, and her no say. While there is time I am going to see a great deal of my grandchild, so they are going to have to see a lot of me. Now my heart beat is a drum roll with sudden long punctuations, as if it is the signal for a trap door to shoot open.

I am outside the entrance, looking down the road, trying to catch sight of him, but with no success.

'Don't worry, it's not you,' comes from behind me. Linda is back from the other direction.

'What do you mean, it's not me?'

'I mean the problem isn't you. I'll come and see you and explain everything. You might have persuaded me, you often do, but he turned up and the time wasn't right.'

'He was the father, wasn't he?'

'The father... Okay...' She launches into something that looks heartfelt, but I can't hear a word because there is a deafening noise. It is neither tinnitus, nor a surrogate nursery. This time it is aerial. A Gulf bound war plane I shouldn't wonder. That'll make me sleep sounder in my bed tonight. 'I shall tell my grandchildren the truth about war.'

'Shsh, Dad, people are looking.' I'd said it out loud. 'I've got a few more minutes, let's sit down again.' Linda is staying longer than she intended, because she'd like to leave me feeling a little happier.

'Your lad wasn't in uniform, was he? That wasn't why you didn't want me to see him?'

'Lad? No, no, that's not possible,' she replies which has me fearing he's disabled in some way.

I order another Americano – I do not remember drinking the first – and Linda and I exchange a few banal nothings, and then she leaves. The extra coffee is a bad idea; my heart is galloping off and jumping hurdles. It's either slump or stroll.

My wife will be delighted with the news. I decide to celebrate in style and go to the supermarket on the way home. I consider buying wine, but decide that the bubbly stuff is what's in order. I go to where it is stacked and am confronted by terror – on the face of a child.

The little girl is an exquisite, plump cherub, with runny nose and gushing eyes. She believes, truly believes, that she is lost and abandoned, and the appeal is to any caring adult. I pick up the blessed little bundle and grab a bottle of champagne.

'Don't worry, we'll find your mummy,' I tell her. She slips into my arms as a child should do, with ease and some reassurance. We both feel it is where she is meant to be. The crying has stopped. As I pass by the frozen food section, cold wafts chill me. I'm heading for a small information help point, but I can't see it. They must have moved it. I hold her high in the hope she will pick out her mother, or her mother will see her. It is taking longer than I thought. My arms cannot keep her raised, and hold a champagne bottle. I plant her on my hip, just as I used to when my daughters were her age. This is one remiss mum; we can't seem to find her anywhere. There is one of those express check-outs near the exit which is in plain sight, so I make my way towards it. It isn't staffed at the moment, and I am going to lean on it. When I do, a suited man grapples my arm, nearly dislodging the champagne. He's probably one of the assistant managers, a plain clothes knucklehead.

'Get your hands off me!' I snap, telling him, 'I know I haven't paid yet, but can't you see I have a problem?' I mean in my arms, and I sure do. It's a stupid mistake, maybe criminal in this strange new era. I have known so well not to do what I have done. I have wandered into a terrible trespass.

By the side of the assistant manager is a young mother who is both tearful and appalled. She snatches the child from me, as if rescuing it from the edge of a precipice. All life in the supermarket has ceased what it was doing and is now scrutinizing me. I am as hot as if I were tied to a stake and set alight. 'Cretin!' is the word careering through my head. Had I seen the child while I still had my intellect I would have known it was not for me to rescue her. But no, I had to reach out to her. I clumsily half mutter, 'She was crying her eyes out. Somebody had to do something.'

39

They clearly see it as the most transparent lie. I should have left it to a woman; they are not under suspicion like men.

'I couldn't hold her aloft any longer. I am only at the check-out to lean on it. Come on this is ridiculous. She was bawling. I had to do something.'

They look at me as much to say, 'Yeah, that's likely, isn't it?'

The mother uses her mobile to take a photograph of me full face, quickly switching round to my side for a profile shot. She then phones, phones I don't know whom, someone to arrest me possibly. The assistant manager takes the wallet I have out for payment and begins to rifle through it. He also makes a phone call. In it he gives my full name from a credit card and then puzzles over an old NSPCC card. There are now two guys wearing security uniforms flanking me. The card was for volunteers visiting kids in care and it is causing the assistant manager a problem. He talks to one of his aides, something to do with a police check. He has got advice he hadn't expected. Finally they accept they are going to have to let me go. I am free to leave, once I dump my unpaid for goods where they are. The goon holds out my wallet to me and I just stare at it. He places it inside my jacket and I wander out.

The cooler outside air hits me like it does drunks, and I reel. It is hard for an older man to know his place in this era - solely on the side lines perhaps. I stand by the exit, breathing deeply. An arm suddenly comes around me, and I am supported down an adjoining alleyway. From what he says, he is the one the young mother phoned moments ago. In response I do little more than shrug and sigh. He is red haired, and red faced with red flecks in his eyes. He is lanky, which means he'll have lots of leverage. I can see the whiteness of the cartilage of the knuckles on his tightly clenched right hand. I might have reacted in the same way when I was young. The brickwork on the wall opposite is poor, but it calls me on. It could solve a problem or two for both of us. I pre-empt his violence and launch myself through the air.

IV

We're breezing up to the mansions of The Bishops Avenue. They look like mausoleums more than ever. Apparently we might still make the hospital on time. Oh joy.

Some while later and still dazed I look upwards for some relief, and back down again. My gaze settles on the cinema across the road where they are showing a film that is a bit of a weepie. If only death could be like it was in old films: dignified, with some touching last minute lucidity climaxing in an effortless au revoir.

There is no holding it off any longer. I go home, march along our tessellated hallway floor to the directories, and look up the number for the funeral parlour. I say who I am and make my request.

'I need to speak to the big guy, the one who stayed behind at Junction Road the other day.'

'D'you get his name?'

'No. He likes a drink.'

'Ah, Jeremy. I'll get him.'

'Hello… I gave it back – to your daughter.' He sounds very edgy and obviously feels he's in trouble.

'Hello there again,' I say trying to project my solicitous smile down the phone line. 'We had a great time. Do you remember our chat? We were talking about dementia and someone who died with the help of his wife. It was undetectable, a perfect murder.'

'Don't know what you're talking about, mate.'

'The family still got an insurance pay-out. We drank a lot of whisky and had a good laugh. I wondered if you fancied a drink. I am interested to hear the rest of that story. It intrigues me. There could be something in this for you.' There's a short pause.

'Ah, I remember you. Alright, but ring me on my mobile,' he says and puts the phone down.

The cut on my forehead should have had a stitch or two, but I am back and forth to the hospital too often as it is. Immediately after speaking to Jeremy I go to the cabinet, survey the congealing blood, whack some gauze and as a big a plaster as I can find on it. In the mirror I notice I still have a plaster on my cut finger. To my surprise my wife is in.

'What on earth happened?' she asks.

'It was stupid really. I tripped up while getting some shopping.'

She takes me into the kitchen, sits me down, removes my poor handy work, bathes the wound and then does a far better job with a dressing.

'You won't go to the hospital, will you?' she says. There is no need to reply. 'Did anyone there help you?'

'Oh yes, there was a nice young fellow who helped me on my way.' He had gone when my head finally cleared.

'Good. I'm so glad you weren't on your own you poor thing. You must go to the doctor's though.'

'I feel okay, honestly,' I tell her, and I add, 'I'm supposed to be seeing them soon about my heart, but it's too late today. There won't be any appointments left for our doctor.'

'You've been lying awake over it. Take any appointment you can get. It's best to get it off your mind.'

I may have been lying awake, but not over heart problems. My wife has been on at me to go to the doctor's. Pulse is controlled by some part of the brain, the brain stem I've read somewhere. The cause is there, quite likely. I look over at the phone, knowing this will be a pointless exercise, and don't budge. Carol has powers beyond mine. She takes the phone and politely let's the surgery believe I am at death's door and have to have an appointment straight away. She succeeds, but the evening surgery doesn't open for some time, so I

43

am at home for a while.

'We're going to be grandparents. Linda is expecting,' I announce to Carol.

'Yes I know. It's lovely isn't it? But it is early days.'

I find an old bottle of champagne that had somehow avoided me.

'Not for me, thanks, not at this hour, and you shouldn't either.'

I have one glass, which I don't finish. I had to wrestle the cork out and the liquid is flat.

What Carol arranged is not truly an appointment. It is more like a seat at bingo. I'll have to wait and hope I'm on to a winner. I seem to be waiting forever. The reception tells me the texts they sent were just for my annual check-up. While I am waiting I read a letter I have brought with me. It is from the Council Tax department. Incredibly it is a threat to summons me for non-payment. I go outside to use my mobile. I am clear that I had set up a direct debit.

I am courteous and careful not to imply that the woman handling my case is personally at fault in any way.

'When did you send it in?'

'Within days of getting your first notice,' I guess.

'We haven't received it.'

'I definitely posted it. My wife checked it for me.' This isn't actually a lie as far as I am concerned. It has the essence of truth, because if it did happen this is how it would have happened.

'Well, it hasn't been received.'

'That doesn't mean I haven't sent it, though, does it?'

She is having none of it. After ten mobile phone minutes of repeatedly demanding to speak to a supervisor, I am eventually allowed to do so. The supervisor asks me the same questions to give me the

same response. Behind the brick wall I first
encountered is a stone edifice.

'Is it not remotely conceivable that the error is at
your end?'

'Check your bank account. Your Council Tax
has not been sent.'

'Don't you think a court summons is just a wee
bit of over-kill?'

'Get your payment in and the summons will be
cancelled. It is on hold for now.'

I am back in the surgery fuming. They had
called me. I have missed my place and will have to wait
longer. Whoever sees me is going to be none too
happy because it will be beyond their normal hours.
Being at the doctors' can be bad for your health; it has
kick-started further unsteadiness with my heart.

My wait is over, and it's someone I have never
seen in the surgery before. I am not a winner. Having
checked my head wound, the locum takes my pulse.
He seems quite concerned. My usual doctor, in the
nicest possible most engaging way, always brushes me
off. He's an interesting man, more like a pal, although
he smokes and that makes it hard to take him seriously.

'Can a brain malfunction that is basic to workings
of the heart be the cause?' I ask the locum.

'I've never heard of it. No, this sort of thing has
nothing to do with your brain, but I think we should have
you checked out.'

I've got to go for tests at the Whittington
Hospital. He tells me I may have something called atrial
fibrillation. I get him to spell it. My medical notes, the
ones about my body for the last five decades-plus,
which I have never glimpsed, apparently already have
mention of an enlarged left ventricle. It must be a
mistake. Surely somebody in the last few years would
have told me. Surely I would have been told at the time
it was discovered. I have to doubt I was told, and then

again, if I was, I have to wonder when. I cannot remember either way, so I'll never know.

'I am more worried about my memory, or rather, lack of one.'

'We can give you some cognitive tests for that, but let's first make sure there's a sound pump house for your mind, shall we?'

Doctors excel at asking patients rhetorical questions.

'When, when can I have these cognitive tests?'

He sighs, and does me a print-off of information on atrial fibrillation. To me it does not look good. I relent. One thing at a time, I suppose. It must be quite significant.

'Do you have private medical insurance?'

The nerve! I am as likely to have that as a second penis. In fact not having a second penis wouldn't be a matter of principle. What is more, no one is going to give me cover now.

To my surprise my wife is still in when I get home. She must have had a cancellation of some sort or another. 'Atrial fibrillation?' she asks and heads for her much thumbed medical dictionary, while I launch out on the web with my ancient set-up.

'It does sound as though you need to get it looked at. Who did you see at the surgery?'

I tell her. Without as much as a by your leave, she once more goes to ring the surgery and catches a secretary on her way out. She succeeds again where I failed: I have an appointment the next day with my own doctor.

'Look at this, you can go virtually any time in the morning to the Whittington,' Carol reminds me of the sheet the locum had given me earlier. 'Get the ball rolling. See our doctor tomorrow and then go there early the next day.'

'They've got these cognitive tests. That's what I

really want. I want my mind checked out.'

'Your brains testing more like it.'

This is sharp. I am ready to cower, because there will be a tirade coming.

'And look, none of this nonsense about not going private. If that doctor says you need to see a private consultant, you are seeing one, and that's that!'

This isn't what I was expecting. She is being firm, but it is considerate. Me, after all I've said and done over the years, I am going to bribe my way to the front of the queue. I'll be spending more money to make myself yet more worthless. There are reasons I shouldn't bother. I could excuse myself by saying I am letting Carol's tempest blow me in whatever direction she decides, but that would be pathetic.

My doctor is a little older than me, and his appointments take as long as he deems necessary. He's a bit of a philosopher and a joker and has nicknamed himself Doc Holiday. That's because he's taken a couple of sabbaticals in recent years, and goes somewhere sunny every chance he gets.

'How are you?' he asks as I sit down in the leather chair and tobacco ambience.

'Fine,' I always answer him.

'How did you get on with that book?' We lend each other books. I guess I look blank, so he offers, 'Monbiot'. It sounds like a French mountain or an organic yoghurt to me, and I haven't a clue what he is talking about.

'Well, I can't see the people in Skye winning. They're brave, but, they're stuck with the bridge, and that toll,' he carries on.

'The atrial fibrillation I've got. Can it affect the mind?'

He checks the computer screen for my recent history. 'Who told you you had that?' He must be able to see it on the screen, but clearly he's not impressed.

He pulls my wrist forward and starts taking my pulse. 'You're going to be a grandfather.'

It doesn't surprise me to find everybody knew before me.

'How do you know?'

'Did her examination, of course.'

Of course.

'New lease of life, eh. You fancy something precious and small and unspoiled that you're allowed to pick up and comfort, eh.'

Evidently his reading of my pulse reveals nothing significant.

'Odd,' I tell him, 'in the period my children are reaching their fecund height, the bottom has already begun to fall out of my sex life.'

'Linda and Sylvia are past their fecund height.'

'I know. Thanks for reminding me.'

'Do you want some help?' he asks, piping up a prescription form on his screen. I think he's set to write me a prescription for Viagra.

'No thanks,' I say shaking my head. 'It's just biology isn't it?'

'How do you make that out?'

'If reproduction doesn't apply, Nature sends the sexes on their separate ways. Boys spend their time with boys and old men spend their time with old men. I don't think Carol and I are up for counselling either.'

'I'm a doctor. I'm here to do something about Nature, you know. However, best to check the arhythmia first.'

'I am much more concerned with a deterioration in my memory,' I start to tell him.

'Well, well, you're going to be the grandsire of a cuddly wild thing,' he cuts me off, 'with volition aplenty. We're born anarchists, you know.'

He's spoken to me before about anarcho-syndicalism, in not so few words.

'Only creatures with wills of iron could survive that journey down the birth canal. It's the most dramatic change of environment humans ever face.'

'I think my intellect is crumbling.'

'No, no, you've got a fine head on your shoulders.' He places the strap from a sphygmomanometer around my upper arm. 'Volition is as essential to life as mitochondria,' he tells me, but I've heard it all before.

'I would really appreciate having cognitive tests.' He appears to be ignoring me, but there is often a time delay with him when he's inflicting his needs on a patient.

'Then we grow up, but there's still a molten core spinning in the centre of all of us.'

I like that image; he's always using it. The strap deflates and he uses the keyboard to make some notes on my record.

'Might need to keep an eye on that. Your pulse is not too bad, nor is your systolic reading. Are you under any stress at the moment?'

'Not at the moment: all the time. That's me these days. What does, "not too bad" amount to?' He hoped he'd slipped that past me.

'It means you haven't got the heart of a young boy, but it's not unusual for a man of your age.'

I'll buy a monitor and check it myself.

As he signs a prescription slip he announces, 'Nitrazepam. Valium to you.'

'Poor man's Valium, more like it. You're trying to pull a fast one on me.'

It is second nature with him. He's egalitarian regarding everything, except the people he deals with.

'It's just shorthand for any tranquiliser,' he insists, which is rubbish. We can have the frankest of conversations until it comes to medicine and my health.

'You gave Carol genuine Valium.'

49

'With her condition she needed something. She can't have HRT, you know.' He passes me the prescription, which I'll bin.

'What about my heart being erratic?'

'No sign of it, but perhaps it's not doing it right now.' It's big of him to concede that. 'It sounds like an ectopic beat. It's not unusual, but you're going for an E.C.G.'

'It says on my notes I've got an enlarged left ventricle. How come you didn't tell me?'

He checks the records on the computer. 'You were told. We sent you for tests and it was nothing serious. You did a lot of sport didn't you? That'll be it. It's going to be checked again anyway.'

He could be lying for all I know. I have no recollection of these tests. The next bit is going to be awkward.

'Carol has told me I have to see a consultant privately.'

He doesn't say a word, gets out a list of names and addresses, and writes me a referral. I thank him and tell him to look after himself.

'I've got the NHS to do that,' he replies. 'See the secretary on your way out. She'll make an appointment for you for the cognitive testing. I didn't know you'd taken to doing as Carol says, but…'

The unspoken end to his sentence is, 'it's only when it suits you, I suppose.'

I've found parking at the top of Highgate Hill where I'm wasting time waiting for the digital meter to give me change. They stopped doing that years ago, when superior new technology arrived, but I keep forgetting. I got here early partly because I couldn't find my papers with the clinic times on, and partly because I was expecting problems parking. I got here at all because Carol had the presence of mind to hurry me along. I repeatedly phone and the cardiac department

50

at the Whittington finally answers my call. It will be open for hours, and I can come any time. Excellent. I have plenty of time for caffeine and cake in Costa Coffee. I am casually filling in a questionnaire for a school kid who's doing a survey for a project, while also looking through the window.

A switch in my head randomly flicks on and I recall Carol's words: 'They are fully paid up grown ups now, something you don't seem to realise. Ring them! They've a right to be told.' She actually meant that I should ring Sylvia, and sitting here is as good as any moment.

'Linda, it's your ailing Dad. It's time for the last rites.'

'Dad, what are you talking about?'

'I've got to have a heart scan. Can you tell your sister for me?'

'Oh yes, Mum told me. Are you okay with this going private? Sometimes you have to these days, if you can.'

'The "if you can" is the wicked thing, isn't it? If everybody could, it wouldn't matter. Anyway, how are you and how is your boyfriend?'

'Father and child are doing very well, thank you. Let us know how you get on. Chin up.'

I didn't want any fuss, but a little more concern wouldn't have hurt. Across the road I can see one of those yellow, rectangular police witness appeal signs. It concerns an armed robbery near here, in Highgate Village of all places; mayhem and malevolence by Pond Square and its Scientific and Literary Institute. Either the miscreants didn't know the rules or desperation has stepped up in class.

Time to head down towards the bustle of Archway and the Whittington. The ranks of ambulances are there, and the smokers are by the automatic double doorway. Some are in pyjamas and one has lost a leg.

51

The antiseptic odours, as I enter through the doors, are nowhere near as strong as I remember from my childhood. I pass some tubular steel wheelchairs that look as though they could have been recycled from armoured vehicles. A crumpled man in one stares blankly and forlornly nowhere. A heart check-up is neither here nor there, if you are destined to be like that. There are not many waiting where I am seated. The usual mags have been donated 'Tatler', 'Natural World' and one I've never seen before, 'Donors': that must be a hoot! There is an old couple in front of me with broad Irish accents. An Italian lady comes out having had a heart monitor fitted. They wish her well and she tells the husband, 'You a lucky man.' A Scot with armpits that smell like an empty pot noodle carton says something reassuring to them, then a young lad comes out and talks to them about an ambulance to take them home. He's helpful, and not patronizing. He's tall and broad, and androgynous looking, with a faultless complexion and smartly gelled hair. There is something almost compelling about him.

My number is on the screen overhead and the well groomed lad comes to take me to the room he is working in. There are lots of cards celebrating his 29th birthday on the wall behind him, so he is obviously popular.

He fits the monitor, and explains, 'No baths or showers for twenty-four hours I'm afraid. You'll be back to normal after we take it off tomorrow.'

It's smoothly done and he is pretty comprehensive in what he tells me. It will be a week before I get the first results, and up to two weeks before the other tests are done. I have an odd desire to stop and chat with the lad, but I am not to be humoured.

As I move to make way for a wheelchair in the corridor, I step backwards on to someone's foot. I am caught in the glare of a woman, making me think that she has spotted something peculiar in me. Perhaps my flies are undone. My next thought is that I might know her, but I dismiss this. These days every new face fits a pattern, looks as though I already know it. I have struck up conversations with complete strangers who I believed I should know, but can't quite remember. Apart from the jet black hair and the shape of her nose, this woman looks white.

She gives me the once over, two or three times, so I ask, 'Can I help you?'

'Hello, Peter. How wonderful to see you. You look well.' While I am asking myself who she might be she says, 'You remember me. It's me, Sam.'

Sam, Sam? I used to know a bloke or two called Sam, and this is no bloke. Sam! She is the hippy rebel who made her respectable Asian-Jamaican parents despair. There she is, a real Caribbean mixture with tons of Celtic blood and some Chinese, as well. We met at technical college where she was re-doing A-levels and I was learning brick-laying. It was she and my wife who got me to take part in a peace convoy during that period. I was young and I had hopes of getting one or the other into bed. She is the one woman I have been unfaithful with, right in the early years of my marriage. That was the single time, or rather, times. It was a week's riotous and unlicensed intercourse, thirty years ago.

She beams at me and I feel like this is part of a recent conversation. We hug an old friends' long, long hug.

'You look good.'

I reply, 'I thought you'd made your home in Devon after years of living half a world away. I've never seen you here before.'

'I've been working here for a fairly short time, but I came back to London ages ago with a sax' player. He's long gone, but we had a gas.'

53

I had always expected to be a bit embarrassed if I ever saw her again. Instead I feel that savoury calm you get after a coital moment. She always did give off an unruffled zestiness, and the mood just adopted you.

'Time for a tea? See you in the cafeteria downstairs in five minutes.'

'Mmm,' I sort of say and smile inscrutably on my way down the escalator towards the exit. This could all get a tad too complicated.

I do not go to the exit. I sit in the cafeteria with its assortment of injured people and anxious faces, glancing through a magazine, which is several months old. When she comes in she isn't pretending to be casual, she is intently scrutinising me. It would be rude not to return the compliment. Her fingers are held up in the old V sign of peace, and it's clear that she truly has not altered.

'Still wearing Indian beads, I see.' She is also wearing extravagant earrings with bits and pieces running all around her ears.

'Always,' she laughs, kissing my cheek. A high pitched whistle is set off nowhere in particular, which no doubt is internal to my own ear. Her clothes smell of incense and I wonder how any person can remain so unchanged.

'So you live up this way?' I ask her.

'Pardon?'

I repeat the question.

'Yes, in one of the houses on the Ladder in Harringay.'

'They're huge, aren't they?'

'It's just a place to crash.'

'I've never lived far from where I was living when we first met. What about you? Make me envious.'

'I lived in Kathmandu for three years. It was the first time they had seen a woman who wore clothes like an Asian behave like a westerner.'

54

'And then some, I would think.'

'I took my son with me, when he was little of course. A lifetime later he got me the job here. He said it was better late than never to join the ranks of the wage-slaves. Telling it like it is, I guess. It's a first for me. Have you seen him?'

I nod slightly and move my shoulders. I am lost here, without a clue who or what she is talking about. I couldn't possibly know she has a son, let alone what he looks like.

'He was in the department you were coming from when I bumped into you.' Well, so were a load of people. 'He's nothing like me or his sister. He's sensible, even wants a career! He got an interview here the day after he finished his degree.'

I go through a neutral response routine and expertly ask questions, such as how old is he, and is he married? Theses are questions, I'd ask about anybody I didn't know, or care for. Apparently he has just had his birthday.

'Oh,' I say, 'the lad with the heart monitors.'

She doesn't really answer and says instead, 'We have unfinished business you and me.'

I do remember that. The final time we had sex, I was drunk, climaxed early and couldn't carry on. Perhaps it was more like didn't bother to carry on.

We talk through the entire hour of her break. She has been in communes in Spain and Goa, and lived in a chateau with a Bavarian noble. I tell her about giving up the tools and my subsequent life in social work.

'So Peter, you are still an activist.'

'No, invalided out when all the changes and paper work choked the living daylights out of the job. Now I am a freed man.'

'Which is beautiful. We must do this again.'

'Definitely!' I agree.

She holds me closely and we kiss on the cheek. I have no doubt about what business she intends. Something in me that was dormant is stirring; old dry seeds in a neglected part of the warehouse are germinating. I can hear my heart, and even see my pulse peripherally in the top corner of my left eye. As usual, when my heart begins to rev up my brain begins to stall. Just what do I think I am playing at? There are more important things I should have in train. On the other hand I haven't found a way forward yet, and I have nothing better to do.

The walk up Highgate Hill is steep. I become breathless and it isn't the sound of Bow Bells that is bringing me to a halt. My heart is playing up as much as ever and I'm slightly dizzy, but the cause is not medical. Inhaling in a paper bag would help. The unfinished business Sam spoke of is nothing to do with any proposed fling. It concerns the product of sex thirty years ago. The dates exactly fit. The child she took to Nepal, the one who had been so pleasant when giving me the heart scan, certainly was striking. However, it wasn't because he was so unusual looking, it was because he was familiar. His high cheek-bones, small rigid ears and, most especially, his nose with its low bridge were what I had seen on every occasion I'd gone to the mirror. He shared some of my key features, but they just hadn't registered. Her son, this kind and gentle and different looking lad is our son, my son.

I arrive home shaken. Instead of pushing the front door itself open, I shove its stained glass, bending some of the leading.

'Present for you,' says my wife. 'Linda dropped it in. She's a thinker that girl.'

She's always buying me things - most recently some Calvin Klein underpants which I can't get the hang of. She has been sweet enough to wrap whatever this is. It is one of those hand held brain training/teasing

56

machines. I go to work on it straight away, hoping I do better than I have with the C.K. pants.

'It is supposed to help brain function,' Carol says.

Before too long I am to be heard shouting, 'For Christ sake!'

'What on earth is the matter?' Carol shouts back.

'Twice, twice I've scored twenty years older than I am!'

'All you have to do is keep doing it. It will improve you.'

I try a placatory tone. 'You must know I'm worried, and this simply confirms it all.'

'Stop worrying and start doing! Linda has bought you something that could help, but oh no, you've given up already. They're not cheap, you know!'

I realize that and I know she doesn't earn much. She's a generous and thoughtful girl. I pick up the machine again. 'I'll give it another go, but first I'll ring Linda and thank her.'

'You know your problem? You've spent most of your life looking out for others. It was your job. It was your hobby as well. It used to drive me mad the way you could work out other people's entitlements, but hadn't the vaguest idea of your own, especially on pay. And now you're retired you have only yourself to be concerned about…By the way, someone from the funeral parlour rang. He sounded like a drunken slob, so watch out for him, he could be a liability. He left his mobile number.'

With that she passes me a piece of paper with the number on it. I go into the other room, ostensibly to ring Linda, but I am, in fact, ringing the man I want to be my mentor. By the side of the phone is our address book. Poking out from underneath it is a form for Council Tax that I filled in more than a month ago and forgot to post.

V

Carol is still keeping her cool. We are now in the doldrums near to Kenwood. A giant lorry and crane are blocking the way. According to hoarding plusher than some houses, luxury apartments will soon be on the plot where they've just demolished a luxury mansion. And me, I am in a sweat. I could walk to the hospital from here in thirty-five minutes. I wasn't sure my wife would be with me today. I suspect I didn't explain why she wasn't at the funeral. She said she was away on a five day trip with one of the clubs she belongs to, which she insists she would have cancelled, except I gave her the wrong date. She says, quite angrily, that she actually came back, as she had believed, early, for the funeral. I don't believe a word. She deliberately keeps her life a mystery to me, and the last thing she will do is admit to it. She rarely lets me to know the details of her comings and goings. I am not certain, but I think she has set up her own bank account. There are phone calls for her day and night, and I do not recognize a single voice. Her answer, whenever I ask her what is going on, is simply to lie and say she has already told me. These days if I come home and find her in, it is a surprise. No, the reason she didn't come to the funeral was because we'd had a row a week before, and she was simply not around, having taken herself off – off to wherever.

The row Carol and I had was over something and nothing; she insisted it was something, but I cannot think what.

I believed I was being considerate when I asked, 'Is there absolutely no hope for HRT?' Half way through the sentence I realised it was a mistake. I pulled the string back, but it was Carol who let fly.

'How many times have we been over that? It was in our early days I know, but you were upset when I had thrombosis due to the pill! So there is no HRT, and

there are no effective alternatives. I've tried them! You know that, you should know it so well. I was in hospital for weeks. You can't have forgotten that. Oh yes, oh yes, you actually can, can't you?'

I set off immediately after the rush hour. I'm soon in a beans and bacon café where the undertaker and I have arranged to meet. He sits opposite me. I effuse bonhomie, but can't for the life of me remember the man's name. I apologise and explain.

He's not fussed and stops gorging himself just long enough to say, 'It's Jeremy, and you said there might be something in this for me,' splattering egg and brown sauce in my direction.

'Of course. I'm not expecting you to help me for nothing. I'm interested in the story you told about the man whose wife helped to kill him. I want to know exactly how it was done.' It looks as though I might as well be speaking in tongues to the deaf.

'I'd had a few, so I'm not sure what I said.' I remind him.

'Ah, I think he died of botulism. He and his missus had seen a programme about a poisoner on the telly. He'd got hold of some botulism, I think it was, and killed business rivals with it.'

'No, I thought the family helped the man to kill himself. There was nothing about business rivals in it.'

He looks at me like he's this instant scrapped me off his shoe. 'That was in the TV programme that gave them the idea of using botulism.'

'Oh, botulism. How on earth do you get hold of that?'

'I didn't say I could get hold of it, did I? Labs must have it. I heard you could get it from tinned food. Weren't there some deaths in Alaska a few years back, after they'd eaten a beached whale?'

My wife had overestimated him; he is no more

59

than a waste of space.

'Anyway,' he says 'what can I do for you?'

'Unless you can get me botulism or its like, not a thing.'

I collect my car and find myself parking in Sylvia's estate, but it isn't her I need to see. I am not up for that, and I haven't come to scrutinize the area either. I am on my way to brood on the waters of the River Lea.

When I get there, the river is less interesting, but more blissful than in its industrial heyday of my childhood. It looks dark and deep and swift running. There are, however, still rainbow coloured slicks on the surface. I can see the odd fish, possibly gudgeon, and glimpse the heavy long weed that still grows at the bottom. It wasn't far from here that I used to go swimming with friends. Back then, on an overcast day we went in as a bunch, laughing and splashing. When we came out again a lad from several roads away was missing. It wasn't until we started a kick-about that we spotted it. We were sure he had gone in with us. We scoured up and down the banks and shouted, but no answer came. We were bemused, but not too concerned. We got on with our game and some harmless pranks after that. In the evening his father knocked on our door and I thought I was in trouble when I was called for. But I wasn't. A day later, police frogmen found his body tangled in the weeds. I have always wanted to annul that day and have never been back to this spot before now.

Some broken beer bottles litter the way, waiting for the soft feet of children. I put them in a bin, and walk back to where I want to go. My shoes and socks are off, my trousers rolled up. I feel more spent than Prufrock. I negotiate the odd sharp bits of gravel as I make my way along the tow path, avoiding nettle leaves. I am going to sit on the bank and dangle my feet in the cold and

60

powerful run of the waters. As I sit down I realize I am the wrong side of the lock's huge timbered gates. The river is far too low for my toes to reach.

An hour later I remain sitting here, as still as the river is constantly flowing. I was watching a fish, much larger than a gudgeon, waiting among thick strands of weed. It was probably a pike. I have now moved on to gazing at the outstretching weed itself. It is leaning entirely in the direction of the river's current, forever moving, but going nowhere. I decide to see if I can hang down over the edge and somehow get my feet in the water some four and a half feet below. It won't be easy. I am bound to tear some clothing, and perhaps scratch myself a bit. It is too far down for safety really, but… And then, from another time and another place, my phone rings so loudly in my internal quiet that I shiver and nearly slip.

'Sylvia's in Tottenham Police Station. Where are you?' It is my wife.

'I'm in Tottenham.'

'Well that's handy. And you've got the car. Why didn't you tell me? I'm getting a cab, see you there.'

The sergeant nods in Sylvia's direction. He's ignored the crowd of others waiting to be served, if that's the right word, and taken us into an interview room.

'She,' he speaks pointedly in the third person, 'won't accept a caution. The alternative is to charge her.'

"She" is sitting in a corner, the two sides of her face looking quite different, almost like she's had a stroke: one half of her face is glum and the other is full of fury.

'You do realise she's a journalist, sergeant. This could all look pretty bad in the press.'

'We're very well aware of that, sir. We're trying

to do you a favour. If you're not interested, go now, leave your daughter with us, and we'll charge her.'

A fat lip couldn't have been more effective. I might as well be a plank of wood, because I can't achieve anything here. Carol talks to Sylvia confidentially. There is whispering and I guess it concerns me. I suspect I am the reason Sylvia cannot make a stand. Words to the effect that your father is troubled enough, without this to worry him, no doubt. Sylvia stabs her signature on a brief document. Carol thanks the copper and we go.

In my wife's direction I venture, 'What was that about?'

'We stopped a train carrying nuclear waste, down by the Hale,' Sylvia snaps. 'We held a paper banner across the track.'

'You were the only one arrested?' Carol asks, knowing there must be more to it.

'No, I kicked a dent in a carriage door.'

I can't help it, I roar.

Carol doesn't, shouting, 'They were going to let you off, after you'd done that, and you refused!'

'I was annoyed. When I gave you as my contact they took one look at the address and thought one of you might be a barrister. There are several in your road. I heard them discussing it. If I were a Tottenham woman I'd be appearing in court tomorrow!'

Back at our house my wife and my daughter make tea to calm down. I imbibe it in a silent toast. The phone goes and Sylvia answers it.

'Well, we're all here. Plenty of support. There'll be no touching of gloves and seconds away.'

'What was all that about Josephine Hill?'

Sylvia replies, but to her mother, 'Linda is coming over with her boyfriend. They want to get things out in the open.'

Within minutes the phone rings again and again

Sylvia answers it. What I hear is completely indecipherable.

'Ooooooh... Really? And that's it. Any other day in mind? Tell him from me he's a big wuss. Okay, okay, don't cry, it's temporary, that's all.' Sylvia turns to Carol and says, 'Linda's not coming.'

'And the boyfriend?' I have to ask

'They want neutral ground,' she tells Carol.

'It sounds more like no man's land to me,' I say. 'I am missing something here, but I am never going to be able work it out. I should know who is involved, and I bet I've been as good as told haven't I?' Sometimes a silent response is far worse than the most outright contradiction.

'For Christ's sake! It's my memory, isn't it? I've met this guy, haven't I? I know him, don't I? My memory is going, isn't it?'

Carol looks at me like I am a lunatic and shakes her head. Sylvia ignores me. I finish my tea, while my daughter and wife exchange warm pleasantries. Sylvia goes, having never drunk her tea on which a thick membrane is forming.

'How did you get on?'

I've this moment returned from going to a clinic at the surgery. This was after another dreadfully sleepless night, mainly due to the discomfort of wearing the heart monitor. The sleeplessness was interspersed with restless impossible riddle solving. In a dream I was trying to get a prescription for an erratically beating affair of the heart, while attempting to recall where I had left my grandchild. I haven't the foggiest what my wife is talking about. I evidently look blank, which is pretty appropriate.

'I mean the cognitive tests at the doctors.'

'Ah, those. Superb, superb. Highest score they've ever seen. Incredible suppleness of mind, and amazingly quick responses.'

'Really?'

'Yes, for someone in their mid-eighties.'

'That was your age score?'

'They don't give you the result, there and then. I'm not sure they do this particular one in ages.'

I pull nervously at the heart monitor straps across my chest. I can see Carol struggling to restrain herself from a terrible verbal violence against me. And then I realise she has lost the struggle. I stand there and take the full blast, as long as I can, and it knocks me back into the chair. She rounds off by telling me, 'You should have some real problems to occupy your mind!'

I would apologise, but that wouldn't work. Whenever I do, it re-fuels her temper. It confirms she has reason and she lays in to me anew.

I spent thirty-odd years coping with the flux of menstruation. I think I mastered it, but now... Well, if menstruation is The Curse, what is the menopause? Utter damnation? Sometimes in the biological mayhem she is the mad axe woman, at others she could be the mother of angels. Right now she is swinging away with the blade more than enough to fell me.

I go for a walk, returning with some flowers, not sure how they will be received. My wife takes them without saying much, but gives them her full attention when putting them into a vase. So there she is, with a mental invalid for a husband, anguished, tempestuous, and naturally without the faintest horny inclination except on high days and holidays – well actually not holidays. We have the maximum opportunity and she has nil desire. Sex as the great reconciler hasn't a chance. Perhaps, long ago, we reached for the sky romantically. These days the propeller's twisted downwards and our relationship is burrowing into the ground. I can't see it ever altering.

'Sam, the arch Hippie, rang,' my wife tells me.

'Oh really? What did she want?'

'She said something about unfinished business.'

'Oh.'

'What did she mean by that?'

The graph on my heart monitor must resemble a cross section of the Himalayas at this moment.

'You know her. You remember how she was. It's a phrase, it means nothing.'

'Okay, if you don't want to tell me.'

And I don't want to tell her. Given the state of our relationship it shouldn't matter, but it does.

As we go to bed, there is no hope. I am prepared for her to launch a second tirade, but this isn't a steady state. Sometimes I am caught out by things being completely normal. Frankly, more often than not I simply can't be bothered. It is impossible. We can't talk to anybody about it and we don't feel able to go to a therapist; we've seen that on the TV and didn't like what we saw. Discussing it between ourselves seems to create more formidable barriers. In the best of times we're politely tiptoeing to some sort of asexual oblivion. If I do not find her attractive, she is hurt, but if I act upon the attraction she runs my ardour through with shards of ice.

If the mood isn't bleak when I enter the bedroom it soon becomes so.

'When are you supposed to take that machine off?'

Christ, I am still wearing the heart monitor. I must have taken it off and put it back on every time I've bathed, and I think I recall that I'm not supposed to bath or remove the monitor. Worse, I've missed my appointment by some distance.

'I'll sort it out for you,' Carol says, and stays turned towards me. We talk a little and still she stays facing me. Although it is dark it is possible to see that

65

her eyes remain open. I can smell her favourite perfume and I am aware of what this means. It is the nearest to a signal that she could be receptive that I could get. However, it is not a risk I am prepared to take, not tonight anyway.

I bring our conversation to an end, and venture a, 'Goodnight'. It doesn't do to be lulled into the comfort of believing she is in a good mood. Storms come from nowhere in these parts.

She waits for moments, says, 'Goodnight, dear,' with a sigh and finally turns her back.

With any luck she will fall asleep in seconds and will hardly move for the next eight hours.

After thirty minutes I get up, eat a piece of fruit and try the brain teaser Linda gave me. Three attempts at improving my score later I throw it against the wall. I return to the bed and lay awake brooding, aware that I am getting nowhere fast with the task of finally superintending my affairs. I get up again to ring Sam who used to be a night owl. It is not quite midnight yet, so she is bound to be awake.

'It's about Oliver...'

'Who is it?'

'Peter'

'Oh, hello.' It is a warm, sleepy and unchaste voice.

'Can we meet? I need to do... to settle things. I can't be passive about this. I am burning to know... I really have to talk to you, to ask you...'

'The answer is yes. Now I'm on earlies.' I hear a mild bump as she lets the phone fall to her bedside floor.

I try ringing Mo.

'Mo, botulism. Do your company's laboratories deal with that?'

'They deal with most things, mate. We work with hospitals. But do we have to talk about this now?

Come on man, it's late.'

I believe I can hear female murmurs coming from alongside him. His mind is clearly on lower things. 'Alright then, when?'

'I'm never gonna let you down, Petey, am I? You've always been there for me. Botulism, though, that's a bit left field. We'll talk tomorrow.'

I let him go.

Bright and early the next morning my wife has rung the hospital and explained - explained what I do not know - and it's no problem. I have a new appointment to bring the monitor in. They can fit me in two days hence. They tell her how to clear the old readings and set it for new ones. I'll have to make certain I wear it for one day only. By the time I rise and my memory trips over itself and causes me to panic, the cause of the panic has been taken care of. Thank you, Carol. I didn't need to give my approval, I suppose.

When you no longer cling to life you have to be alert and careful, because no matter what, it still clings to you. You need purpose and strength to loosen its grip.

VI

As a result of a tailback from an accident not far ahead we have been stuck now for half an hour in the short stretch leading up to the Spaniards Inn. Without as much as a by your leave Carol drives on the wrong side of the road, past all the stationary traffic, for one hundred yards plus, and pulls into the car park of the Spaniards. Immediately she gets on her mobile and rings the hospital.

I am on my way back round to Mo's. With any luck his girlfriend will be there and I can catch him with her. Part of me still wants to tackle him over his absence from my aunt's funeral, as well. It's crazy I know, but as I believe I have said, I am not in control.

'Mo, you were going to look into this botulism business for me. What have you found out?'

'I've got my hands full at the moment, Petey. It can't be that urgent, but I am working on it.'

'Mo, it is urgent for me. You used to be such a straightforward sort of bloke. What on earth is going on? I am asking for some help here.'

'It's complicated. I am working on it, believe me, but there is another problem that won't wait. I need to get it out of the way first, because it is getting me down. I need some advice, some help.'

This is nothing new. 'You want some tips on your love life from an old hand? Positions, etc?'

'Shut up will you!'

'Okay, what is it?'

He looks down, so I do. He is wearing an expensive pair of trainers. When I look back up, he says, 'Cool, eh?'

'You want to talk about those, instead of botulism? I don't get you any more.' He picks up a box of identical new trainers.

'So?'

'I've bought a van load.'

Mo is no business man. He always pays the full asking price, wouldn't know a bargain if it threw itself into his TSB account, and he has no enterprise in him whatsoever. I do not know what to say, so he carries on.

'I am helping a pal out. He didn't have enough cash, but it was buy the whole van load or not at all. It was a fantastic deal: ten pounds a pair. They're over one hundred pounds in the shops. We could either take them, store them and sell them as and when, or, alternatively, we could have them delivered straight to a market trader and he'd give us twenty five quid a pair.'

'Mmm. You opted for the latter, I take it? Who arranged this?'

'Yeah. You remember Bob Nayar, played midfield for Spurs back in the Seventies when you had a season ticket?'

'Nope, can't say I do.'

'You do. You loved him.'

'No, but it hardly matters. Go on. How did you meet him?'

'Watching a youth training session over at Chigwell. The thing is, he isn't answering his phone. I don't know if I've got the right number, if he's changed it, or if he's lost his phone.'

'And you've given him a lot of money.'

No answer.

'What do you want to do?'

'I've found out where he lives. I want to know if he's playing me around, or if there's something else going on. I don't want to be dissing him otherwise.'

I feel like hitting him for this new language he's adopted.

'Will you come round and see him with me? You know, talk to him, and tell me what you think. I'll pick you up tomorrow.'

I could tell him what I think right this second. The trouble is, if Mo finds out he truly has been conned, it'll come to blows. 'What's wrong with doing it now?' I ask. 'We'll sort this out and then you can concentrate on my problems.'

'I didn't want to hassle you, but if you've got the time...'

I've got the time. 'Okay, but on one condition. No violence.'

It has never occurred to him, apparently.

We drive over to Epping in his new car, one of those little sporty convertible MGs. New clothes; new language; new car. I don't know.

We arrive at an impressive detached house with a long frontage. There is a 'Sold' sign by the gate. Mo gets out of the car, and is steaming up to the front door, before I have got my seat belt off. He has a vicious looking claw hammer sticking up from a tool belt he is wearing and his hand is moving towards it.

'Whoa! Stop right there,' I say as I catch up. 'What have you got that for?'

He is mystified, takes his hand off his hip and looks at me, declaring, 'I forgot to take it off. I've been hanging some pictures.'

The tool belt off and safely back in the car, Mo knocks on the door. A lady answers. She tells him that she and her husband are the new owners, that it is a re-possession following a divorce, and they don't know where the former owner lives.

At my suggestion Mo rings the estate agent. He then glumly reports, 'They say he's done a runner, and any money left over went to his wife.'

Driving back, Mo concertinas between loud anger and silent dismay. 'He's completely dicked me over. When I find him I gonna walk up to him, say, "Hello, remember me?" and then chin 'im!'

'Think about it, Mo. You don't have to get your revenge. He's lost his wife, lost his house, and lost any friends and respect he ever had. He'll owe money everywhere. What's a black eye compared to that?'

'That's not what you'd have said when I first knew you.'

'Let me take your mind off it, Mo. You're not the only one with a new love life, and you're not the only one with problems.'

He is not the best person for advice, but I can use him as a sounding board. 'I've met an old friend, a woman. Her name is Sam.'

'Sam. Of course, I know her. She's an airhead who doesn't wear knickers.'

'That's a bit harsh. Well, I bumped into her and I think we are going to go out … On a date.'

He looks alarmed. 'Get real! You can't do that. What about Carol?' He's a huge Carol admirer.

'Hold on! You can't go back to being old-fashioned on me right now. There's more. She has a son and I think I might be his father.'

'What are you talking about? When did you have this son? How can you do this to Carol? I wouldn't like to be in your shoes if she finds out.'

'It's not absolutely certain he is my son,' I admit.

'Are you telling me you are going to date her without knowing if he's your son? Don't worry about the botulism. I'll get some and force-feed you with it. How can you do this?'

'Suppose I am wrong. It'll ruin my chances if I ask beforehand.'

He looks at me like I belong under a toilet rim.

'Alright I'll do it, I'll do it. I'll ask her first. Who knows how much longer any of us is going to be around? Aren't I entitled to some fun in the meantime?'

'You're not going to last any time at all, at this rate, mate.'

71

'It's fine for you to be getting your leg over, I suppose.'

'That's not what's happening, that's not the way it is at all, Petey.'

'Tell me about it then.'

'I'm not going to dirty it with a conversation like this one. Some other time!'

'Really. Ready when you are.' Great, isn't it? I am getting a lecture from someone who was a virgin in their late forties on sensitivity in matters of romance. 'We've all got problems, apparently. You've had some help with one of yours and now it's my turn. Come up with this information on how to get hold of botulism, and don't take forever about it.' My parting words are, 'How hard can it be?'

For Elizabethan poets death was a metaphor for orgasms. I could be heading for both, but the interim that is now my life has acquired some compelling elements. Some are for the future I may not be having, but at least they are for the future. I might salivate at the thought of Sam, but I am beginning to feel a strong affection for her lad. Anyone would for their lost and found son. There are reasons for me to be in a hurry, especially where the boy is concerned. If he is to remember me, I'd rather it be as someone who is of some interest, someone who is not a brainless ghoul. As for the sex, well, I just feel with my diminishing responsibility that it shouldn't be a problem. Don't misunderstand me, I love my wife and will always. It is possible to say that there is a sort of passion there, namely compassion.

Sam rang me this morning, before I could ring her.

'Is your wife there?'

'Carol? No. Are you available sometime later this week? – after my check-up, that is.'

'Far out. With a little notice I am sure I can swing an afternoon off. We can have some fun.'

"Fun", that's intriguing. Asking about the paternity of her son may well end any hopes of "fun", but I suppose it has to be done. We are to meet in the pub just outside her workplace. She is unattached, although I would guess that she is attached loosely in several different directions, able to slip any tie she wants to. And me, why my decision to plunge in? There's only danger in the long run when complications get a chance to build up, and I have no long run. Besides, it isn't as though I'd be being unfaithful. I am not in a viable relationship.

Today is a big day. I found an innocuous parking space, half way down, no yellow lines, bays, etc; it must be unique. Descending Highgate Hill, I pass Waterlow Park in sunlight sprinkled between the trees. I go by St Peter's, and the school is emptying. Two little lads are embracing as they walk. Some Horn of Africa kids sway by with tall, slim elegance. Their grandparents are thousand of miles away, yet they are thriving without them.

As I get nearer to the Whittington, it is as it so often is, teeming with traffic wardens and I think what an absolute mess modern life can be. The pavements here are about a foot above a road that is usually hectically busy. I carefully step down, close my eyes and wander out. There is a screech of air-brakes and a hooter. I carry on over the road at a point that is exceptionally wide and where virtually no one crosses. It is impossible that I won't be hit. I have scared a lorry driver and he is cursing me. Somebody is calling out 'Lunatic' and I hear a scream. I can smell the exhaust fumes of a motor bike as it swerves from one lane to another to avoid me. I am almost curious enough to open my eyes. On I go and suddenly, wham! I am sent

73

flying. There is pain and a sense of shock. I am definitely conscious.

My shin is gouged where I have tripped over the edge of the pavement on the far side. One or two passers-by are heading to assist me. I take a look behind me; the road is virtually empty of traffic. I smooth the odd crease, remove some dust and limp towards the appointment I must keep. The world is full of opportunities to kill yourself, but they're frequently not good ones. This would have been a little premature and I don't believe I was serious. I wouldn't do that to any driver after all.

At the hospital my intention is to feel my way with the lad. There is no point in antagonizing him. What is more, I should not get carried away: I've got a grandchild in prospect and that sense of procreation could be colouring my belief that I have a son. After all, his mother always had lots of different affairs and casual liaisons going on at once. Statistically I am not likely to be his father.

I don't know quite how I'm feeling as I enter the clinic, so much is going on. It may be promise is there.

Sam's son comes to get me from the row of linked metal chairs, and calls me by my first name, which may be unique. Once I'm in the treatment room he greets me, repeating my name.

'You know my name then.'

'It's on the forms, but actually my mother told me you used to be pretty close.'

'Very, in fact. Did she say much more about me?'

'Only that you were worth my while knowing, and that I could be seeing a lot more of you. We don't talk much.'

'What's your name?'

'She said you would want to know. It's Oliver.'

'You must talk more than you think.'

'Not really. It's usually a bit of shouting and then we avoid each other for weeks on end.'

I am a driven man, so I ask, 'What do you argue about?'

'Oh, just about everything: paying your way, being grown up, taking responsibility.'

'Far be it from me to interfere,' which is always my foreword to interfering, 'but she probably has got a point you know. I used to say much the same to my own children.'

'Not me! Her! She's the one getting the advice and I am the one giving it!'

That stings. Conversation stops, and it is awkward, but he breaks the silence.

'So you have a family of your own?' I believe he's as driven as me. 'I'm sure you have children, haven't you? I bet they've had a conventional upbringing. You will have given them a solid and stable home, and no doubt they'll have had normal, ordinary schooling.'

'We've tried to do our best.'

'Exactly. You will have been worthwhile parents.'

"Issues". I think that's how they say it. The lad has got issues and he is sensitive.

Going about his business, his manner is informal and reassuring. He knows what he is doing. I don't know why I thought him so androgynous looking; it's only that he's youthfully handsome. I notice the hands that he is going to lay on me. Like me, he has an exceptionally short little finger. Those hands are strong enough.

As I lay on the trolley he says, 'Let's just turn you around shall we?' It is to get a different angle for the scan. 'I'm sorry about the gel; it's a bit cold I'm afraid.' He seems to be relaxing more in my company.

'It's freezing, but that's just tough luck on me.'

He is having to lean over at an awkward angle with the scanning device.

'That must give you a backache,' I say.

'Don't worry, I'm used to it.'

I am feeling self-conscious, but push on, 'So your mother told you we are old friends?'

'Yes, she said you knew each other virtually up until the day I was born.' With that he puts down whatever instrument he was handling, turns and stands staring intently at me. A countless number of short breaths from me, and he is still staring right into my eyes. On his face there is an excruciating look. My tongue might as well be in an iron clamp. This is the opportunity I most wanted, and I will have few others.

'How does it look?' I ask, referring to the scan.

He is lost and then recovers. 'Look for yourself,' he says turning abruptly.

I focus on the screen; it looks marvellous. There it is, pulsating away, the heart I might never otherwise see. Best of all, the valve looks frayed and fragile.

'Don't worry, Peter. It is fine; you'll live a long time.'

This news does not depress me, because of the way he delivers it. His tone is more than kind, it is caring.

'Don't you have much to do with your mother?'

'We might work in the same building, but no, I don't. I don't see much of her or my half sister.'

'You don't live at home?'

'I've got a room in a house on a corner of Muswell Hill Road.' He gives me the number and tells me to call round if I get worried over my heart. I imagine that is a first.

'I'm only ten minutes from where you live,' he tells me, 'and I'm kind of doing my own studies, examinations, you know.' He's obviously taken the trouble to read my notes carefully. I doubt that I'll be able to put the question now, but round at his place might be the spot.

'I suppose you don't go round your Mum's house often.' I'm making chat, wanting us to be on casual talking terms.

'No way. I went round there once with a girlfriend and it was crawling with all sorts. It's a drop-in centre for anybody from far and wide. I was so happy to get away from there. You couldn't organize your life in that place. Never again! I have things I want to do and being there would hold anyone back.'

That didn't go well.

'Girlfriend, you say?' It had occurred to me that he could be gay. 'Surely with family it's worth a second try.'

He breathes in and lets out a sigh big enough to fill a sail, and stares at me again. This is a discussion any father and son might find difficult. 'I've a new girlfriend who is a bit special and who has problems with her father. I don't think it would work for either of us to be lumbered with meeting each other's parents at the moment! I'm on pretty heavy evening courses at college too, so there's no time for humouring impossible parents.'

Am I one? I could be irritating him.

'I am going to do a medical degree, although I might have left it a bit late to be a doctor.'

He looks like a teenager. Then again, everyone under forty looks young to me these days. 'Nonsense, you are only just about old enough. People who go in for that sort of thing with a bit of experience behind them, and real desire, get the most out of it.' That pleases him. 'Your father must be proud of you.' In for a penny, in for a pounding. But he doesn't bristle. Quite the contrary, he looks so forlorn I want to embrace the lad.

'Even if he were here now, how could I be sure

I'd know him? I think I am narrowing it down. At one stage I thought there was a queue of candidates crossing several land masses. Sometimes I just think I'm okay as I am. Do I really need a cavorting sperm donor from three decades ago?'

His face says he does, but it hurts to hear him say that. It could be he is deliberately having a dig at me. For a moment I was at the tiller, but I have beached myself. There is no chance of pursuing this any further at the moment.

'So what is your next move?'

He is happy to tell me he is going to run the department at the Royal Free; he takes up the post in under a week. It is a step forward and will look good on his c.v. His smile breaks into a grin revealing a gap between his two front teeth, identical to my own. He goes into greater detail than I need about the individual stages of his career. I want to say more to him, but it has become too awkward and I could make myself look a gibbering idiot, something I excel at. Finally he opens up the subject I am not here for.

'My mother clearly sees you as a boyfriend. I've given this advice before and it's been useless, but I'm going to give it anyway. She's worthless and she's trouble. Save yourself the grief.'

'She's different, that's all,' is the best thing I can think of to say.

'Yes, totally different. Are you still with your wife?'

It's not on my notes, so I tell him I am.

'She will tell her. She will you know. It's her version of being free and liberated.'

I understand why he is bitter, but I knew his mother long before he did, and she is simply not that vindictive. That is what my memory is clearly telling me.

VII

My wife blesses me with an unsolicited pint of Adnam's ale. There's a golden half light in the Spaniards Inn with a warm smell of venerable beer slops ascending from the carpet. You could be certain that sufferers have come here ever since yeast met hops and sugar. Instead of her usual glass of mineral water, Carol has a gin and tonic. I am grateful, but curious,

'What's the occasion?'

'I rang the hospital to tell them we could be an hour or more late. The consultant can't wait, but he will fit us in same time next week.'

'That's good of him…I expect he has to see his private patients now.'

'That makes no difference at all. I thought you'd be pleased with the pint.' I tilt my glass to her. I wouldn't mind a reprieve, but this is just a brief stay of execution. I do not understand the workings of her mind, or her body for that matter, but my wife has been a rock in all this. Yet it had little impact when she told me she was leaving.

I could not swear to it, but I think when my wife turned to me the other night she might have meant to make love. We had not had sex for months and when we actually did it was as it always was. The manner of it simply confirmed the state of our relationship. More on-tepid than on-heat. The morning after the deed she had joked, 'Did the bed move for you, dear?' That about said it all for me: I produced poor quality goods. She and I both know the score: below average in our case.

Alright, her leaving will not be forever or to the ends of the physical world. It is only to go on a course in France for a few weeks, but as far as our emotions are concerned, there has been a continental drift taking place for some time. All that while back the sex we had was a close cousin of a one-off. I am not sure my wife enjoyed a climax. Who knows, I can't tell anything in any way any more. It is not a blow, it is not news and I'm pretty used to it. I'm not sure where we are on the orgasm count anyway. As often as not I've been faking mine, once Carol has had hers. It has occurred to me, however, that she might have been faking hers when she thinks I'm set to have mine. It could be that all we've been engaged in is the occasional bout of polite sexual shadow boxing, going tamely through the motions, but never making a connection. Perhaps I should have taken the risk, and responded to her. On the other hand, I don't mind her going; she is not the sole seeker of different scenes.

The bell goes and my daughters enter.

'Hi,' says Linda and hugs and kisses me while Sylvia walks past.

Carol announces, 'Don't forget I am leaving tomorrow, and don't forget...'

She's going to tomorrow. I knew that was the day, did I?

'...Linda and Sylvia are around, if you need help.'

'Staying here?'

'Don't be silly, but they are not far away, are they?'

It's a wonder they haven't got power of attorney over me.

'You've hardly listened to a word I've been saying, have you? Well, if you look in the kitchen there are post-it notes for using the washing machine and the dishwasher. By the telephone there are notes on paying bills, especially the electricity, which you've forgotten twice already. You are going to have to ring them and make a card payment ASAP. You'll be in trouble if you forget again. By the computer there are details from Dell and P.C. World for a new set-up. Remember you've promised to take that old thing to the recycling.'

'The cooker?'

'No, the computer. There's nothing wrong with the cooker. It's pretty new.'

I believe I was aware of that. 'I actually meant what about using the cooker?' I am lying. I am annoyed, though, because she may well be taking advantage of me here. I don't believe I agreed to do anything about our computer.

'There are post-it notes there, too.'

I turn to Linda. 'Did you know your mother was going to France?'

'Yes!' snaps Sylvia.

'Great, isn't it?' Linda says.

'Yes. Yes, I suppose it is. Good for her.' I try to sound enthusiastic.

'Now listen,' Carol commands, 'I spoke to Julie, your cousin. She is taking a break after all this time. You might like to keep track of your uncle in that home. The number is in our address book.'

She couldn't be more wrong. There is no way I would "like" such a thing. I thought I had told her I have already been, but perhaps not. As if I'd want to go again so soon. If I do decide to go, that will be up to me.

I don't know about the heart, but absence makes my mind grow distracted. My wife and I pecked a kiss goodbye, and off she went on Euro tunnel. It felt oddly final, in spite of her saying, 'I'll ring, and don't forget...' For once I was aware of not listening.

My wife rings when I have dozed off in front of the TV. It is a little after midnight, gone one in the morning where she is. I can hear a voice or voices in the background.

81

'Where are you?'

'France, dopey, in my bedroom.' She sounds tipsy. I am glad she has rung; I am feeling a little lonely.

'What can I do for you?'

'Remember…,' I think she is pausing to sip something, 'Remember your appointment with the cardiac consultant. Do you know when it is?'

'Two o'clock tomorrow?'

'Right time, wrong day.'

'My heart's been fine just recently. The next day? The following day?'

'Go and check the calendar. It's on there. Make sure you go to the appointment, and let yourself sleep of a night time. You'll only lie awake worrying over what it might be otherwise.'

And then we said goodbye.

I get to PC World and back within an hour. My mind wasn't on it, so I've ended up without a printer. You get sucked in at one price, only to find out an entire package is half as much again.

I'm trying to set the thing up, so I ring Linda for some assistance. Her advice is clear, but she is called back to the work she was doing and I make little progress on my own. I have to ring the help line. The fibre optic must be glowing with all the different options I have to select from. Eventually I pay fifty pence a minute to speak to someone an alphabet or two away. They are amazingly third world restrained and polite. What they enable me to do is limited, but it is part of what I am after. I summon up the web and type in "botulism". The first entry on a long, long list is from E Bay. They apparently do it cheaper than anybody else. Having discovered this to be untrue I spend some time going down the list. The nearest I can get to a supplier of botulism is someone offering a vaccine. Instead I type in suicide and E bay comes up first again. Once more there is not much of interest except for one entry which says:

'DON'T DO IT. 'I've been there. Life is good. With God's help I'll show you how. www. strongfaith. net.'

If God indeed existed, he'd be to blame, the giver of life no matter what its quality.

I press loads of keys in disgust, the screen goes blank and I can do nothing with it.

I resort to the only truly reliable help line I have. I ring Linda again. She takes a break to come and see to me.

'Don't worry, Pops.' She has it working in no time and sticks in a CD to give me word processing. 'Let's have some bagels while that loads.' She has bought them at the deli. 'Looks like you might need some more software. I can fetch it from work, although not today. It's illegal, but that's just up your street isn't it? When I come I'll set up your email properly'

'How's the baby?'

'So, so. No probs, not really.'

I'll always regret not pressing her on that. Instead I ask, 'And are there any developments with the father?'

'You never know. I could be moving in with him soon and then the mystery will be over won't it? Now, eat the bagels I brought.' They are smoked salmon and cream cheese. Delicious. After too short a time, she kisses me and goes back to work. I have time to spare so I pick up my father's diary which has become my favourite reading (one thing amongst many others you will probably find me repeating). He seems to have forgotten his former handwriting style and everything is now in upper case.

MY SON SAYS HE CANNOT UNDERSTAND

WHY FLOWER POWER FAILED AND INTERFLORA FLOURISHED. YET WHEN HE WAS A LAD HE WANTED TO JOIN THE ARMY. I DO NOT KNOW WHAT HE IS TALKING ABOUT. I DAREN'T TELL HIM THAT. HE WILL THINK I NEED TO BE PUT IN ONE OF THOSE HOMES.

The final s is smudged, twisting like a faint blue snake down the page, because at some stage a tear had fallen on it. He no longer understood me; around about that time my daughter ceased to understand me as well. I remember her protests, 'You cannot do this, Dad, this is just not right.' Well I went and did it, and it turned out to be a terrible thing. Immediately after I did it she told me, 'I will never talk to you again.' Morally she has kept her word. What is more, I can hardly blame her. I acknowledge I committed an awful wrong. All I can say is that it was out of character and, given the chance again, I will not repeat it.

Certainly I will not allow it to be done to me. I do believe I will find the way out before too long. I hope that I can hang on until I see my first grandchild, but there will be no point if I can't grasp that it is my grandchild.

I've had the rarity of a goodnight's sleep. Fifteen minutes to go and I am unsteady. I can detect my pulse in my mouth with my upper teeth knocking against the bottom. It is racing, foundering and racing again. I'm too old for this, but hell, I'm on my way out so I have little to lose. If I am not careful I will begin to tremble like a pubescent youth. I am waiting in the pub for Sam to arrive. Queen's I want to Break Free is blaring out, while I sip tomato juice with tons of Tabasco. I am musing over the life I have with my wife. It is like one of those slow exposure photographic slides of night traffic.

84

You can trace every route taken, but can erase one path only by turning off the power to the lot.

My mind is totally lust skewed. Am I thinking consequences? Family? Hardly. I have overdone the Tabasco and it is burning my throat. I'll have to start on wine. I normally avoid drinking at lunchtime - it ruins me, especially in the bedroom. First I have to go to the gents.

I carefully zip up and slowly wash my hands. I am waiting for the instant when the toilet will be empty. I hold the door open for an old boy with a stick to go out. I feel like a perv hanging around the condom machine. The second coin goes in, and sure enough in comes a youngster. He looks at me as though I don't belong here doing this. He offers, 'As long as she is a good clean woman.' It's an Irish accent. What a fecking eejit! The machine is dated and when the handle turns the noise is incredible. I collect some Mates and read the legend on the front of the dispenser, 'Feeling is everything.' It will have to be, because thinking is neither here nor there when it comes to sex. Sexual passion is a form of temporary insanity. Compared to it, love is quite logical.

While I sip my drink, Sam rings to tell me she'll be here in two minutes. She wants me to wait at the doorway in order to see her in to the pub. She arrives wearing a waisted, short black leather jacket with some studs and chains on it, a medium length black skirt, black leggings and black leather boots. Sex and death; she could have had it tattooed on her knuckles. It works for me. She looks so complaisant, and sways Gauguinesque hips at me. As she gets to the door and its etched glass, she turns, deftly manoeuvring me between the two sides of the frame. It's clear she wants to kiss, so now we have to. It is not muscular, but I can feel it all the way to the back of my jaw. We are not grappling; our hands are hardly upon each other. The

85

doorway is a master stroke, because it forces our bodies close against each other. She is pressing against me. The kiss goes on; I can feel her body, and she must be able to feel mine. Blood swollen parts are reaching out to each other. Two men are trying to come in so we squeeze through the entrance, me avoiding their eyes and her not caring less.

We come to a table and I nearly knock a chair over, but she manages to catch it. She leans over, smelling powerfully of a scent that must be all pheromones, and puts her right hand on the top of mine. I am gently eased down with a kiss on the neck. A circuit is made and the charge runs through me. I mean to ask if she wants port which used to be all she would have. Instead I am struck dumb with lust, like a nervous teenager wanting to be carried away on a sea of seminal fluid. My left leg is shaking.

'Don't move, Peter, I'll fetch myself something.' I pass her a fiver, and she brings back an advocaat with a cherry in it. It ain't sophisticated, but it is evocative. It is thick and mucousy yellow, with a blob of red; primary colours of the body.

'This always was my favourite,' she says. Must have been someone else who used to like port, my wife perhaps.

'What is that?' I ask, as I reach over and fumble at her lapel. I'm referring to what looks like heather in her buttonhole. 'Gypsy luck,' she laughs. 'An old lover started me on it.'

I don't mind the mention of old lovers. Our knees nuzzle each other under the bench.

'You have a lover, don't you? You must have because you can't stay married so long without one. Everybody has a lover.'

'Do they?' I can't say no, it would make me look like a sexual simpleton.

'I can't believe you're still with that woman.

What was her name, Carol? How long have you been together?'

'For two grown up children and a lot of years.'

'I thought she'd go off with that big handsome young guy who was a friend of yours. She must have had lovers.' It had never occurred to me. 'I could give her a ring. It'll be a gas.'

'What for?'

'I'll find out for you if she has had lovers. No, just kidding. She's an old friend.'

It's true; Carol has known Sam at least as long as me, going way back to when they were mates in the sixties. I fiddle with the condoms in my pocket, and can hear a high pitched whistle, coming from no particular direction. Blood pressure is affecting my inner ear. I am a novice here and try to substitute having nothing to say by saying almost anything. It's mostly nonsense. She carries on along the track she's already started.

'Getting together is in our stars, you know.'

I hardly know what star sign I am, but I accept I have to climb on board if I want to go on this trip. 'We're not star crossed lovers I hope.' She doesn't seem to catch that, so I ask, 'Would you like another drink?'

'I'll finish this one first,' she replies.

I am blundering here, but she is all smiles and appreciation. Somewhere in there she slips in a tale about her multiple orgasms.

'Have you ever had a multiple orgasm?'

I have trouble with the single version, but I am relaxed now, so I can reply, 'I am more of a giver than a receiver.'

Sam doesn't respond directly, but comes out with come-hither wit of her own. I am ready to follow her lead. I don't know the path at all well, but I can see the gate to it is wide open.

My phone bleeps with a message from Mo. In the subdued light of the pub the screen of my mobile is bright. 'Ask her!' it says. Sure. All it doesn't do is tell me how.

'I saw Oliver for a heart scan. He is your son isn't he? That is him, isn't it?' Romance may lead to offspring, but talk of offspring can kill any prospect of romance. Every bit as bad, I've reminded her of my health situation. No woman finds the idea of an under-par man arousing. 'He gave me the all clear, by the way,' I quickly get in.

'Heart scans, did you say? Everybody is having those scans these days. They're just a precaution, but I don't believe in them, anyway. You can tell if someone is ill by their aura.'

She seems to be reluctant to discuss the lad, so I ask yet again, 'The good looking lad doing them, he is your son, isn't he? I have got it right, haven't I?'

'So you did notice him. He's uptight about loads of things. Did he look familiar enough to make bells ring when you saw him?' She's making this easier than I thought.

'Should he be familiar?'

She doesn't seem to hear me and simply says, 'He'll get himself together, sooner or later. I can wait.'

'Do tell me, why should he look familiar?'

She doesn't answer.

My volume goes up. 'Do I know his father?'

She hears me and so do the half a dozen drinkers in the pub. 'Can't tell you if I haven't told him yet, can I?' she says, leading me to wonder if she is playing silly games.

I am about to be even more direct when my phone goes again. It is Mo sending the same text once more. Stuff him!

'All this is too heavy for a day like this,' Sam says and places her hand on my leg. 'Do you spend a lot of time apart from your wife? Perhaps I should ring her and swap notes.'

I do not know if she hasn't heard me or is avoiding the subject. If I wasn't light-headed with desire I might think harshly of that, but right now it has no impact. If she can ignore my awkward questions I'll ignore hers.

'Love, it's important to have passion. I must have passion,' she carries on.

It's facile, but I match her. 'Yes, the world needs love, and peace of course.'

She is pleased with that, picks up the baton and runs with it, telling me about her travels. 'I lived with a shaman in Ecuador, once…'

On it goes and I lose track. Geography and affairs pair up, as though there is a filing system somewhere so they can be cross referenced. There are tons of characters from her love annals and it is easy listening. I vaguely imply that I've had the odd liaison. She takes my hand again, and again her touch is high voltage.

'That's your love line. See that?' she laughs as she runs her finger along my hand, stopping at an indentation. My own fingers curl and close on it for a moment. 'Do you know what that shows?'

It actually shows where I accidentally stabbed myself with a screwdriver years ago. I am hoping she sees something deeply sexual there.

'It would be very naughty to tell you what that means,' she says.

'No, don't stop there!'

'It's a stallion's hoof mark which means you are beautifully hung.'

By the neck until dead. It's a thought I won't dwell on. Like I say, I stabbed myself with a screwdriver. If she could really read palms she'd see an abrupt end to the life line, but I'll go happily with the love theme for now. I am clear: I am desired. This confidence allows me to rattle on in a pretty entertaining

89

way. I am looking forward to slaving over a hot woman.

My phone bleeps once more. Mo has re-sent his text, with additions, 'Ask her! Ask her! Ask her!'

That's become a low priority. I am not going to risk the probability of tremendous sex, for the possibility, and that's at most what it is, that Oliver is my son. Mo really is annoying me.

I have to get a glass of wine, but she won't have another one, which should forewarn me. Still, I'm committed. Booze may lower my pleasure, but it enhances my performance.

'Do you smoke?' she asks, producing a joint from her handbag.

I knock my drink, spilling some, and she laughs. Goodness knows how much she would laugh if I actually did something funny.

She puts her joint away saying, 'I shouldn't, not right now. It's for you and me on another day.'

I don't understand what she is talking about, and attempt to retrieve the situation.

'Come on, you must have something. There's not much harm in a second drink, is there?'

'Slimline tonic, please. It's a drag. I couldn't swing the time off. I'm covering for a friend, so I'm doing a double shift.'

I come back without Sam's drink and have to ask what it is again. She tells me to leave it; she has got to be at work in ten minutes. The imminence of this leaves me forlornly squeezing the condoms in my pocket.

'Don't worry,' she assures me, 'we'll get plenty of chances. You can see me out, if you want.'

I do want because I know there will be a repeat manoeuvre in the doorway.

We separate, otherwise she will be late. 'See you – soon,' she says and goes. I return to my seat to sip what's left of the wine, but before I can start the phone rings. It is Mo yet again, but this time in person, urging me to do the right thing.

I have nothing to lose so I rush outside, but already Sam is too far away for conversation. 'When? When? When will we meet?' I shout towards her.

She cups her ear and shakes her head. 'Give my regards to Carol,' she mouths, and then she circles the palm of one hand with the index finger of the other. Of course I'll ring.

That night I fall asleep unusually quickly, but not for long. The phone wakes me. Before I can speak, Sam asks, 'Is that Carol?' Then she laughs, 'That got your attention.'

The reception on her phone is terrible. Her friend is going to return the favour by doing one of her shifts. We struggle, but finally make another arrangement to meet.

I am a daylight optimist, and night is never a good time for me, but a disrupted night is truly bad news. If an insect flapping its wings on one side of the world can cause chaos on the other, what can an affair do to personal relationships? The strain could shatter my family bonds once and for all. All night long I am in and out of dreams where characters with blazing lights come to interrogate me. The only thing missing is water-boarding.

Morning comes. I put my feet on the floor and stagger forwards. My sight is early morning bleary and any threats are dulled. Why worry? Butterflies don't live long and neither should I. Practically, I don't have a wife to lose and in this new relaxed era there is no need for my grown up daughters to over react. There needn't be consequences, especially when I've got condoms. If I do have sex with Sam, and lust is posting excitement all over my body, there is no reason why it should go any further. She is a grown up woman for whom loving and moving on with no fuss is a way of being.

My mobile is making one of its annoying noises.

It is a new text from Mo.

He's text, text, text these days. 'Dd u ask her? Wt was ansr?' He's doing it like my daughters do. Using my best non-predictive text I reply. I give the subject due weight and consideration, 'Bllcks, dd I!' I could have added that I intend to get to it very soon, but didn't.

What I also could have texted to Mo was a demand to know when he would meet me with the information I've asked for, but I'm all thumbs and thumbs when it comes to those little keys. Exceptional enjoyment is shortly to be mine, but I am not stupid, not entirely, not just yet. There is no recovery from Alzheimer's, merely the odd and temporary respite. If I am to do more than randomly feint at a decent end, I need help, and he could be in a position to supply it. I ring Mo back and make my demand. He has clearly got other things to occupy himself, so he gives me the briefest assurance, 'Yeah, yeah. I've got it covered, bro,' and signs off.

I have nothing better to do, so I pore over my father's diary. After a point, each succeeding page has just one line. I read:

> F'ING HAVE LEFT IT TOO LATE
> F'ING FANTASY, F'ING, F'ING
> LEFT IT TOO LATE
> F'ING NIGHTMARE   F'ING LATE
> TOO LATE   IT'S TOO LATE

Somehow he must have worked it out, knew what I was going to do with him. Whatever memories of mine fade it will be a blessing if this one goes.

Even if it does, there will be Sylvia to remind me. 'I'll never forgive you. You will never forgive yourself,' she said, and she was right.

VIII

We are spending a long time in the Spaniards Inn, largely because I am dragging it out, savouring it as long as possible. If I had the power of reflection I wouldn't care to go into Carol's kindness and tolerance towards me whilst we are here. With any sense I would realise that this is that unsolicited unilateral giving that only occurs with love. If I have become a diminished man, then how much less will I be without her?

How I handled my first crisis after she'd gone to France is an indication.

If you think you have got a good memory then try finding your way around your own home in the dark. My wife has gone and so too has the electricity. It's happened before. The board or whatever they call themselves these days usually don't take long to get it up and running again, so I sit here waiting for the power cut to finish.

After two hours I go over to the window, open the curtains and look outside. Everybody else's lights are on.

'Carol,' I say, having rung her, 'we've got a problem with the wiring. Our house is blacked out and nothing is working.' She is there, but all I hear is a sigh. 'Carol, Carol can you hear me?'

'Oh yes, yes I can. Making yourself heard is not a problem for you, though listening to others is.'

I've done something wrong, I guess, but this really isn't the moment to be telling me.

'You were supposed to ring the electricity supplier and make a card payment, and you haven't, have you?'

I'm damned if I know. If I've forgotten, I've forgotten.

'I'm sure I did,' I lie. 'Anyway I don't know what

to do now. What do I do?'

'There are always emergency teams. You'll have to ring them and see what can be done. Just plead age or illness and see what they'll do. Tell them you're a pensioner and you're getting cold. That should do it.'

I thank her for the advice and put down the phone. It is useless: I don't even know who our electricity supplier is. It isn't like the old days when there was only one. In the dark I'll never be able to find the relevant papers. I go to the gas hob to boil some water for tea, and send the ironing board and iron flying. I also knock the scab off my barely healing shin.

I give up on the tea and carefully feel my way back to the sofa, nevertheless tripping over a small coffee table. I lie flat and think in the pitch black, a light I can always examine things more clearly in. What a low state I have been brought to. I still remember nothing of the electricity supplier or any contact I am supposed to have made with them. I doze off and have dreams that agitate me. There should be some hot water, and there is, so I run a bath. I'll never find my clean clothes, so after the bath I put on a dressing gown hanging on the bathroom door, which happens to be one of my wife's. I lie on the sofa again. After some tranquil time there is a knock on the door. I go down the stairs warily, because there was a spate of violent burglaries a couple of years or so back, and this is not a good time of night to answer the door.

'Who is it?' I ask as I peek through the fisheye lens in my front door. The face does not look to be one I know, but then nobody's would through one of these. I am able to spot he has something heavy in his hand though. The voice answers and I do not recognize it. It is a stranger. 'Just a minute I say,' and make my way back up the stairs. I am looking for something: a weapon, houses are full of them. Fifty per cent of the

94

stuff could be handed in at the police station under any amnesty. I crack my shin again, and settle for the iron. That should crease any assailant.

I open the door and sure enough a big guy is there with something in his hand, and it looks heavy and it could in fact be a truncheon. He sees blood, literally - because it is trickling down my shin. I raise my iron and he smiles and reminds me that I helped him a year ago to find a job. It doesn't sound likely; I don't have those skills any more. He explains that I helped him by giving him money to travel for a job. He has been made redundant, and now sees no alternative but to go back home to his own country. He is selling paintings. Other people have bought some and he doesn't need much more money. He looks me up and down in the street light. I put the iron down, search the pockets of the dressing gown, which only produces a shower cap and a bra, and tell him I don't think I can help him. He looks at me quizzically and steps forward, his nose almost touching mine. One tilt back of his head and a quick forward thrust and he will butt me.

'Hey, no problem,' he says, 'maybe next time.' We shake hands, and he says, 'Take care,' looking at my weeping shin as he goes.

I pick up the iron, struggle across the kitchen, plug it back in, fail to find the board and curse as the iron smacks on to our wooden table surface. Me, my lumps and bumps, the iron in my hand and in a woman's dressing gown; obviously I was in no position to help him.

'Say I've got dementia,' I suggest to Linda. I'm bored by the dark and have rung her for help, confident she'll know which company we're with. She makes the call. Not too much later an emergency crew has done something, and the lights are on.

It is now late, but having dozed I am no longer able to sleep. I change, and leave without tidying the

95

mess I've created. I go for an aimless stroll, limping and rubbing my forehead wound. As for sending the ironing board flying, I had not long been ironing a shirt there, so I should have realized exactly where it was. There are bright lights in a late opening pub and I am drawn towards them. This one will actually do me a cup of tea.

Following my tea I make a circuit of the walk home and manage to laugh at the lumps and bumps I have given myself. Then, suddenly, it hits me: I've left the iron as it was! I have a habit of putting the iron down still switched on. That iron has now been face down on the table where it fell for more than hour. I start to run, but can't continue, so walk as quickly as I can.

Too late. As I near home I hear sirens. Too late it may be, but those sirens are not for my house, whether they are needed or not. I rush up to the door and can definitely smell burning. Inside an alarm is screeching and acrid-smelling smoke fills the house. I struggle past obstacles to the sink and fill a bowl with water. I throw it over the iron and the smouldering patch of wood it is on. Bang goes the fuse and over goes the imbecile who is the cause of all this as I try to head for the fuse box in the dark. I've been there so many times I should be able to do better.

IX

Sometimes I just don't know. More than sometimes. The journey back from The Spaniards should have been, if not joyful, then balmy. I had been lavished with three pints, which were mellowing away inside me, and I'd been saved the showdown at the hospital. What do I want? An easy get out.

I haven't yet shaved and showered, but having replaced my iron I have pressed my shirt, and feel pleased with the job. I stand naked in front of the wardrobe mirror. My flesh has so many lumps, bumps and blemishes that my skin is starting to feel like bubble wrap. With a specialised cutter to trim hair nurseries in my ears and nose, a razor and some deodorant I'll have to do my best. I'll take some sugar free gum for my breath, the condoms, some tissues and some indigestion tablets as a precaution. Some of the lust is disappearing beneath a logistical exercise. 'I've a duty to do.' I tell myself, 'and I am going to do my best to meet the challenge.' It's all quite honourable, really. I wonder if the older Casanova staggered to a liaison, simply looking to put in a good performance to preserve his infamy. The real trick will be to manage a slick enough ruse for returning to my own bed. If I am to fidget, fart, medicate and agonize over what is done, I want to do it there, unencumbered, and in dedicated terrain.

I expect my journey to Leicester Square to be an excited one. Instead strangely subdued spirits carry me to the hollow noises and low voltage light of my local tube station, where I join the shuffle down the escalator. My heart is beating erratically. I wander in, choose my spot and perch with my toes over the edge of the platform, swaying slightly. After initially glancing at the

97

two dark holes at either end of the platform, I finally look down at the glistening live rail and wonder. The risk of any true adventure is the possibility of annihilation. As the rail begins humming I start singing the Hobo's Lullaby. I guess I've been letting things drift slowly by and still am. I am swaying more and there is a draught on my face, which could as well be the last breath of leapers from Beachy Head. In fact it is the breeze of the train entering the station. I see the driver looking at me with terror on his face, but he's got it wrong. I wouldn't do that to a working man.

I step backwards and then mount the carriage. I read a science article in the Metro that is on my seat. Life is amazing; there aren't any final paths that you can't be dislodged from. The article reckons that electrons can shift from one circuit to another instantaneously. I am not convinced, but if it is only partly true, then what can happen for one part of the physical universe can happen for another. The doom of the years, the daunting tumble downhill, can be set aside by the ability of life to detach anyone in particular from the given path, for no matter how short a time. I have reached a hiatus, and it is no ordinary hiatus. It is so long that it is close to being definitive; it is nearly an end, and therefore nearly a beginning is conceivable. Anyway, I am here now. Well not quite. I can't precisely remember where we are supposed to meet.

I meander from place to place, but can't catch sight of her. She'll have to spot me. I buy yet another Big Issue and sit down to read it while I wait. The café I am at is the most probable candidate, being across the road from a cut price ticket office. I haven't exactly forgotten about Oliver, but the rush of blood to my loins will let that idle for a while longer. I don't care how many times Mo rings me, I won't be asking her today. Not, that is, before the coital act anyway. There she is. She's wearing a headband with, with…

She sees my face. 'Flowers in my hair,' she announces. It's a good job we're in theatre land. 'Do you remember the girl who put a flower down the barrel of a trooper's gun?' she asks.

'Yes, that picture went all round the world.'

We kiss and she sits next to me. We look at the menu and it all feels very continental.

While she fiddles with her exotic earring, I offer, 'That was a great statement for the peace movement, when...' I am inexplicably breathless for a moment. And then I am going on to complete what I am saying, but can't because she cuts across it.

'It was a great personal statement.' She puts an index finger to her temple, and says, 'The revolution is in here.'

I buy tickets for The Rat Pack.

'Sinatra and Dean Martin. This is music to screw by,' says Sam, and I am not arguing. 'You always did have broad taste,' she tells me.

We've got an hour until the show, but we'll get there fifteen minutes early. We're having salads and wine. I'm a little restrained, but Sam has reached under the table and is doing things I could go to prison for.

'There is an offer on a hotel just down the road which has a sauna, whirlpool and a *water bed*,' I inform her. I pay up and drag Sam towards the hotel I have in mind.

'No, no, too boooourgeois,' she says as we reach it. 'Besides, I've got the best spot for a love-in; we're going back to my house after the show. That's where to get it together.' Apparently the house was ceded to her by an old lover.

Conversations with her are strange. I thought we'd just agreed on the hotel. I had a pretext for leaving a hotel by midnight, but now I'll have to ad lib an excuse back at hers. I hope Oliver doesn't change his mind and drop by his mother's. That would probably be the end of

99

my ardour.

I buy a couple of rounds of drinks in the interval. Sam and I have been necking as she calls it. The mohair suits and casual smoking of Sinatra and co look chic, and the Burelli Sisters, who are the backing group, have my attention. At the end, Sammy Davis Jnr renders, What Kind of Fool Am I. I am primed.

'Zowie, my daughter, is cooking,' Sam tells me on the way to her place.

'Zoe?'

She just gives me a look and says, 'Zowie.'

I can't believe this; her daughter is going to be there!

We arrive at a huge, under-tended looking building. The door is ajar. There is a guy in his thirties going up the stairs, and a woman at the top of three flights having a loud conversation with some others on the landing. I stare.

'They're friends.'

The voice is that of a young woman who has to be Sam's daughter.

'Yours?'

'Some are Sam's, some are mine, some are friends of friends and some…we don't know.'

'Exactly how many are here?' Mother and daughter both shrug their shoulders. We go up past unofficial bed-sits to an unself-contained flat.

The daughter kisses me. 'I'm Zowie, Peter. How was the show? Sam says you're a friend from way back.'

She knows all about me, and probably what I am playing at.

'Come on.' She takes me by the hand and sits me down. 'Would you like a drink?'

Sam has disappeared for the moment. I don't want to appear boring, but I can't have more alcohol, yet. 'Oh something herbal,' I say. The room has an old

Indian carpet on the wall, a hookah in one corner, two prints on the opposite wall, and a huge poster of Jimi Hendrix with the line, "There must be some way outa here", along the bottom. Pinned on the adjoining wall is a ragged cover of a record album. It is Transformer, an early one by Lou Reed. There is a black abstract sculpture in a corner; it is unmistakably a tribute to fecundity. And hell, where is Sam? The settee I've been left on has old style Habitat covers. I don't know how much longer I can sit here. I want to pace the floor. I feel like I am the only one who has been neglected in the waiting room of a brothel. Let anyone come and fetch me. There's a slightly decrepit joss stick smell from every direction, as though it's been used to disguise the scent of endless copulation in the place. The daughter is at the fridge. She is wearing a strip for a skirt, which is not only very short, but also very low with the waist band resting on her pubic bone. She bends over, deliberately presenting her backside to me.

'Mind if I join you?' she asks, sitting down.

I hope she doesn't see herself as the warm up act. Whether or not she does I daren't sit here like this for long. I go to the toilet, which is separate from the bathroom to discover lit candles there. By the bath yes, but in a toilet? It doesn't seem right; crap by candle light.

The situation is too awkward for me to sit back down. I pick up a book from the coffee table and stand. The book is The Orgone Energy Accumulator.

I ask Zowie if she has been reading it and she replies, 'No, reading doesn't work for me.'

A cat comes in and saunters over to me. It winds around me and then, when I finally sit back down, stays nuzzled against the shin with the scab on it. Christ, they're all at it!

'Where is…Sam?' I almost said 'Your mother' but nothing so normal goes in this house.

101

'Oh, she won't be long. She always disappears like this.'

Sam has gone off to the bedroom to slip into something more comfortable. I am hoping it's a divan, and that she'll be ready soon. The infusion Zowie gives me is cannabis, which I feign sipping at. I don't need it; my brain cells are struggling enough. The daughter snuggles up beside me and then giggles. Sitting there hasn't ceased to feel dangerous.

'Oliver, your brother, seems like a pretty nice lad,' I launch a conversation beyond romance.

'We don't see much of him, especially now he's got a new girlfriend. Sam said you'd be interested in him.'

'Did she? Why?'

'She says you were all friends back in those days. You must have known his father.' This is naiveté, not irony, I think. It's odd; I actually have a clear and comprehensive memory for that era.

'His father? Does he say much concerning him? And your Mum, does she talk about it?'

'No, she's bored shitless by the subject. Oliver plagues her with it. They've had so many rows; she refuses to discuss it. It's the only thing she ever loses her cool over.'

'I got the impression Oliver doesn't care,' I lie.

'Oh, he does. He sometimes pretends not to, but he does.'

At some point I really have got to play a part in putting the lad out of his misery. Not right now, however.

'Do you like the hand on the ceiling?' she asks. Oliver's paternity is obviously of little interest to her. I wonder if her own is.

'I did notice it.'

'I did that, it's an orgasm.'

An abstract representation, or an athletic product

of the real thing I ask myself.

'Hi!' Sam comes into the room and glares.

Her daughter jumps up, saying, 'I'll bring the food in.'

Sam is wearing a long corduroy skirt with an offset full length split virtually to the top and a low-cut blouse, but it is my chest that is heaving. I am breathless, trembling and transfixed. She sits in the spot still warm from her daughter, her thigh pressing against mine. The split in her skirt has somehow shifted to the front. It is now an arrow pointing in the only direction I can take. 'You don't mind, do you?' she says and lights a joint.

'Yes I do. I can't stand smoke', I say, adding, 'But go ahead.' And she does.

The daughter is still around. She returns from the kitchen area and places what looks like a macro-biotic meal on the coffee table. We both lean over and gobble at it. I rush my meal down and put my arm around Sam. It's obvious it is high time for the daughter to exit. My mobile goes. It will be Mo telling me to, 'Ask her!' again, so I ignore it. My mind is fevered with what to do next. Years ago I must have handled this situation more than once, but now, with an arm around Sam, any further move looks impossibly awkward. My memory won't supply me with any techniques. Sam's daughter puts the dishes in the sink and exits.

I'll save you the details of what immediately follows, except to say that the action is essentially one of Sam leaping astride me and throwing herself loudly all over the place, while I try to hold on.

'Jesus!' I shout, and halt as I literally withdraw. Never has a pathological memory felt as bad as this.

'What's wrong? Stop worrying. You're doing fine, it's beautiful.'

'Maybe, but I have forgotten the condoms.' - along with the indigestion tablets and gum, that is

103

'And?'

She apparently never uses them, refuses to.

What happens when an irresistible force meets the immovable object? I crumble and do what I swore I would never do. My hope has to be that she knows what she's doing, which should make it simple. Even at this moment I am aware, of course, that simple can be just another word for stupid, but my loins are calling me on.

I've worked it out: orgasms don't exist to persuade us to have sex. Even without orgasms, sex still feels so good that something definitive is needed to make us stop. Otherwise we'd carry on forever.

Not long after we uncouple I murmur, 'I've got things to do. I do have to go,' planting a kiss on her.

She looks at me. She has missed it, so I repeat myself.

'Of course you do, because I am on an early shift.'

It is so trouble-free that as I leave I nearly let out a cry of triumph. It wasn't one of those occasions where parallel lines meet, or two into one will go, or where heat can go from a cooler to a hotter, but there were orgasms aplenty, and although it was a struggle I managed to have a sort of one. The alcohol performed its function, and I went like a steam train, passing various stations for Sam, finally puffing into my own stop at the very last.

On my way out I exhale a sigh and feel a deep ache. I've had these before. It will go in a minute. It's cold and raining, and the air slaps me in the face. The blood has made its way back from my appendage to my head. My phone bleeps, and I know it will be Mo pestering me again. The question is who is the idiot, me or him? I'd had my fun so, with nothing to lose, I could have pressed Sam about Oliver. The cause is not lost, however. There isn't anything preventing me, so I can actually undo this: I can go back and ask.

I turn, meaning to knock on Sam's door, but as I do there is an excruciating pain deep in my chest. What is more, with each step the pain increases. I knock repeatedly, but moving my arm hurts like mad.

Eventually, a guy I've never seen before comes to the door. He takes one look at me and says, 'Oh, one of Sam's.' He fetches her and she stands there, not inviting me in. My chest and stomach are verging on agony.

'Who is Oliver's father? Am I the father?' I am finding breathing hard, and I barely wheeze it out. I have to hold on to the door frame to stand up. I am gasping and I don't think she is fully catching it.

'Oliver? Are you on something?' She knows I've been drinking.

'Am I his...' I can't finish the sentence.

'Oliver? I don't get it. That's too far out, too heavy. You know I've got to be up for work soon. You look terrible, Peter. Come in and crash if you need to.'

'You alright Sam?' It's the voice of the guy who answered the door. He arrives and stands by her. He is huge, and is glaring at me, clearly thinking I'm a threat. I am in pain, more than I can cope with. I turn, nearly falling and stagger away, getting no distance before I am bent double. I flag down a cab, and the pain down my arm is even stronger.

'You alright, mate? You look bad.' The cab driver helps me into his cab.

'Hospital,' I manage to gasp.

He gets me to the Whittington rapidly and supports me as we stumble into automatic doors that don't open quickly enough. It's almost empty.

'I think it's a heart attack!' he shouts at the receptionist.

If I wanted to die, I wouldn't want this pain.

Someone comes straight away and shoves an aspirin in my mouth. Then I'm on a trolley and a small

105

team of medics is examining me while every breath is agony.

> 'What have you been up to?' asks the only doctor who is now with me.
> 'I've just had sex and I've got this terrific pain in my chest.'

She takes my pulse and my blood pressure readings, and then listens to my chest again.

> 'Where is the pain?'

She presses around while I agree to the spot where the trouble is. It seems to have shifted a little lower.

> 'That's your stomach,' she says. 'Did you eat not long before having sex?'

One Rennie and an hour later I am clear to go home. I feel wide awake, pain free and pricelessly stupid.

When I get home there is a radiating glow in the lounge; I have forgotten to turn the computer off.

I have mail. I am getting better at this and bring it up at once. It is from Linda and it simply opens, 'Daddy,' not, 'Dear Daddy,' which is what she'd always put on any form of mail. 'Didn't you get my text? I'm bleeding.'

I start shouting, cursing, 'Jesus! Jesus!'

When was the email sent? I haven't set the computer clock properly, and she's not answering her phone. I'll email her; see if there is a response. My fingers can hardly manage it. The damn thing won't go. My hands are shaking. Precious minutes are spent fiddling around on it. Another help-line call suggests I can receive emails, but can't send them until I change my broad band account. I sprint out of the house.

In the car I pray aloud to no god in particular, but to the slightest possibility that there might be something out there with the power to help me.

I get to her place which is in a breeze - block

estate. I go up one slope, down another, past several locked gates and press an entry phone buzzer repeatedly. One flat mate is in.

'Where is Linda? Is she okay? Do you know what's happened?'

She tells me what I really hoped I wouldn't hear. 'They all went off in an ambulance.'

'They? Where?'

'Linda, and the other two who live here. I wanted to go, but Linda said to stay in case you made it round here.'

'Where, where have they gone?'

'To hospital.'

Christ, she is like the nightmare of a help line.

'Which one? Which one?'

She doesn't know. I go to the North Mid which is two minutes down the road from her, but she isn't there. They suggest I try the Royal Free. Insane! It's thirty minutes away.

'Please, can't you ring?' I ask.

They try, but A and E can't give an answer. 'If she's there they probably won't have processed her yet.'

I am on my way. Finally I get into the A and E at the Royal Free and rush around in a demented way, seeing if I can spot her.

'Can I help you?' It is a porter.

'Oh, yes please, please!'

He escorts me to the desk. They have her and he takes me to the precise spot.

She is lying on a trolley in a cross between a side room and a cupboard. As I enter a figure leaves through a curtain on the far side. A tall Asian doctor, I think. He's being called elsewhere. The sheets are bloodied and it is obvious we have lost the baby.
'I'm fine, honestly. Don't worry.' She takes my hand, and I begin to weep. I take my hand away to put both hands up to my bent face and turn to sobbing.

107

'Dad, Dad, it's alright. It happens. You've started me off, now.' That brings me to a halt, and she stops in response. 'Here, have one of these.' She shares a box of tissues with me. Linda is as strong as her mother. She tells me, 'I'll be going up to a ward when there's a bed, and I'll have to have a D and C, which is a nothing procedure. You have to have one on these occasions.'

We cuddle. 'I'll stay until they take you.'

'It's not necessary, honestly.' But she can see I need it more than her.

'Okay, okay. You might as well make use of yourself, then. Got your phone? Know how to use the reminder on it? Give it here, I'll show you.' She puts in notes to ring Sylvia and to ring her mother, and next puts in a separate note about the ward and hospital number. Finally she shows me how to set alarms for the reminders. 'It will change your life, Daddy.'

I think she's right. I get a chair and slump on it, clasping her fingers while a colossal weariness like six feet of earth presses down on me.

'Tell Syl she can come as soon as she wants, but do tell her I'm fine.'

We are such a contrast, she must be in some discomfort, but is so upbeat.

'As for Mum, wait until tomorrow. I am having the D and C as soon as they can fit me in. You can ring up, find out how I'm doing, which will be fine, and then you can tell her. Dad, Dad, listen. Do listen. You must tell Mum there is no need to come home. I am fine and I will be out of hospital before she can get here. Tell her it will only upset me if she makes a bigger deal of it than it is.' With that she wipes a tear away.

I squeeze her tightly. 'Look, I know, I can see you're a big girl now, an authentic grown up woman, but you don't have to act as though you're so strong when you're upset. Of course you're upset.'

'Honestly, Dad, I was, I was even scared a little, but my mates who came with me were terrific, and everybody here was as well. You know how it is with Mum. If she rushes back, if I see her, we'll both bawl, and that would be daft. She paid a lot of money for that course and has done a lot of preparation. It really isn't necessary. I'm fine, I'm fine.'

'I really will do my best to remember. I will do the things you say, sweetheart. Wow, it makes you think about your priorities, though.'

'Never mind those, just remember I'm fine, I'm fine.'

I'm in the lift, which is a bit cramped, with her, a porter and a nurse. We are holding hands. The nurse is tolerant. We kiss goodbye at the ward door. I stand there waving through the window, until they pull curtains around her.

Everything is, "fine, fine".

The sun has risen when I leave, but the roads are still clear. When I get home I am exhausted, but I know I will not be able to sleep. I had expected the sleep of a hero, but any sense of triumph has now gone. I am still here and the baby has gone. What is a shag compared to this loss?

It is either the sex, or the shock. I have some kind of rogue hormone in me that isn't going to let me nod off yet, so I put the TV on. I don't have the energy to flick around, and find myself watching something I would normally give a miss, the sort of program women can take. It's about the medical treatment of kids with terrible facial deformities. Some have had a series of operations, and you can see they know more pain is coming. Their parents are hugely strong, amazingly brave and discretely full of worry and tears. Sooner or later we have got to take matters out of God's hands. He's just not up to it.

About eleven a.m. I awake and ring to see how

my daughter is. She has had the op', and is awake. I am allowed to speak to her. She is bright.

'I'm fine, fine. Mum's classes don't finish until five this evening. Texting wouldn't be a good way to give her the news, so ring her after her class. Don't forget to ring Syl.'

They could let her out this afternoon, after the doctor has done her rounds.

The sole universal constant is no law of physics, it is Sod's Law. Apart from calls from fools you answer your mobile every time you hear it, respond to every text, and look what happens the one time you don't respond.

I ring Sylvia who is much more concerned about her sister than her sister is. All she says to me is, 'I'm going to see her.' I start to say that I don't think she'll be allowed until visiting time and that Linda may shortly be discharged, but she has already put the phone down. Then I set the reminder on my mobile to rouse me and make sure I'm ready to go and collect Linda the minute she calls.

X

"We're on the road again." It's playing on the radio which I've put on because of the silence in the car. There is no "we", however, because Carol has absented herself. I don't blame her, not after the meal we had with Sam – more of which later. I've got a terrible headache, which has now got a grip on my neck as well. Stretching it in a noose might help. I'll soon hear that I am brain dead, but unfortunately it's not terminal.

A reminder on my phone sets me ringing my wife.

'Linda has lost the baby, she's in hospital. She's had to have a minor op',' I blurt out.

'I know. Sylvia has not long rung me.'

'Linda says she's fine. The hospital says the same.'

'I know. I rang them too. They let me speak to Linda. I had just paid for a plane ticket when I spoke to her, but she wouldn't let me come. Even raised her voice. She insisted I stay where I am. I had to let her hear me tear my ticket up. She said if I came it would upset her, and I know it would. We'd both have started bawling the second we saw each other. What a love she is. Her sole thought was for me, that I should carry on with the course. She did seem perky, I must say. She's talking about the next time, but I told her there is no hurry. How are you taking it?'

'I'm slaughtered. It is such a shame. The poor thing. It puts everything in perspective.'

'It would have been lovely to be grandparents, but perhaps it was too soon. Don't forget I miscarried the first time and worse after that, so these things do happen. Some doctors say it is often for the best.'

'They would, though, wouldn't they? Where are you?'

111

'Revising for a practical.'
I can hear background noises again.
'Don't forget the consultant.'
I promise I won't.

My cousin's return from holiday has been
delayed by an emergency operation for appendicitis, so
I cannot avoid visiting my uncle again. Sunshine
Homes doesn't look any different, but it feels different.
Personnel on reception and on the way in generally
seem to recognise me and look apprehensive.

I come across my uncle in the corridor. He is
shuffling along giddily and he cannot support his head.
It is lolling to one side, half resting on his shoulder, half
on his chest. I can't help myself and rush up to him
crying, 'Uncle, uncle.'

There are staff close by and they are observing
this. Once more I can't help myself, and shout out,
'What have they done to you?'

They descend on us, repeatedly use his name
speaking warmly, and attempt to take him away by the
hand. I am having none of it and grab him. I am told
that they need to discuss my uncle with me somewhere
more suitable than the corridor, so I let him go for the
moment. In the office they explain that this is probably a
form of Parkinson's, which can happen with dementia
patients.

Unfortunately Sunshine Homes is no longer
appropriate for him because he will need more
specialized treatment.

'How can this have happened? He can't have
gone downhill that quickly! What have you done to
him?'

There are four of them, two wearing white and
the other two in uniform. I am deliberately
outnumbered. They tell me that naturally things like this
are very sad, but they can and do just happen, and

when they happen it can be very sudden.

I'd like to tell them, 'You're not getting away with this,' but I am too crushed to say much at all. Instead I insist on spending time with my uncle. He is no longer capable of games or paper folding. He is a long way gone, not responding to a word I say. Nevertheless, I promise him, 'You were doing fine, uncle. This isn't right. They are not going to get away with this.'

As I leave, my intention is to ring his GP and find out what has been going on and take up the battle from there.

Driving back I say to myself, 'Too right he won't be staying there.'

I badly oversleep, awaking with dribble coming from my mouth, sweat on my eyelids formed behind my sleep mask, a sore throat and blocked nose. It's a cold. It always happens with stress. I quaff some Day Nurse and a Lemsip.

I manage to ring my uncle's old doctor, but he subtly and steadfastly defends his colleagues and the home. It is a brush off.

After going to the library for advice, I spend the rest of the day using the phone and an internet directory. I manage to get some useful information from Help the Aged and from the Citizens Advice Bureau, although the latter emphasises that I need to make an appointment to see an expert or a lawyer.

The suggestion is that my uncle has been put on drugs that are meant to calm him. They have the effect of making patients less mobile, and can cause Parkinson's. Apparently their use simply to render patients easier to handle has been known. As far as immediate action is concerned I fail to make much progress, but I won't let it rest there. I have to put this aside for the moment however, because I am going on what has become a regular visit to my daughter in hospital.

Linda has been in longer than expected because of a number of minor things; there was the high temperature, then her blood pressure was too high, next it was too low, and the following day she had a raised temperature again. They are "keeping an eye on her".

I infuriate myself by being delayed because I get the route to the hospital wrong. As I drive past a set of lights coming from where I shouldn't be, the Archway Road, there is a double flash. If I was above the speed limit it can't have been by much. Sometimes a man just feels beat.

The Royal Free car park is a torment. It's all backed-up traffic and impossibly tight bends. I believe at last I've found a non-paying spot. I've brought my rucksack with grapes and some magazines for Linda in it. There are different coloured lines straggling along the floor like huge linguini. I follow this essential guide and manage to find the right ward.

My daughter looks good. Any tears are long behind us. I won't be describing my uncle's condition to her.

'How are you? I hear you're talking about the next time.'

'I'm fine, I just want to get out of here. They reckon it could be tomorrow. How're you keeping on your own, Daddy? Your forehead isn't healing that quickly.' She wants to mother me.

'I'll come round and do you a meal or two, once I'm out.' She adds that some of her friends have visited earlier.

'Has the culprit who got you in here been?'

'Of course! He loves me.'

'And you love him?'

'A lot of the time I think I do. Of course I do. Please don't ask me when you'll meet him. It's not so urgent now, and it's complicated. I'll cry.'

That stumps me.

114

She carries on in her jolly way. 'Syl has applied for a sabbatical and is going to see an old friend who's teaching in New Guinea.'

Sylvia is off travelling again. She's thirty! There used to be a lot of talk of second childhoods, but these days it's second teenagerhoods. I think I can understand it - just. I could say that young people travel because they have no place to go, but that wouldn't work. Linda wouldn't accept that, let alone her sister. Sylvia will go, and Carol and I will put ourselves on a sort of stand-by. Should she get into trouble we'll be ready to go at anytime, anywhere, as the first emergency service.

'I won't kiss you,' I tell Linda, 'because I've got a cold and a cold sore coming.' We hold hands and then let go.

'Don't forget to ring up early tomorrow to see when you should come and get me. If not, don't worry, I'll get a taxi.'

'I'll be there, that's for definite.'

I stand at the ward door and look back. I know it is hard for her and her sister. Our generation is to blame. We promised so much, and delivered so little. We showed them a distant horizon and crammed the path to it with obstacles that grow year on year.

The hospital kiosk is closed, so I can't get some paper tissues for my streaming nose. I can feel a rasping cough building in my chest. Outside the air temperature has dropped and one of those penetrating drizzles quickly soaks me. I struggle to remember where I have left my car. Ah, I think I have got it, and sure enough it is there. But that is not all. Even from a distance I can see clearly that a bright yellow triangular snare is wrapped around one of the wheels. It is clamped. This has to be a mistake. Yes, it is. No it's not. There may be no yellow lines and no notices on posts, but there are stickers on the wall. I have parked

115

in a spot reserved for chemotherapy patients. The entire bit of road is free, and they don't do chemo' this late in the day. I would never knowingly park somewhere like that because I might need special parking concessions myself one day. My mind was on my daughter. They should know that when people arrive here they are bound to be distracted. That would work wonders with any appeal, wouldn't it? If I had an angle grinder I'd cut the bastard off and I'd also go for the bastard who put it on.

I'm not putting up with this! I go to the boot, and fetch out a jack and a wheel brace. I've seen it on TV; you can get these things off. I jack the car up and depress the valve to deflate the tyre. As I do I get gut ache from bending over. I sit down in the damp and realise that there is now grease on my trousers. I loosen the first nut and go to take the hand brake off, so I can turn the wheel to get at the other nuts. Can't be done because it's got to stay in gear, otherwise the whole thing will roll forward, possibly over my leg. I am breathing hard, feeling dizzy and not getting far. I cannot be dealing with this. It's impossible, pointless. I drag myself up and in the glare of neon lighting I see that there is a CCTV camera pointing straight at the car and me. To someone somewhere this will be hilarious. I lock the car, pick up my rucksack and leave. The only other thing they can do to me now is tow it away. Let 'em.

Cab or tube? I'll walk in the direction of the latter up the moist slope, find a bar, have a drink and see if I want to get a cab. It's dark and the pavement is slippery. I am not surprised there are few people around.

A young man nudges against me saying, 'Excuse me do you have time, please mate?' Strange accent.

I don't have a watch. I am cold, tired, soaked

116

and I really don't want to be asked, but he is young and a stranger to these parts, so I do the social thing. There is a clock on my mobile which I peer at, press a button to light it up and offer him a view. At first he's not interested because his hand is inside the flap of my rucksack. But now, he grabs the phone, as a rust heap of a car pulls over with another guy in it. He gets out and starts pulling at my rucksack. I expect a kicking, but I don't care; half my brain has evaporated and the other half is sizzling in a steamy anger. I've had enough.

'You want it? Piss off or fight me for it, you arseholes!'

They wrestle the rucksack from me. My wallet is in the front of it; it's safer than a trouser pocket. They are speaking mostly in a foreign language, but partly in English. 'Quick, quick.....fuck........careful, careful.' The one with the phone jumps into the driver's seat, while the one with the rucksack is getting into the passenger side at the back. The front door won't open because it's got a huge dent by the lock. It almost seems as if they are trying to be gentle with me.

'Get lost, arseholes!' I think I've been shouting during the whole assault.

I grab at the rucksack as my mugger tries to close the door. He closes the door, with the straps still sticking out. My hand remains wrapped around them. The car starts to chug away, slowly picking up speed; I am still holding on. 'Bollocks to the lot of them!' One of my shoes scrapes against the road and comes off. I am being dragged and couldn't let go if I wanted to. Flesh is coming off my foot, my hip and my elbow. All I can feel is the adrenalin. They slow and the window comes down.

'Let go, please let go.'

Oh sure, "please" makes all the difference. It's definitely a Slav accent. 'Fuck off!'

The car stops, and they try to untangle the

117

straps from my arm. I am half on my knees and they are lifting me. I am fighting them and they're not winning, although my flailing around is mostly bruising the air. There are people emerging from somewhere, so the two Slavs jump back in the car and start to pull away. I am still holding on. My head cracks against an obstacle, and then it grates against something else. The wound in my forehead reopens, and there are some bits of concrete sticking in my skull. I see a radial with hardly any tread on it rearing towards my head. Bang! The car stops. That same accent, 'Sorry.' They release the rucksack and shoot off.

      Me? I feel strange. There's sharp, prolonged soreness somewhere and nausea, but also tranquillity bordering on euphoria. Mission accomplished! I am dying, and it's not at all bad. Real pain begins, but it's odd, like it's hurting someone else, not me. I can actually gauge how much pain there is and think, 'Hmm, that isn't at all good.' The pain carries on and it now feels more like it is my pain. This is pain to die for.

XI

The walnut on the dashboard and doors and the grey padding could have been the interior of a wooden coffin. The fact of the matter is that the journey and the car I am in feel empty and bare without Carol. She had her reasons for not being here, but how much more strongly would she have felt if she thought I had the clap?

I often get things in the wrong order. I should have described my humiliation at the private hospital before the violence that was done to me. If I had told you it would have gone rather like this –

My father's diary has become my favourite reading, but I'd no sooner picked it up than the phone rang.

'You're not doing it, Dad. You're not going private. You're not going are you, Dad? Tell me you're not going.'

It was Sylvia and she was calling me, Dad. Who did I want off my back the most, her or her mother? In their own ways they were both right. This was the nearest thing to a conversation I'd had with my daughter for years.

'Look Sylvia…,' I began, but she interrupted me.

'It's not for you. Don't go, walk away. That's what others do. You can still put up a fight.'

'Head case, old me?...' I'd whined, but she interrupted again.

'That's pathetic.'

'Fight where, alongside whom? What is more during the period I've been resisting, the resistance movement first dwindled and then signed up, leaving me stranded. Everybody else bought in while my health has reached a point where no private medical scheme would take me on.' I knew that was feeble. 'Look Syl...,' I started to protest, but she put the phone down. Thank goodness, because it wasn't an argument I thought I could win.

Since my antacid episode I've been less interested in the state of my heart. My problem has never been there. Going to the consultant felt pretty much a waste of time, although I didn't quite realise then that it was shortly to become a complete irrelevance. The appointment was in a lovely building down a beautiful road near Highgate golf course. It was so plush there should have been a concierge. There appeared to be fewer patients than personnel, one of whom immediately offered me a beverage of my choice.

'Hemlock,' I said, but they didn't get it and of course neither did I.

I didn't like the privilege, I didn't like the debonair senior staff, and I didn't like the well-heeled clients, most especially me. In health terms I'd told myself that in going there I was trying to keep my head above water, but the truth is I was taking a dip in moral sewage. My wife wanted me to be there, but that was no excuse. On the other hand, they'd still have charged me whether I turned up or not, so I wasn't cancelling.

While I was drinking the tea they had brought me, Linda rang. (I wasn't going to accept their strictures here about turning phones off). It was then that she had told me of the delay in discharging her.

'I'm fine,' she told me.

When I said goodbye, I hadn't realized that the next time I saw her could be my last.

A doctor in a pinstripe suit came to take me to his office and seat me on a sumptuous leather chair. It was less like a surgery there, more like a large booth in a gentleman's club. First he shook my hand, as though congratulating me.

'What can I do for you, Peter?'

He was half my age; I would have thought a 'Mr' would have been appropriate. I started to reply, 'I'm paying for this time, you're a cardiologist, so I'm not here for my piles. Interpret the charts for me, and soften the bad news,' but he began moving on before I got beyond the first clause. 'Let's see what the hospital had to say about you, shall we?' he had interrupted.

As he read my notes I brushed them to one side and insisted, 'I've a dodgy heart and I want to ask you something related to it.'

'There is a little irregularity here, but it is not out of the usual for your age.'

'What about an atrial fibrillation? It was suggested I had one. Isn't it possible that it wouldn't necessarily show up on any particular occasion?' Apparently anything was possible, but this was unlikely. He asked if I smoked, had ever smoked, how much I drank, how much I exercised and about my family medical history. He had all this information already.

'Do we have to go through this rigmarole? I've already told doctors the answers to these.'

'Ah, but you haven't told me,' was all he could reply. He carried on, essentially reading from a questionnaire. Then he totted up a set of marks he'd given me, looked at the charts from the Whittington and declared, 'There's no great cloud on the horizon here, Peter.'

I went there specifically about me, but he was giving me this epidemiological rubbish that applies to everyone in general and no one in particular. I'm a novice, but I'll bet I could get one of these questionnaires and the marking scheme off the internet.

He looked at his watch and said, 'I think we should examine you.'

Oh, really? My half an hour must nearly have been up.

He took my pulse and blood pressure, and got

121

me to lie on a couch. I suddenly saw that the lamp at the side was plugged in and had bare wires, and that the switch was on. It was within my reach. I stretched towards it. I could almost see the sparks and feel the hot and icy bolt there and then, but he snatched the plug from the socket. It was done at a speed only normally seen in his sort if they are young bulls on the floor of the Stock Exchange. He smoothly joked about how bad that would have been for my heart and applied a stethoscope to various places. When he tapped my chest at the end it seemed no more scientific than water divining.

'Can a dodgy heart cause or contribute to dementia? That's what I really want to know,' I asked.

For one moment he looked nonplussed and then he gleaned something. 'Well, yes it can. It is not at all uncommon. The condition is called multi-infarct dementia. It's actually caused by strokes, I believe. Kills off brain cells en masse. You did mention atrial fibrillation, didn't you? Well there is also recent evidence of a strong link there. Neither is my field I'm afraid.' He took a considered pause and fully surveyed the business opportunity. 'I do know a chap who's an expert. I can arrange for you to see him, if you want.' No doubt he'd be on a percentage.

'I may be losing it, but I am not giving it away,' I told him, but he suavely ignored this.

Finally he passed me a prescription for statins and blood pressure pills, and promptly saw me to the door. If he wasn't careful we would have run over time. I had gone in like a lamb and come out like a slug.

Strokes can be fatal sometimes and aren't they painless? I can't think of a reason I would want to stop one of those, except that it would be my luck simply to be left paralysed. I went to a chemist, got my pills and washed them down with Italian coffee.

In bed later, I didn't sleep well. I scratched what

modern advertising might call a masculine irritation. I
began to wonder how many strokes I might already
have had, and to what extent I had been damaged. I
bet that even if the strokes were stopped, the dementia
would continue to develop.

The phone interrupted my morbid whimsy. It
was twelve-thirty in the morning, and there was noise
and hilarity in the background. Someone was talking,
yet I couldn't catch a word. I talked back, but they
couldn't understand me. Either the speaker at the other
end had an exceptionally deep voice, or it was not
female. I put the phone down, and because I didn't
have the number, tried the call-return button. It didn't
work, so I gave up.

Two hours later the itching had got worse and
worse, and I was coming up in welts. I tried the call-
return again. A man responded in French.

'Can I speak to Carol, please?' I asked.

I swear I could hear her in the background,
asking if it was for her. He, apparently, could not
understand me. I put the phone down and instead rang
Carol's mobile. I didn't expect her to answer, but she
did. It was obvious she was quite merry. She was
completely up to date with Linda's situation, so we
exchanged the usual pleasantries. Actually I did the
talking and she let me.

There was still a background voice, or voices, in
French. That was one demanding course. She would
normally have been asleep long before then.

Sleep and I are not good bedfellows. As
darkness and my head rejoined the pillow, black
lightening struck and worry was all there was. I fidgeted
and scratched, something I often do in bed. I've heard
this is a condition which involves some sort of nerve
deterioration. I've forgotten the name for it. Anyway, I
was awake, shifting back and forth, and scratching and
scratching. A third hard lump of the sort you get with

Dupytrens Contracture was forming in my hand. I was fretting about things I must do: I had to find the way to reconcile Oliver with me as his father, mend my relationship with Sylvia and persuade Linda's boyfriend he had to meet me. I had a mnemonic to help me remember this inventory, but I was struggling to recall it. How on earth was I to complete these tasks before I lost all ability?

I wanted to tear my flesh off and was scratching so much that I started to bleed. I couldn't lie there any longer. I decided to run a cold bath and see if that eased it. On went the lights. And there it was; the Scarlet Letter, the Mark of Cain, not even the Stigmata are as well recognized as that. Exposed in the wardrobe mirror, bubbling, blistering and crimson, was a rash. It was all over my inner thighs and my genitals. It looked as though I'd been beaten with a meat tenderizer. One time in thirty years, I strayed, just one time I had extra marital sex, and this was the price: a sexually transmitted disease!

It was at that point that I realised I wasn't quite ready to give up on Carol. What would she say? Hell hath no fury like a woman infectiously spermed. I'd have to tell her. On went the computer. I knelt because I couldn't bear to sit on the stool. An NHS Direct number came up which, when I rang, directed me to a twenty-four hour Genito Urinary Medicine department, G.U.M. for short.

A cab took me there. I couldn't drive; I needed both hands to scratch. I had expected low lighting and an atmosphere of confidentiality, but this place was well lit – too well lit. As discretely as possible I stuck my head around a door. It was pretty well all young people, some of whom were under age. I spotted someone nearer to my years and was about to enter when I realised he was in fact a doctor. I would be the only old perv in there. I couldn't face it. I got a cab back, then took some paracetamol and ibuprofen, and swigged them down with best part of a bottle of Baileys. I hate the stuff, Carol loves it, but it's all there was. I couldn't stay still for one second, so I was up and down, with the liquid slurping around in my belly. Now I felt sick on top of the itching, and I'd have to stay that way until morning when I would see a doctor at the local surgery. And all the time the rash was spreading rapidly.

Eight o'clock on the dot I was ringing the surgery. It was urgent, and it had to be a male doctor. I was there prancing up and down, by the reception desk, out on the external steps and back inside. Over and over again.

Thank God, it was Doc Holiday. He got me standing, shirt open and trousers round my ankles.

'Is it the clap?' I asked man to man.

Doc Holiday, sun tan and all, looked me up and down. 'It's one hell of a performance,' he laughed, 'but not an occasion for applause.' Sometimes I don't think much of his sense of humour. 'Stranger things have happened,' he answered, 'but no. This is probably either the statins your private consultant put you on, or it's the blood pressure pills. It's an allergic reaction. Nobody's fault, but we'll need to change them.'

It felt like a come-uppance. His amber stained fingers wrote out a prescription for different pills and a steroid cream. Then I set off towards the chemist.

Mo was waiting for me outside the surgery.

'Want a lift?'

'How on earth did you know I'd be here?' I was amazed.

'Not at home and too early for coffee. You spend almost as much time at the doctor's as you do at those two places.'

I accepted a lift after I got my prescription filled. At my house I didn't pause for pleasantries. I went straight in the bathroom and plastered myself with the

125

cream.

'Petey?' he pestered me.

'What? Look if it's any more of that "Ask her" drivel, forget it! I'll do it in my own time, at my own pace and when it makes sense to!'

'No. No, it's not that, although now we're on the subject have you thought about talking to the lad direct?'

'Of course I have, but it's a tad difficult isn't it? Let's leave my love life aside, shall we? Life's a lot simpler for you, Mo. What, about all your sessions in the boudoir? When I came round there was someone in the bedroom, wasn't there? Gagging for it, no doubt.'

'You've got the wrong end of the stick and I can't talk to you about it. Every single occasion you bring it up all you're looking for is porn.'

I don't understand his problem. He used to love to talk dirty.

'Alright mate. You stop texting stupid instructions to me, and I won't be so tacky. Agreed?'

'Okay. Anyway, I've got some mags you can take to Linda tonight.'

I put them in my rucksack with the grapes I'd bought. I picked it up by its straps when I left for the hospital that evening, not thinking how easy it would be to get my hands trapped in them.

XII

You know the attempted mugging has convinced me once and for all: dying is not bad. I'm nearing the hospital and my appointment, and I am missing Carol. In the past she would have been shoulder to shoulder with me on a day such as this.

I haven't a clue who I am. There are eyes above me and the big disc with four white lights hovering over me looks like a craft for alien abduction, and yet I have seen it before. Has it come to take me back to the mother planet?

They're smiling and saying someone's name. 'Peter. Hello Peter.'

Some strange noises and a buzzing near my face. Is it take-off? Then it is all blank white. Some indistinguishable time later it is still all white, but somehow it is different. There are some familiar faces, except I am wondering who they are. I know! It's Carol and our eldest daughter. And it is becoming clearer that I am Peter. But they shouldn't be here. One should be at work and one is in France. If I am conscious, I am delusional. Then again, they had obviously thought I was dying, so one has risked the ire of her employers and the other has rushed back from her Gallic capers. See, dying has its good points; the mere fear of mine has conferred pricelessness on seeing me.

They smile, so I smile. That hurts, as do my hip and elbow and foot. I wonder aloud, 'What happened to the car?'

They are dumbfounded, obviously feeling it is of no importance. They are right. Perhaps I'll get off the fine this way, which would make it almost worth it.

Apparently I am in the local paper and in the nationals. "Hero sees off asylum seekers", or something along those lines. They want to interview me. Let them, because once they hear what I've got to say they'll shelve the story.

My youngest daughter enters the room. Shouldn't she be in bed in a different room in the self same hospital?

Mo is there too. I squint at him and he gives me the oddest look, some of which is sympathy. He looks solemn and it could be he is close to distraught. He's not the man I used to know. The only emotion he used to show was as occasional anger and frequent belly-laughs. He's going down hill faster than me. I'd have expected him to rib me about my exploits, that's what blokes do. The, 'Think you're a hard man, eh?' sort of jibe. Instead he comes forward and smiles, and gently asks, 'You alright, mate?' He wants to shake my hand or ruffle my hair, but the bandages and clotted blood prevent him. He retreats looking awkward, probably because he doesn't like hospitals.

I feel as though all this is happening in the third person. It's a bit akin to a dream you can observe yourself in. My family members say I saw them last night, and nights before that. That is news to me. I try to twist to look at what is on the bedside table, but my neck is agony. Everybody seems to believe I know what they are talking about. All I take in is that there are grapes - bare stalks mean some have been eaten - and cards, and copies of all the papers beside the bed.

I've been stitched, and had my nose set, they tell me, but the doctors want to do more tests. Of course they do. They've already found I have high cholesterol and lipids, and they are not happy with my blood pressure. I thought that cardiologist was supposed to have sorted that out. Oh yes, that rash led me to bin those poisonous pills he prescribed. Mind you, I'm sure my GP gave me some others. Knowing me, I probably thought better of taking them. My family have been up here five consecutive nights; I was properly conscious

128

only for the last two. That's what they think. I am tired and they are going, or did I say that already?

Carol ends with a kiss and the jolly news, 'Oh yes, Sam rang. When you get out we are all going to go for a meal together, including our children. Won't that be lovely?'

One of the great things about being ill, and I don't mean a cold, is that you can sleep, yet I am woken the next morning at a silly early hour.

'Tea love?' I nod and it hurts again. Breakfast is due soon after the tea is served by two jolly ladies. One of them apologises for there being no milk. 'If it was up to me you could have a biscuit as well.'

It's warm and it's wet, and I am too groggy to miss the milk. I drink half and lay back thinking of the cluster bomb Carol dropped last night. There could well be innocent casualties. I don't believe I dreamed it. Ah, of course, she knew Sam before I did, they were friends from college. That is one thing I am confident I've said before. But I can't see how contact had been made; it's not as though this hospital is Sam's workplace. It may be through Oliver who could have moved here already. I've been ill and I can be let off anything. No matter how I try, I'm not going to succeed in kidding myself that's true. The meal smells good, but the trolley misses me out and that is ominous.

There is a tempest raging in my bowels, which has me leaping out of bed and rushing for the toilet, but I don't know where it is. I call out loudly to a nurse who reacts by telling me it is where it was the last time I used it. I find it, and let loose. I will save you the details except to say that if it was a storm it was all wind and rain. As a result of my trip I discover the toilet is as familiar as the nurse suggested, and that there are lashings of Vaseline around my sphincter. I am weak and collapse back into my bed.

A doctor comes in.

129

'Time for your colonoscopy. An engineer has been working on the machinery and there was a bit of a backlog, if you'll forgive the phrase in this context.'

He thinks that's funny, but I haven't a clue what he is talking about.

'After that you can have some rest before we send you for more tests on your neck and head.'

Surgery on my head and neck wounds, yes, but a colonoscopy... 'Look,' I say, 'I don't see any point in this and I don't want it.' I left out that the NHS could do without the waste of resources.

He looks at me as though I am cussedly awkward. 'You signed the permission letter, Peter. What is more, if I recall, you were enthusiastic about it. You said something about missing out on the sunrise on Mars and that this would be the next best thing.'

I would think he was making this up, but I remember the day pictures came back from a Mars probe. I was shattered because I realized, for the first time, that I would never get there. I am, after all, from the generation that saw moon landings long ago and expected humankind to be commuting the solar system by now. So I probably did say this. Nevertheless, I must have been drugged up to have agreed. He has rung someone and he passes me the phone.

It is Linda who says, 'Just think Jules Verne, Dad. It'll be a bon voyage.' I get it: Journey to the Centre of Myself. She says a little bit more and finishes with, 'I love you.'

In the meantime, the doctor is shooting the second of two hypodermics into a port in my hand. He sees the question in my looks and answers, 'Pethidine.'

It, and whatever else they injected, has me drivelling to a nurse, 'In my youth, space shots were aimed at exploring new worlds, now they are about weapons guidance and spying.' She is not phased.

Tests: I can't seem to get away from them.

Hopefully they are relaxing me, not sedating me. I want to remember this.

After I was mugged it didn't take the hospital long to contact my daughter, and she got hold of Carol who came back from France. The hospital has been incredibly thorough. I've already had kidney, liver and most other organs checked - I can't remember all they said - and repeated further scans all over. There was no food for me because I have to be completely empty, but nobody told me the colonoscopy was imminent. Of that I'm certain, but then again, I can't be certain of anything. They have been making a lot of detailed measurements of my head and face, to check the nose and nasal passages, I suppose. They've even taken a cast of my head. I do not remember any of this, nor do I remember the series of talks doctors are supposed to have had with me.

I have been wheeled to what must be one of the older parts of the hospital, because the ceilings are higher. There is a fantastic large cubed clock with four faces hanging there. Seeking donors is a priority here too with a sign saying, "Transplants save lives." It's a wonder they are not playing 'Why not take all of me' in the background. I had a donor card once, which, ironically enough, I lost along with a jacket, when giving blood. My mind can't be bad, this is all so clear to me.

We pause before going into a spot which is not as spacious as a surgical theatre. It's more like a video room, much more intimate. I should be embarrassed over hands around my anus, but I am not. Maybe this is how geriatric patients feel about the help they get with faecal matters. I study a poster of photos and charts of my inner-space helpfully displayed on the wall beside my trolley. Shame I can't take notes: anus and rectum, yep I know those, and the lovely little appendix. Then there's the Dentate Line, the Transverse Colon, the pinky yellow Sigmoid Colon. There is loads of it, with

131

some reminiscent of a scene from Alien. Is this a glimpse of where my true core is, that hidden hot spinning thing that can be solely detected by the path it creates and the effects it has? I am ready, I am kitted up and the ground crew of two technicians is here.

The lead guy explains, 'We will be inserting a small camera for a little look at your system, just to make sure everything is in order.' By way of what I think is conversation he asks, 'Do you have mucus in your stools?' I must look bemused, so he says, 'You would see mucus on toilet paper you had used.'

Did I, had I? I answer, 'No, not unless I blew my nose on it first,' which does not go down well. I try to tell him that I want to watch, but it is partly garble that comes out, and I think he has lost interest in me verbally. I may have got it across. When he gets me to lie on my side I am facing the screen on which pictures of my journey will unfold. I peek at the long black craft being readied to enter me. It is much bigger than I thought, but I am not fussed. It is a struggle to stay awake, but I have got to remember this.

I am not sure when I lost awareness, there was a bit of fading in and out, but I properly woke up several hours later in my bed. I felt my sphincter; no harm done and no intestinal gripes. I am battling to recall the various names of the parts I have beheld. The various differently titled colons I can manage. Not bad for mister no-memory-man. I sleep again. It is that hospital-bed-sweetly-drugged-without-a-care-sleep.

Then I awake thoroughly, exceptionally rested and alert. I go over the whole procedure and revise any parts I have forgotten which, as it happens, is a lot. I still have some unforgettable images, I think.

Carol has met Sam. Are they coming here together tonight? I don't think so. I believe that I heard that Sam's son transferred here and visited. All these tests. It is not too surprising to me that I don't remember the days in this hospital, and what should have been unforgettable bowel movements. And that is it; I am back in it, the fear of dementia. There is definitely something wrong, and the confirmation is that doctors keep coming to look me over. They are coming in twos and threes, all poking around the wound in my neck, where a procedure was carried out. I cannot understand what it is all for. They are here again, this time with someone from palliative care, asking me about any previous treatments and operations. 'How do you get on with codeine?' 'And with opiates?' 'Have you had those before?' 'Did you have any adverse reactions?'

He looks odd when I assure him, 'My face isn't that sore.' They obviously know something is wrong, but can't work it out. They need to identify the site of some pain and they can't, because anguish doesn't show up in that way. I know my conduct is weird, and I know the break down in my brain is the cause. They don't understand because they haven't got the inside information, which I am not going to give them. I am not giving it to them because I do not want anyone treating me as if I am unhinged. They are not confiding in me, so there is no reason I should do so with them. It's my particular twist on patient doctor confidentiality. They do the usual expertly, superficially chat to me, even joke, look at my charts, and feel around my areas of pain. Then they retreat a couple of feet beyond the end of my bed and discuss me quietly enough for the sense of it to be lost on me. The one word I think I can catch is, 'urgent.'

I shout, 'It's rude to whisper. Haven't you heard?'

Apparently they haven't heard, not in the past and not me saying it now. Doctors suffer from a special condition: selective professional deafness. Then they all come back, stare at me as though I am something in

133

a petri dish, and move off having thanked me. The ideal subject for them would be someone in a persistently vegetative state. That much passivity must save a lot of having to speak in half whispers and play silly games.

At night Carol arrives with my eldest daughter and a stranger. I think I might have dozed off. There are light kisses all round because my face, in fact, still hurts.

Carol says, 'Scars are not a problem on men; they can look more manly with scars. Look, someone special has come to see you.'

Then I recognise that there is no stranger, this is my elder brother.

'There is definitely something wrong with my brain.' I say it aloud and they laugh. It is the sort of laugh that avoids having to give a pertinent response. I should know my own brother. He has flown back from New Zealand where he spends chunks of his retirement. It must be serious for him to come all this way; he doesn't do anything spontaneously.

Meanwhile they air light-hearted matters in a manner I've seen before. It is the same old tragedy-in-the-background-humour-to-the-fore phenomenon. Blithesomeness never did much for me, but they mean well. We discuss his deep suntan and his expensive sunglasses, but avoid the subject of his dyed hair; he wouldn't tolerate that. It's probably as well the pethidine has departed, otherwise I wouldn't be able to resist it. 'I've come to cheer you up, and to help sort out aunt's estate.'

Bless him, he never paid her much attention when she was alive. He must know something I don't, or he thinks I don't. He is giving lots of good news regarding his own children.

'Have you heard the one about…?' He reels off a few jokes with perfect delivery. He's always been a comic. This, I remember, is why I like him so much.

134

I can't hold it back any longer. 'Have they said anything to you at all about my state of awareness?'

My brother steps back, it is obviously not his place to comment.

Carol says, 'Of what? What do you mean?'

It may well be the doctors have enlisted her. It is probably part of the protocol the medical profession follows. You know that keep-the-patient-in the-dark-we're-hands-on-on-their-condition-not-them and if-we-let-a-relative-in on-it-they-will-have-to-keep-it-to-themselves approach. Or perhaps these are the paranoid ravings that dementia brings on.

I can't be dealing with this. 'Alzheimer's, dementia, off my bloody rocker, going stark staring doolally, losing my marbles!'

For a moment she stares at me as though I am an advanced case. She knows this is a terror of mine. She breathes in and composes herself to deliver as much as she can, as coherently as she can.

'They've not been saying anything on that subject. The way you were knocked around, and all the tests they've had to do, they've got enough to contend with.'

Oh yeah.

'They are concerned with your head and neck injuries. You've been through it. They have to check it out, especially where anything to do with the head is involved.'

They are going to do more tests and they want me in again within a fortnight. I interrogate Carol further, but she could earn money as an expert witness in high court trials. She coolly gives me every detail she wants to - which isn't much – marshals her reason, smiles understandingly, and gives nothing away.

I've lost the ability to argue, so I just say, 'Alright, alright, I'm reassured.' She's too strong for me. I might have been hoodwinked, but I'll have plenty of time in the

135

small hours to hold the matter up to be illuminated by the dark. I'll spot it. I'll know where to look for the threat, because already I know it is there. If this is garbled what do you expect? Let people out of kindness try to soothe me. The evidence is I will need to act before long, and my hope has to be I'll remain able to tell when that time has come.

My brother slaps me on my sore arm and reels off a whole load more jokes. The subject is mental illness. Some are funny.

They go and a nurse who spots me fidgeting brings me tea. I am not going to trouble her with more ravings. Instead I lay back and start stark musing.

Carol mentioned that the doctors wanted her to be with me when I returned. There was no need, she would have insisted on coming anyway. I can guess their game: I am no longer capable of taking myself places. I will need emotional support after I hear what they have to tell me. I used to have to go with my father on these occasions. What more do I need to convince me?

A couple of doctors come to see me. It can't be a ward round because they take place much earlier. They have a student with them who is making notes. One of them is a specialist of a peculiar sort I've never heard of. The other is not wearing white and asks, 'Do you remember how you got the old wounds on your head and shin, and that scratch on your finger?'

I tell him and they ignore me while discussing what sounds like "vision motor co-ordination".

'You made a lot of noise in your sleep last night,' says the suited guy, 'and kicked out, knocking your blankets off. Is that a normal occurrence?'

It isn't entirely unusual I let him know.

Ignoring me again they ask the student something I can't hear, and he says something about, 'Sleep Behaviour Disorder.'

'And I gather you've lost weight,' the suit says to me.

I think I am supposed to respond so I tell him it could be hospital food, and all three of them laugh. There is some examining of my head, some chat and then the two senior men go, leaving the young one to talk with me.

'The one in the suit,' I say, 'he's got to be a psychologist.' He is in fact a psychiatrist. 'And the other one?' I ask. Apparently he's an Otalaryngologist, which is what I'd thought I'd heard.

'To you that's a head doctor,' the helpful lad tells me.

He can see I am alarmed, so he puts his papers on the end of the bed and sits down to spend some time with me, chatting away amiably. He shows interest in my family, even asking their names and ages. I, of course, struggle with Carol's age which seems to especially get his attention. He asks me questions regarding hobbies I might have had. When I tell him I've given them up he returns to his papers to make a quick note. He comes back with a game similar to noughts and crosses, which we play while talking. We discuss my weight loss about which I can remember no details. I think he was anticipating me being foggy, so he is very forbearing towards me. His whole manner is very reassuring. After a very pleasant period he goes.

He has forgotten his papers. I lean forward to get them, but am too sore to make it. Among the papers is a magazine, so my path is easy. I ask a nurse if she can pass my mag and the other bits and pieces to me, and she obliges. The magazine turns out to be from the Alzheimer's Research Trust. The papers belong to the student, but I don't say so and am rifling through them at a pace. There is stuff about MRI and CT scans I have had. I am going to be recommended for Reminiscence Therapy, and there is stuff about

137

weight loss that I don't understand.

I call a nurse over and ask her about the student. At first she looks perplexed and then says, 'Oh, he's not a student. He is a doctor who is studying to be a specialist.'

'In what?' I ask. She checks with a colleague and returns to tell me, 'Geriatric Psychiatry.'

Immediately she goes I carry on with the papers, but am not getting any clear sense from them. My hands are shaking as I pick up the magazine which I pore over. There is an article in it which lists factors that indicate a greater risk of getting dementia. The list could have been specifically designed to describe me. It puts in no particular order herpes, raised cholesterol, raised blood pressure, blows to the head, excessive alcohol consumption, and certain forms of disturbed sleep. Sudden weight loss also features in there as a symptom. There are hardly any other factors. The final article I read is written in a very positive tone about the efficacy of some therapies. The one it is most enthusiastic about, and this doesn't come as a surprise to me, is Reminiscence Therapy.

The young Geriatric Psychiatrist suddenly appears, looking worried and asking for his papers. I pass them over and it is clear I have been reading them.

'You know what I've got, don't you?' I say. 'It's Alzheimer's, isn't it.'

He says nothing.

'Haven't I?' I demand.

He moves his head back and forth, in neither denial nor confirmation, and says, 'I am sorry, I am not your doctor and your condition is really not for me to say.' With that he rapidly retreats.

XIII

It's stop-start along a narrow stretch hemmed in on either side by heath on my way towards Jack Straw's roundabout. The silence in the car is an anthem of loneliness. I never envisaged making a journey such as this on my own, and yet here I am, less than a mile from meeting a medical Judge Jeffries. I thought Carol might turn out for this one for old time's sake, but I haven't heard from her in days. When we did speak she cut me dead: 'Do you ever wish you had a son?' I'd asked. 'We did for a few hours, or have you forgotten?' I believe if I was a woman I would have nothing to do with me.

I am driven to adopt a boy. For how long? For just as long as I've got.

Nobody was happy with me walking out of the hospital. They were refusing to talk sense to me and denying the obvious, so I told them that they, like me, would have to wait a couple of weeks until I came for the meeting with the big chief consultant, and they could play straight with me then.

Under pressure from Linda I subsequently agreed to go back for additional scans. My foot is healing, so I've cut up a shoe and strapped it on over the bandage and some extra padding. I believe I can now walk pretty normally, although a severe headache is back. It's the worst one yet, and it has spread to my neck and along my sinuses to where my wisdom teeth used to be, where in fact it is strongest. Before I set off to see Oliver, I am taking refuge in a coffee house. I've got his address written just above where I've noted his shift patterns on the crepe bandage that is wrapped around my left arm.

One coffee, one FT and the usual kindergarten later, and I feel it is the likes of me who are to be seen and not heard in this era. I'm not sure, however, about the "seen" bit. My foot has started throbbing, but the delaying is over; I must now set off to see Oliver. I've locked myself out and don't have keys for the car. The car would have been handy, but I'll have to do without it. I haven't a clue where I have put my house keys either. I have a distinct memory of putting them in my trouser pocket, but they are not there.

The sun is shinning and I am determined and ready. I've drawn an imaginary starting line stretching from St James' spire on my left to the art deco style Odeon on my right. I get a nod from a local down-and-out sitting on the pavement playing something unrecognizable on a guitar. We've often shared some of my change. I'm off towards Highgate.

The walking gets me to the right temperature. On another day I might have felt good, but today I don't. Either the bright light or my facial injury is giving me a bit of a migraine, only the fifth in my life. I recognise it because I get a waviness in my vision, as though looking through rising hot air. I stop in the newsagents and ask for a bumper size box of paracetamol. They don't sell packets with loads in anymore, so they are no use beyond helping with headaches. I work up some spittle in my mouth and swallow three. I am racing towards the huge place in which Oliver has his bed-sit.

As I approach the next corner I see a young man in trouble. The plaster on my forehead has slipped a bit and is impeding my vision in one eye, but I recognize the figure: the darkish complexion, trendy shiny hair, the height and the smart dress. It is Oliver. He is in deep trouble; he really is staggering.

'Son, let me help you,' I say as I reach him, but it isn't him. It is a clean shaven lad who has on an expensive designer coat. He turns and looks me up and down, and it is clear I have passed a test with flying colours. He has difficulty speaking but persists when showing me a piece of paper.

'Do you know where this is?'

On it is neatly written the address for North Highgate Practice on North Hill. 'Where is this?' he asks again, leering and swaying.

'Easy,' I assure us both. 'Straight across at the lights, fifty yards and straight on at a mini roundabout, two hundred and fifty yards more to the next roundabout and turn right. That's North Hill. If you can't find it, ask up there, it won't be far.'

I have kept it simple, but it might as well have been an extract from quantum physics. 'Thanks,' he says ever so politely. I look at the numbers on the buildings; I am only a turning away from Oliver's. He'll go to work shortly and I'll miss him if I'm not careful. Off the ailing lad goes towards the lights. When he reaches them he slumps against the end of the railings. Heavy traffic is tearing by and he is in danger of falling into the road. I go and get him and have to take him by the arm or he'd collapse. He is getting worse by the minute.

'Come on back to the bus stop, I'll put you on the right one.' I tilt him against an electrical sign in the shelter, advertising a store that closed months ago. I'll have to pay, he would not be able to reach into his pocket and get his hand out again. He is like a little child, just going where I lead him.

'I've got M.S.' He is trying to make conversation, not get pity. Well that explains something. A relative had that and it's a terrible disease.

A bus comes, but it is not going to North Hill. Neither is the second one. A third one arrives. I get on to ask, and am told it is turning left, nothing goes straight on. I look at the lad; there is definitely something of the Oliver about him. 'Come on,' I say, 'I'll walk there with you, it's not far.'

His face is deeply tanned like someone back from a long Caribbean vacation. Either that or he spends a lot of time in the open air. He is uncannily similar to the figure I glimpsed being rushed from the coffee house by my daughter. This boy's either got tons of gel on his hair or it is naturally oily. As we walk along, he is becoming more dependent. I am now using my good arm to keep him from falling. People on both sides of the road are looking at us weirdly, but not antagonistically. There is me limping, bloodied and part swathed in bandages, with someone who is manifestly far worse off.

'I haven't always had M.S,' the boy tells me as I look down noticing he has no laces in his shoes and no socks on.

We pass Oliver's place, but I have to go on.

My foot is hurting, but it is only about a hundred and fifty yards to go to the top and the roundabout. The going is slow. The trek is like the days when your first child becomes a toddler; suddenly everywhere you look there are dangerous obstacles. In this instance it is the corners of head height brick columns, railing spikes or the half collapsed poles holding estate agents boards. In fact it is anything hard and with an edge to it, and I am having to hold him tightly.

I ask, 'Where do you live?'

The answer is Finsbury Park, so his local surgery cannot be round here.

'Why are you coming here for a doctor's?'

'A lady wrote me this,' he says holding out the same note as before. 'I need Phenobarbital.'

Now I think I understand. 'Isn't that a barbiturate?'

He doesn't seem to notice what I have said. I am sure it is prescribed for drug addicts who'll use it when nothing else is on offer. I believe barbiturates are also the weapon of choice in the Swiss self-service suicide clinics. It is gone twelve and any surgery will now be closed. Besides this, they'll refuse to take on someone not on their books who is in this sort of condition. We're reaching the top.

'The surgery will be closed,' I say. 'We'll go to the hospital instead. It is the opposite way down the hill.' I thought he would protest, but he passively follows my lead.

'Can I...,' he says and stops.

'What?'

'No,' he says boyishly and with a bit of a smile. 'I was being cheeky.'

'Go on, ask anyway,' I say.

He wants a cup of coffee. He is virtually sitting down every few steps with each paving slab inviting him to rest. I am almost dragging him along in a crouched position. He isn't going to make it all the way down the hill. It's impossible, short of rolling him down there.

'I've got to get money from the cash point,' I tell him. 'There is a coffee bar there. We'll get coffee and a taxi.'

He looks down and asks, 'What is wrong with your foot?'

'It's constantly out of step,' I tell him.

'What's your name?' he asks. I've often noticed before that people you help want to know your name. 'Is it the Good Samaritan?' he offers in an insane style of laugh which turns into heavy coughing. I rub his back and can feel his spine.

'Peter.' I tell him. A Good Samaritan, I don't think so, no. Me? I'm a sometimes bleeding heart. 'How old are you?'

'Thirty-two, but I don't look it, do I?' He says it with a grin. There's a little devilishness in there somewhere. He's not ready to join the angels yet, so there is some hope. 'I come from Eastbourne. My Mum and Dad are still there. I did a degree in pharmacology.' He enjoys telling me that he and his mates used to produce, and consume, everything from ethyl alcohol to

143

LSD. I am still holding him up.

I've prepared myself for it, and I really do not want to miss Oliver today, so I guess I'll have to catch him at work. We turn left onto the top of the hill, and head the few yards to the cash machine. I glimpse Canary Wharf way off, through the pollution haze. He is still talking. Some of it is jumbled and he is more unsteady than ever, but he leans on a wall and manages to communicate one thing by holding out his arms, one hand in front of the other. It is as though he is holding a long horn, but instead of blowing, he is sucking. It is a deranged exaggeration of a thing I've never seen first hand, but I know this is someone who smokes crack cocaine. There is briefly a look of wild glee on his face. He's incapable of standing while I go to get some money from the machine, so I sit him down on the steps of Costa Coffee. Remarkably no taxi has come by. It may be this is a bad spot for them.

'Just wait there, I won't be a minute,' I say, as I enter Costa's to get his drink. At that moment a taxi with a turbaned driver pulls up in traffic.

'We'll get the coffee in the hospital,' I say, grabbing him and dragging him into the taxi. The driver can see what a state he is in, but is fine about it. He only charges three pounds fifty. He has made a sort of contribution, and he won't take a tip.

It seems as though I've never been away: hospitals and dentists' chairs are like that, and the lad seems to be feeling the same.

'The security guard won't let me in,' he says.

'It's alright, you're with me. I know somebody who works here.'

I am ready for an argument and I am on solid ground. It is difficult to see how entrance to a hospital could possibly be refused to someone as clearly ill as he is. No problem going through the automatic doors.

'This lad's not well, he has MS and needs

Phenobarbital,' I tell reception.

Without hesitation they send us into A and E, which must be the sole way of getting treated without a letter from a GP. We go by the seated crowd to its desk. People are staring while I support the lad, telling the desk the same as I told reception.

The two women both look at me, as though they don't know what to do on an occasion such as this. One asks, 'And what about you?'

'Oh, I've been seen to, I'm fine,' I say.

Her co-worker turns away and starts to busy herself with something else, while she goes to get someone who will know what to do. This has to be unusual, but then I suppose the lad is unusual.

From behind closed doors he emerges: no more than five-ten, wide-shouldered and barrel-chested with his belly catching up on the chest, a panoramically broad cleft chin, a bomber jacket with badge, and a marine's haircut. He has come from scrutinizing the closed circuit TV screens. He is the very essence of a security guard. He sizes me up, raises an eyebrow, believes I am no physical threat and is happy to ignore me.

He speaks only to the lad. 'There's nothing here for you. You are a nuisance, so go away.'

'There has got to be something that can be done for him,' I say.

'You can stay if you want, mate, you look like you need it, but he's discharged himself twice and there's nothing we can do for him. He gets people on the street to help him and takes them for a ride.'

Obviously I am one of these people, but I come back, 'He has asked me for nothing.' I understand this scene. This man has a job to do that needs doing; sometimes it can be bedlam in here, crazed and violent people coming in at all hours, and women on the desk badly exposed to danger. I wish Oliver worked in this

145

department; I could do with some support. 'I do not disagree with a single word you are saying, but something has got to be done for him. If I take him out of here I might as well lay him down in the middle of the road outside.' I am pronouncing every word fully and correctly, trying to sound as though I could be someone important, a QC, for instance.

The guard runs his eye over me again, head to toe again and shakes his head. I am a total pain. He knows he cannot touch me and that I will resist him physically removing the lad.

'There must be somewhere here for him.'

'There's nothing here. He can go to the Walk-in Centre in Soho.'

'Fine, that'll do.'

The guard has done more than the job he is paid for. I have heard of this place. I'll get a taxi.

I take my crack addict over to the coffee bar and sit him down. I tell him, 'Don't go anywhere, coffee is on its way.' He looks terrible, and can't grasp what is going on, but is trusting. If I were to say, 'Let's go to the railway bridge, and throw ourselves over it,' he'd follow. I constantly feel an urgency, as though any second he'll wander off to disaster. Everyone is gazing at us, but it is not inane curiosity. He appears younger than he is, and they are looking with concern. I come back with coffee and a cake and tell him, 'Stay there while I ring a taxi.' He is fully occupied.

On reception there is a phone line, put there for this purpose. The taxi firm tells me they'll be ten minutes. When I get back to him he has poured loads of sugar into the coffee. It is boiling, but he has, largely, downed it. The cake, one of those big muffins, was a bad choice and now it is everywhere: all over him, all over the table and all over the floor, mixed with the dregs of spilled coffee. I curse quietly, although I think he hears me, and go and get some serviettes from the counter. I wipe down the table and the floor as best as I can, all the time looking over to reception to see if a cab has come.

A lady from behind the counter comes over with a wet warm cloth, 'Need some help, dear?' She's everybody's mum.

I wipe his hands and his coat, asking him, 'Where did you get this coat?'

'A beautiful woman gave me it.'

I give him the cloth and tell him to wipe his face.

'Don't move. I'll check for the cab.' I stand over by reception facing the doors for any sign, while trying to keep an eye on him.

Where's my lad going? The toilet, which could be for the best. At reception I ask if I can get a message to someone in the cardiac department. A woman there picks up the phone. When I ask for Oliver she says, 'Are you a relative?' I can't give a reply to that, so I just tell her, 'I'm in Casualty and it's urgent.'

'He's...,' she begins, but I have to abandon the phone because the cab is here. I tell the cab driver we won't be long. He'll wait just outside. I get a piece of paper from reception and write, 'The Walk In Centre Soho,' on it. He is still in the toilet. Suddenly, I recall that this is the addict's favourite spot for self-medication. I've got to have him able to stand. I go in, but he's fine, sprucing himself up in the mirror. It is all other-worldly. He must have thought I was annoyed and that he looked terrible. He has wiped himself down and put water on his hair, running his fingers through it.

'I look better now, don't I?' he says.

'Yes, great,' I assure him.

His hair is standing up, as though several hundred kilowatts are running through him. I hook his arm, saying, 'Come on,' and we go out to the cabbie.

'He needs to go to this place.' I show the note to the cabbie and then pass it to the lad. There are two

147

additions on it, my number and my address in case there are any problems. Not wise, I know.

I give the cabbie the fare and a two pound tip.

He tells me, 'Don't worry, it won't be the first time I've taken someone there.'

Now the lad finally does ask, 'Have you got some money, for food?'

Food. I can't refuse that so I give him twenty quid, the last note in my sparse wallet.

'If there is anything I can do for you?'

That's unreal and I am equally unreal. 'Yes, when you've eaten and when you are feeling better, put the change towards getting a coach back home to your Mum and Dad in Eastbourne.' I wonder if they would thank me for that.

Of course I made a mistake, I don't suppose the money will be used for food, but that is the trouble with being a bleeding heart, you can't control the flow.

I'd set off to see Oliver, to talk over things, things that had to be settled. Dealing with this other lad will have been easy compared to what I am anticipating. If I had resolve, most of the vitality has now drained from it.

I am late and he is probably not free, but it is worth a try, so I go to the clinic where he did my scans. I've been here twice fairly recently, but I don't know if they've re-decorated, because it looks entirely different. Even the layout has changed. The clinic desk was surely somewhere else, and the rooms seem to have been switched around. I know it is not possible. It is eerie. I go over it in my head: where I entered, where I sat and which directions I went in.

I go to the desk and try to find the woman I had not long phoned about Oliver, but nobody there recalls such a conversation. I look for a familiar face or two, but there are none, and certainly no sign of Sam. It's not eerie, it's just me. I want to toss my head in the air and catch it with an almighty kick as it comes down.

'Excuse me,' I ask, 'Could you tell me where the heart monitors are fitted?'

Now I know where I am. I hover outside the room where Oliver operates the machine, but when the door opens someone else is working there. I look around, failing to spot him anywhere. I go back to the desk.

'Excuse me, I'm looking for Oliver. Has he started work yet? Do you know where he might be?'

'Who?'

'Oliver, a tall good looking lad who's not long had his twenty-ninth birthday. Works in heart scanning: the room over there.' No joy with this, but someone else, with a stack of folders under her arm, arrives. She's the one I spoke to on the phone earlier.

'Can I help you?'

No one can help me, but that's beside the point. I explain what I am after again.

'Ah, he's not here anymore. He's working at the Royal Free. It's not too far from here, near to the mainline station in Hampstead.'

I thank her. Much more of this and I will not be able to remember who I am, let alone who my newly found son is. I knew full well he had moved hospitals and I knew full well where to. Oliver may have been the priority, but I am done for. The Royal Free is only a short taxi ride away. All that is left in my wallet are the condoms I thought I had forgotten the other day and as far as I know taxis don't take cards. I've dealt with a son of other parents and that will have to do for today. Yet I know I cannot possibly leave it much longer.

A klaxon is sounding deep inside my ear. I again take three paracetamol, thinking bucketfuls wouldn't go amiss, and attempt the trudge back. My foot won't have it, so I sit on a seat at a bus stop and loosen the ties around the shoe. I get on the bus, say I'm only on it for a few stops and argue about the cost with the poor driver. It requires most of my remaining change. The bus does not turn where I had expected it to, which I believe I knew already. So now I get off, bend over and re-tighten my shoe, and dodder back to my empty home.

XIV

The car is idling, but my mind is racing. I should be focused entirely on what is facing me, but the "success" I've had sorting out some of my affairs feels almost as lamentable as anything the hospital will reveal.

'We're going to Dalston. I did tell you that's where it is.'

If I didn't trust her entirely I would believe that Carol was playing games with me. Not much longer and I'll be convinced.

LMNT is the name of the restaurant that Sam has selected. When we arrive I can see from the board outside that it is not cheap. The menu reads pretty modern. This area has been coming up while Tottenham has been going down. What a strange ogre the market is. It can leave one place as the scraps while its like elsewhere is turned into a delicacy.

'There's plenty on there you'd go for, Dad,' Linda tells me. I must have done something good to deserve her.

Sam arrives, barely acknowledges Carol, and embarrasses me with an excessively warm greeting. Everyone is polite, making no reference to my cuts, bruising and bandages.

I have had my paracetamol fix, but still have aches. As we go in, I am lacking lustre everywhere. Unfortunately, inside we are seated intimately, but at least I am next to Oliver who is giving nothing away. On his other side, cramped up close, is Linda.

'How's the new job going?' I ask Oliver.

'He is going to enrol in medical college before long,' replies Linda who must have been chatting to him outside. Sam and her daughter make a point of sitting opposite me and before long I feel a foot, with the shoe slipped off, shoved in my crotch. I let out a half suppressed yelp and it is withdrawn.

The conversation is going surprisingly well, mainly due to daughter number two's efforts. The extent of her skills has never occurred to me before, although I should have been able to work it out. Firms have rapidly promoted her, even when she has gone as a temp. Led by her, the talk has moved on to medical matters. This has the attention of Oliver and should do the same for his mother.

Sam is not participating and for the same reason I am not. Her concentration must be on what is stirring below decks. The foot is back and I assume it is not her daughter's. We order and Sam, I notice, is completely ignoring her old friend, Carol, and saying things like, 'I really fancy something fruity,' while running the circle of her joined index finger and thumb up and down the phallic neck of an empty bottle which holds a candle. Perhaps everything we have done together is this crass and ridiculous. Nobody else seems to spot any of this. Sam pushes her foot further and bruises my left testicle.

'Agh', is all I can manage; it is conceivable that she interprets this as pleasure. I react, reach under the table and shove her foot away so forcefully it makes her rock back in her chair.

I guess she is trying to engage me when she launches into stuff about the Maharishi, Tantric Sex and Transcendental Meditation.

'You can put that hocus-pocus in a barge and scuttle it.' I actually spit slightly as I say it. Sam should be stunned, but she isn't. She carries on with the meditation nonsense.

The wine arrives, is passable, and is soon followed by the starters. Portions are small, but the food is good. Carol decides to head to the toilets and I take the opportunity to shove the foot, which has been reasserted, away again. At that, Sam gets up, calls out,

'Carol, hold on,' and follows her.

The two women are gone for an excessive time. Sam returns looking slightly flushed, but there is no sign of Carol. I swear I hear Zowie, who has failed to speak or acknowledge a word at the table, say, 'He's a good screw.' I nearly fall off my chair. It can't be me she's talking about. Nothing comes of it. My phone goes and it is Mo. Extraordinarily, he is outside wanting to talk. Out I go.

'Mo, we can fit you in inside; there's no need to hang around out here.'

'No, this is just for you and me, mate. You have been asking me and I've been wanting to tell you...'

'Look, something has happened in there, something that could be very bad and I should get back and see if there is anything I can put right, or, more likely, take what's coming to me. You've been telling me I'm acting stupid and you're right. I'm afraid someone else could have taken a real blow in there, as a result. It would be fine if it were only me, but I think someone who really doesn't deserve it at all could have been hurt. Christ what a mess!'

'It can't be as difficult as what I've got to do, Petey.'

He has no idea. I take a deep breath, look him up and down, and then it strikes me. My oldest, in fact my only friend, a man who is dear to me, stands there with his shaved head, tight jeans, trendy trainers, a white tee-shirt, and now a pencil moustache and goatee. It's almost a uniform, and I am not so out of touch that I can't spot it. And I get it, I truly get it: those effeminate briefs I saw in his flat weren't a woman's, they were his, or his partners. The bedroom door he closed so surreptitiously didn't have a woman behind it, but a man.

'Oh mate, it's not a problem for me,' I tell him, although it won't be easy. On the contrary, it changes

153

our relationship fundamentally, but I am not a Neanderthal, I have caught up with some things. 'I know what you are about to come out with,' I go on, 'and it's okay. We are mates and that is the way it is going to stay.'

He is unable to say anything; he is looking at me, unable to believe I've worked it out, so I finish the job for him and tell him what he was struggling to tell me. Then I add, 'I can't stay here much longer. I think Sam has been talking to Carol and I need to get back in there for some damage limitation.' I hold out my hand to him. He stares at it as though I'm offering the contents of a pooper-scooper.

He shakes his head, not in denial, but in amazement. He doesn't accept my hand, but simply says, 'I'm sorry, it's something I can't talk to you about. Neither of us is up to it, sorry. I thought I could, but...' There's nothing to be achieved here, so we part.

Inside the restaurant, Carol is not in her seat. I go in search of her. She is not in the corridor, so I take a risk and check to see if anyone is in the women's toilets. One of the cubicles is locked, but doesn't respond when I call out her name. I walk through the rest of the restaurant, but can't see her anywhere. Shortly after I return she comes in from the street entrance, sits down, pours wine and lifts her glass to me. I look at Sam but she does not respond.

While her sister is deeply back on the subject of medical vocations with Oliver, my eldest daughter has noticed her mother has become silent, and turns to her and chats. Carol is doing a good job of acting unperturbed, but if you knew her as I do, you would see that there was a tremendous upset there.

I cannot eat and I cannot even drink. The time is passing excruciatingly slowly. A piano and a singer have struck up. I believe I can make out Linda saying something about student accommodation to Oliver.

'It's cheaper if you share,' she tells him. 'You could help me. It'll be fun.'

I should be perplexed, but my mind is elsewhere.

There have been no more feet in my crotch and the bill is split, with Oliver paying for his mother and his sister.

I ask Oliver, 'How are you finding the Royal Free?'

'Oh, fine. I hear you are coming in. I will pop around for a chat or two, if you want.'

So he knows I am ill, too.

Outside, Sam attempts to turn a goodbye peck on the cheek into lip on lip contact, but I turn away. It's about as desirable as an anal fissure.

'D'you want to come over to our place again?' the daughter interrupts, and I become like one of those dog puppets in car back windows. My jaw flaps back and forth, but nothing comes out. The damage is already done, but this won't help matters.

Carol stays apart from it all and there is no pretence by Sam at a fond farewell. There are a few hugs and the girls all peck each other and Oliver on both cheeks. It's pretty standard fare, except for some prolonged words between Oliver and Linda.

'Oliver is nice, isn't he?' Linda says to me and laughs.

Carol remains forlornly apart; Sylvia goes and stands by her and the taxi. Oliver is going on somewhere, but stops, turns and comes back for a few more words with Linda. Over my shoulder I gaze at his height and breadth of shoulder. He has a tight, tan coloured, bonnet style hat on his head. I am too busy admiring him and walk straight into the hard surface of the obvious, and it sends me reeling. It almost goes without saying that I hadn't gleaned right. Oliver's dimensions together with his skin tone were there to be recognised. He is precisely the silhouette I saw slink

155

away in the coffee bar. I suspected I knew him, I even said so, I'm sure I did, and I actually have known him, for a little while at least. For once I'd got something right, more's the pity. Of course I have been slow to see the clearly evident. There already existed an easy connection for Sam and Carol to arrange tonight's get together. That connection is Oliver and my daughter. She won't be at college with him because she is going to do a medical degree. I had misheard. She will be with him, but for altogether other reasons. I don't understand why it has been hidden from me. Perhaps they didn't want to give someone in my condition bad news. No that makes little sense because it presupposes they knew what underlies their relationship. I can't work it out. Each time I return to the problem it looks more opaque. The more I consider it, the more bewildered I become. The sole clear thing is that Oliver is the man I caught the glimpse of when Linda whisked him out of the coffee bar. They chatted so easily and intently tonight because they are boy and girl friend, lovers in fact. But why avoid me? They cannot possibly have the awful knowledge that I have: the sire of her failed pregnancy, the father of my miscarried grandchild is my probable son. My son and my daughter, carnally together! But they have no idea, so why keep their love from me?

This is too much and too bizarre and too Victorianly gothic for the new millennium. I cannot become the patriarchal monster standing over them and forbidding them to meet ever again on no declared grounds. Impossible. Moving area is not on, and the extreme of emigrating wouldn't guarantee separating them either. Yet I must be the barrier to their love, if love is what it is. It is a problem of a century and a half ago without the means to resolve it that existed then. When I see the lad I am going to have an appallingly difficult discussion with him, but it has to be done. I am his absent father and he is forbidden to see my daughter. That should do a lot to cement my relationship with him.

I have not forgotten Carol. She sits in the taxi opposite me, and looks straight into my eyes. She is not quite crying, but her eyes are moist. She keeps it up the entire way home and I owe it to her at least to return her gaze. It is wordless, yet I can hear it, and it is a telling conversation. She knows each of my flimsy excuses, and totally rejects them. She can anticipate each of my apologies and vows about future conduct, and totally rejects them also.

When we get indoors she packs her case.

XV

My injured foot still has some difficulty in pressing the brake peddle, and it could be I am a danger on the road. Certainly I have been a danger to those who have travelled with me in recent times. I have run them down and now the most important journey of my life is to end alone.

I open the front door and start when Carol shouts from inside, 'We should talk.'

Oh, yes please. I'll take this one chance and do and say whatever it takes. At that very moment my mobile rings. After Linda's miscarriage I will never ignore it again. 'You're sorted. We need to meet.'

'Who is this?'

'Jeremy.'

'Who? Ah, yeah, I've got you.'

'Can you make it down to Harringay in an hour? I've set up a meeting. You'll need two grand. I've worked the oracle and come up trumps for you.'

Then it dawns on me; he's found someone to supply the toxin, botulism. Anything is possible in London. 'I'm on my way,' I tell him and close the front door behind me.

I keep failing to refill my wallet. Since it was emptied I've been living from a card. Two rings and three knocks later Carol opens the door to me. 'I'm sorry, truly,' I say. 'I really have to go somewhere; I need some money for a cab.'

With a shake of the head she fetches me some notes from her purse and slowly closes the door. I would have preferred her to slam it. A few seconds later I am back at the door, rushing in as quickly as possible to get my passport - it's always in Carol's dressing table.

First the cab stops at the bank where the passport isn't enough and I am interrogated on the need for my own cash, which I explain is to buy a bargain car.

Eventually I am down in scintillating Harringay. I go past fruit and veg stalls selling those tasty little curly cucumbers the supermarkets reject and past some of the best cheap cake shops in the world to wait where I have been told. In my inside pocket is a fat envelope. I am expecting a long wait, because people don't work on Greenwich Mean Time down here, but they are right on time.

Looking me up and down, Jeremy asks, 'What happened to you?' He has the company of a Mediterranean with a nose that wouldn't work on white people.

I don't bother explaining. We're not meeting here, apparently, but I make it clear I am not up for much walking. Fortunately we are not going far. They take me to a sort of cafe which has obscured windows and claims to be a social club. The sign outside says, Laci F.C. Inside there are middle aged men and older at the back, some playing a board game, some a card game, and gambling on both. At the front is a man who stops scooping up something with pitta and welcomes us. A few words and he brings a litre bottle of whisky with a duty free label on it to the table and three glasses, and then returns to his bread and dip.

We knock back a triple and the business begins. I get the envelope out and the swarthy guy's hand smoothly reaches out and glides it back to his side of the table where he meticulously counts it. His hand is lumps and bumps and as rough as mine used to be long ago, which has me thinking he simply doesn't look the part. Every time I go past a DIY store in the morning I see dozens of him crowding outside for work. The gang masters charge £20 a day for them. I fix him in the eyes and follow this by doing the same to Jeremy. Nothing. The package I have just paid for is not produced and it looks as though I could wait a long time, forever in fact.

159

This could be a con.

'Come on where is it?'

The man, who turns out to be Albanian, stands up and looks set to make his exit.

As he turns away, I push him and then swing him round by the shoulder, noticing just how big his shoulders are. I hold my hand out. 'You're going nowhere until I get it. Where is it?'

He looks astonished and as though he'd certainly like to give me something, but still nothing is forthcoming.

'Come on, when do I get it? Where is it?'

'We've got to arrange that,' says Jeremy. 'These things don't just happen.'

My patience has gone. 'You get me down here in a hurry and I have to get that sort of cash at a moment's notice, and then you tell me you've still got to get the goods! Does this guy have a package of botulism or not?'

The Albanian doesn't speak very good English and Jeremy is stumped. I know he is a piss artist, but surely he understood what I wanted.

He whispers and I have to draw close to catch it. 'You want someone killed, right?'

Now I'm completely stumped. 'What we talked about was an undetectable suicide where my family can claim the insurance.'

'Gobsmacked!' is all Jeremy can manage. He turns and chats to the Albanian who nods repeatedly. 'They'll do it,' says Jeremy. 'They'll top you. He's got someone with a shooter who'll do it.'

I look over my shoulders left and right to see if they are talking to anybody else. 'Do you mean shoot me? With a gun?'

'Exactly. In the back of the head.'

The Albanian says, 'Bang,' which coincides with the noise of one of the players at the back slamming a

160

counter down on a board.

Jeremy adds, 'It doesn't come much more painless than that; if it's the insurance you're after, who could argue against that?'

I swig another triple, but don't pour them any. I have a variety of aches and feel worn out by it all. I'm running out of other options and they are deadly serious. I probably wouldn't know anything about it and he's right about the insurance, but I've crucial things I have to do first.

'Alright. When?' I ask

'You won't know. They'll drive up behind you on a moped and pop, you're gone.'

Apparently Somalis will be involved. It's the same the world over: once you've parted with your money you've lost control. "Pop." That doesn't sound too bad.

'Okay, if I do go along with it, I need to know roughly when it will it be. I don't need a specific date. I can see that might not be a good idea, but I need to do some tidying up. A couple of weeks might do it. I want to check the insurance for one thing and I've got a son with problems for another.'

They look at each other. 'We'll do our best, but it won't be easy,' explains Jeremy.

The Albanian is looking at me. He has clearly decided I am weird and he doesn't like me, but he eventually nods. The deal is done except for the contractual formality: they insist on shaking hands. When the Albanian gets up to leave, I notice cement and mud at the bottom of each of his trouser legs. He could probably do a good job of seeing me off with a spade. And that is it; my future is taken care of.

They leave swiftly, but as I prepare to go, the pitta-muncher comes over to me with an astronomical bill for the whisky. He will settle for half, given that there is quite a lot of the bottle left. I shell out and finally part

161

from him to find a cab. As I do I can hear a moped slowly tracking me. I attempt to sprint, but can't and so hobble across the road and hurriedly raise my good arm to flag a cab.

I've got to ask myself how much time I have left. I don't trust Jeremy and the Albanian. I ring Sam and repeatedly ask to meet her, but the reception is terrible and she is hardly able to hear a word. As far as I can make out she is at home so that is where the cab is taking me.

When I get to Sam's, her daughter opens the door. There she stands, Venus de Milo with arms, in a micro skirt, and in no need of an uplift bra. 'I've arranged to see Sam,' I tell her. She warmly takes my good hand, brings me in and sits me down.

'Wow, have you been in accident? Let me make you a drink.'

'Yes, please, a tea, an ordinary tea, please.'

'I don't do that often,' she says, as she puts the kettle on. While we're waiting she lights a joint, puts on some music and sits as close to a man as her mother does. She's too close and I am uncomfortable. There is a tocsin ringing in my ears. The girl isn't that good looking; she has tattoos and piercings that make me cringe. Yet here she is, turning into a piece that passeth all understanding. I have thought of women under thirty-five as little more than old enough to have stopped peeing in the bath. And how old is this girl? Eighteen? No more than twenty-four, surely. The whisky, or the paracetamol I've taken more of, has eased the throbbing. I am tired and the sofa feels so comfortable.

'The kettle's boiling,' I tell her. Where is her mother? In the bedroom putting on her seduction outfit possibly. It will be wasted on me.

Zowie brings over the cup with tea leaves floating around on the surface, having paused to put on a burgundy coloured lipstick.

162

'When you've emptied the cup I can read these for you, if you like – the leaves I mean. It's what I'm best at reading.'

I could have got the arrangement wrong, because there is no sign of her mother. Zowie takes a long drag on the joint, snuggles up and turns her head, to blow away the smoke. When she turns back it is stunning. Her eyes are wide, and glistening, her pupils huge and dark, and her skin is faultless and shining.

There's a danger that my judgement is pulsing towards my pelvis. I have had to deal with problems like her in my working days, so I exert myself to summon up some survival techniques, some wisdom from my experience, or some restraint at least. I am exhausted and restraint asks a lot of a man's energies.

Zowie is half turned and leaning against me. Her lips are full and moist. If they open I swear I will follow the air she breathes in.

'Where is your mother?' I demand. 'She is supposed to be here.'

'I don't think so. She won't be here for a while.'

She is leaning more heavily against me. Could any normal man turn away from this? It is so marred and yet so compelling. I know that if I touch her she will melt and coo. The blood flow to my loins is robbing the supply to my intellect. Yet I should be proof against illicit longing. I catch a glimpse of my scarred forehead in a wall mirror. I rub the stitch marks in my neck and grind my heel against the scab on my shin, and the throbbing aches are back. Zowie has her head on my shoulder and I feel sorry for what I have done to Carol, and I feel sorry for this girl.

And then I hear the word "Daddy". It isn't Zowie, nor is it a recollection of any particular moment with either of my daughters. It is an echo of the vigilance that men somehow learn informally and imperfectly, and which I am supposed to exercise. I believe the ability grows along with the size of prostate glands in older men. The likes of me are not made of wood, so how do we resist? I suppose by not letting pleasure get in the way of feeling good.

On my way out I ask Zowie, 'Seen anything of your brother, recently?'

'He was round here for the first time in ages last night, but it was the same old, same old. He brought a form with questions about his parents' names and his birthplace on it, and they rowed.'

'Oh, yes? Was it about anything or anyone in particular?'

'I think it started off about you, but I try not to listen.'

'Me?' I ask, re-entering the main area of the room.

'Yes. Oliver said to leave you alone, to stop mucking you around. He said you were the solid sort and that she should be straight with you. Then I think he was on about who his dad was, again. I think he won. I think she's given up. She said she would arrange for him to meet his father, or something of that sort. I don't know.'

'What exactly did the form ask?'

'I don't know. Reading it wasn't for me. It was for work records or something. It will have been information about his birth.'

'Were there any names? Did my name come into it?'

'Yes, of course. I've already said they rowed about you.'

'I don't just mean at the beginning. I mean did my name come into it, you know, under the subject of fatherhood?'

'Fatherhood? I don't know. I told you, when they start arguing I try not to listen. This isn't fair; last night was really bad. The louder they shout, the less I can hear. You'll have to ask them.'

'Why isn't your mother here?'

'I told you she'll be a while, hours as it happens. Didn't you know?'

'She said she was here!'

'You must have spoken to her on her mobile. She's having problems with her hearing aid, especially over the phone.'

Well, that explains a lot. Sam doesn't finish until ten p.m. and hanging around here with the daughter would not be a good idea.

'Thanks for the tea. Tell her I called. I'll be back tomorrow night when she's finished her shift.'

'That's not a good idea. Unless you've spoken to her and she's agreed to it, she'll please herself. Ring her first and make sure she's heard you.'

'Why?'

'If you don't, you'll find out.'

'I'll see myself out.'

I ring Sam, as Zowie suggested, but it's a pointless effort. I have to leave a message. 'Sam, where were you?' I ask, and then I come to the point, 'I need to ask you who Oliver's father is.'

Carol is not home when I get in, nor does she return that night.

Eleven the next evening and I am back at Sam's. I knock and there is no answer, but it doesn't matter because, as usual, the door is not locked. Up I go, hoping I bump into Sam before her daughter bumps into me. I knock on the door to her section of the house and again there is no response. Don't tell me I got the time of her shift wrong once more, or she's gone straight off elsewhere.

In I go, hoping I'm mistaken, and I hear sounds that are definitely from Sam. It's a noise I should recognise.

165

I shout at the top of my voice, 'Sam! Sam! Did you get my phone message? I must talk to you. I have to know about Oliver.' From the bedroom she emerges without a stitch on. She doesn't even have her hearing aid earring in.

'Oh hi, Peter. Now's not a good time.'

'I need to discuss Oliver with you. Am I his father?' I don't believe she catches a word. Not quite true.

'Oliver? Oh, he can be a bad trip, sometimes.'

She is turning to go back to the bedroom, which gets me shouting again, 'Well, don't you think there is something we should discuss before then?'

At this point the big lump from the other night emerges, wrapped in a towel that is barely concealing his formidable erection.

'Man!' he says, and glares at me. The one word conveys a mixture of "Get a life" and "Get lost"! Sam is back in the bedroom.

What a twenty-four carat idiot I am. I was there, drooping with world weariness, while he stood there with the imperial majesty of a hard-on. Sometimes I want to put my head in a vice, and spin the handle. The daughter had all but told me what to expect, and this is Sam, the Sam I've always known, but it still feels bad. Well, she's in the bedroom with the prize bull, and deaf to anything I might have to ask, so there's nothing left to do but leave.

XVI

The car has a mind of its own, which normally is something to be valued. No matter how little pressure I am able to put on the peddle, it races long. It sweeps left down the side of the Heath, and past some splendid old buildings, including Boy George's house.

I have a few days leave left and there are things that have to be done. I am constantly looking over my shoulder which, with the state of my neck, is difficult. I never knew there were so many mopeds. The wounds in my foot and my hand are healing well. By contrast, my vocabulary is deteriorating badly. It is coming down to half a dozen catch-all words: thingybob, whatyacallit, wotsit, and whatsisname, interspersed with lashings of y'knows. I can hardly string a sentence together any more.

When my father got to this stage, his favourite general noun was dildo. Only those who didn't know him laughed. Whatever I report from now on will be an abridged version, with as much gibberish removed as possible.

After I walked out to meet my assassins the other day, Carol has hardly been seen and hardly been heard, not by me at least.

'It's a letter from France for you.'

Carol, who is back in the house for the minute, takes it from me, opens it and puts it in her pocket.

'What's it about?' I ask.

'It's from the chef on the course.'

'What's he want?'

'Recipes. Nothing that should interest you.'

I don't believe a word.

She must see the look on my face and tells me, 'You need something to lift you. We're going out.'

I can't believe she is prepared to spend time like this on me. In the past I might have protested, but I will grab this and any opportunity. That she is so temperamental is something I'll have to bear with, especially when it's in my favour.

On the back seat of a newish car is the most recent copy of the Alzheimer's Research Trust magazine alongside its predecessor.

'When did you start subscribing to that?' I ask.

'Oh, I picked that up from the bottom of your bed in the hospital.'

She is lying. I would have noticed it before. It's the dual deception that takes place with dementia: the victims won't publicly admit to having it and their nearest and dearest try to shield them from the truth of it.

We're not going far, to Hampstead High Street, but she has plans and is enthusiastic.

Carol parks at the top of a wide road in Hampstead and we get out and watch masses of high and low cloud scrolling overhead. She turns, puts my arms around her, stands close and kisses me. It is the earnest kiss that speaks of the long playing love, fidelity and commitment that only the recently unfaithful can give. It resonates in me. Call it a leap of lack of faith, but I think it confirms she has strayed. There is reciprocity now: we have both strayed.

I have noticed that one of the capacities Alzheimer's victims lose is that of being jealous. I can't quite have reached that stage yet.

'What exactly were you up to in France?'

'Speaking French and cooking. What do you think?'

'You seemed to take friends back to your bedroom.'

'What are you talking about, Peter? You have got a nerve, and now you're in danger of spoiling a good thing today. I made friends in France. Of course some

168

things happened... Oh, it could have been more...
Anyway, it is none of your business any longer.'

'Are you annoyed, I mean furious with me?'

'I've been angry with you for years, and it hasn't always been your fault.'

'Are you going to leave me?' I ask.

'It strikes me that we started leaving each other a long time ago.'

'Where do we go from here?'

'I haven't decided, but we should try to be sensible about it, no matter what we do. There'll always be a "we", we've got children and a history, but we may decide we don't want to spend that much time together. I don't know to be honest, but I am not going to do anything rash. We've both got options.'

Fair enough. It is hardly surprising if I mistook her smile. And then I get it. I do get it. I do recognize the look. I have seen it at certain weddings that have followed not long after funerals: the weddings of devoted partners who met someone new surprisingly quickly after the prolonged illness and death of their loved one. And I understand why it happens. It is because they had been grieving for so long, possibly years, before the terminal moment. They couldn't share their grief with their partner and it would have been improper to share the loss that for them is already real with anyone else. They have been alone far longer than anyone else realises. This is the way it is for Carol. She knows part of me has been extinguished and the rest is going that way. No doubt my conduct has diluted any grieving. Now she is at the stage past bereavement. She may not have done the definitive deed yet, but there is someone out there who can replace me, someone with whom she is prepared to be intimate. Provoked or not she doesn't have to leave me, because I am already far into the process of leaving both of us.

169

'That sounds reasonable, but can I ask if you will go back there?'

'I will go back to France. I have been back, but I'm here today because I want to be here. I have my two daughters here, and (is she going to say a husband?) a life here. Now let's just concentrate on today shall we?'

'You mean enjoy my faculties while I've still got them.'

'If you want.'

I tell Carol there is a pub around here, an old favourite of mine. We're still searching twenty arid minutes later, but it's gone, if it was ever there.

'What was its name?'

'I think it was The Fallow Buck.'

'The one with the big plastic deer out the front?'

'Yes.'

'That's one we used to go to in Hertfordshire years ago, but it's an easy mistake to make.' She takes over. In a shop in the plush and quaint High Street, she tries on a couple of dresses which make her look slimmer. Actually she is slimmer, but not too slim.

Carol has booked us a table in a restaurant with live Irish music – my favourite. She sits me down as though I am an invalid and I swallow a pint of porter in one.

'You'll make yourself ill.'

'I am ill.'

She frowns at me as I order a second. 'Don't worry this isn't the threat to my brain cells.'

Outside it has clouded over completely, so they light some candles. Failing eyesight may be one of Nature's kindnesses, because we can't clearly see all the ravages of age. Here, now, candle light is the finishing touch. It's burning off the years and smoothing the hollows. As I look across at Carol, she looks beautiful, different to how I remember her from years ago, but beautiful. I am sorry for what I have done and know it is probably irretrievable. You have considered it and you have waited for it. It is that moment when you can tell an older woman she looks beautiful and this is it, but it has already passed because the right to it has been foregone. The band turns from the foot tapping stuff to singing Carickfergus. I look at my wife, and listen in agreement:

> "But the sea is wide and I cannot swim over,
> And neither have I the wings to fly."

When I get home there is a letter from the hospital with the details of additional appointments. They want to repeat some of the scans before the climatic meeting.

Carol is upbeat about it. 'Oh, you have to go. They are finding out more and more, and there are more and more new treatments, new drugs, you know.'

I can see little point. It is clear that most of what has become available recently delays the full onset of the disease, no more. I'm not convinced this is better than nothing. It would merely prolong the dread, which can be the worst part.

I am getting constant mood changes, much the same as those I've seen in the past in stricken relatives. Even the up moments are a symptom of disintegration. I don't see why Carol should be lumbered with my mood swings. After all, I tolerated hers poorly.

I take myself into the bathroom and shout, 'What the hell are these scans for? So what if my neck and cheek bone are sore, I'll get over it, and my headaches respond to pills.'

Carol must be able to hear, but she ignores it. It's the sort of restraint that is reserved for the ailing. I was going to shout out again, 'And what's the game with that colonoscopy?' I've guessed the point there,

171

however: all my father's family had gut problems as well as Alzheimer's. It will be what the medical profession calls a marker for the disease. I am half a mind not to go for any more scans.

When I finally emerge, Carol says to me, 'We both know there is an important appointment looming. You need something practical to occupy you and I've got just the thing.'

It is like distracting a child who is crying, something I remember that she is good at.

XVII

The possibility of losing your closest friend is bad enough, but losing a child is the most terrible thing.

****

Apart from traffic and engine noise, which do not register, the car journey feels an even more silent one now. I pull the car over half way up on the pavement to let the traffic squeeze by, and weep. I do not think I can put things right.

Another day, for most people, is a chance for a fresh crack at things. For me it is a further recognition of time running out. I've done a mental list of things to do before I die. I don't know if I've already said it, but I have a mnemonic that I can only remember part of. Also, I am sure the list of things is getting longer. Regardless, this isn't the normal type of to do before I die list, you know: go paragliding, swim with dolphins, see the Taj Mahal. Key things on it are: assure my best friend I am okay with his sexuality (did I tell you Mo is gay?), reveal myself as the long lost father to a boy, while simultaneously forbidding him to see the girl he loves ever again. I am sure I am missing something out here.

Carol and I have never had the talk she said we needed and it may be things have moved beyond that. Obviously she hasn't left me yet, although I am getting the impression that she feels if anyone is to go it should be me. She may well be right, but I'll be gone soon anyway, so that one is covered. As far as my infidelity goes, I cannot tell quite where I stand with her, but I really don't feel I can make amends. I don't think she wants it for a start. She's constantly out doing things, which doesn't suggest she wants to spend much time with me these days.

173

I need time, but everywhere I go I hear mopeds behind me.

'Sam, it's Peter. We have to meet. I really do need to talk to you. I need to see you.' There is a long pause, which could be a problem with her hearing aid. 'Can we meet?' I shout. 'We need to discuss Oliver.'

'Of course we can meet. Where?'

I don't think we'll handle a pub well. 'How about coffee, just up the hill from your workplace?' If she suggests her house I will refuse. I can't do trial by orgy any more. Hopefully she'll accept my proposal.

'Why not in our cafeteria at the hospital?' It is an entirely inappropriate spot, but I agree and it's settled.

Sam no longer attracts me. I was propelled towards her, but now I've swung past her at twice the speed.

It is a first, going into a hospital and hardly noticing the institution. I wait in the cafeteria. Once she arrives I go to get what she wants to eat and drink before sitting down with her.

'I am surprised at you with Zowie, Peter. I though you'd be too uptight for that. Still it's cool, she's a grown woman.'

'I don't agree, and either I've got the wrong end of the stick or you have. Anyway, that's not what we're here for. Look, there is no smooth path into this Sam. I need to ask you about Oliver. He is a smashing lad. I know his age and his birthday, and what is more I can see an awful lot of likenesses between us. Am I his father? Is Oliver my son?'

'Peter, you and Oliver are such heavy, troubled people...'

Another thing we have in common.

'He hasn't stopped hassling me over this, and now so are you.'

'And so? You should bring this to a conclusion because it just isn't fair on any of us.'

'I'll tell you what I told him, which is as much as I can. Don't get uptight, because I suspect you won't like it. I told him we got it together in Brighton.'

That is how I recall it, and I am sure that she has got it exactly right.

'He was a light-skinned Trinidadian I met at a party. You know how it was in those days.'

I remember how it was for her.

'And you and Oliver don't look anything alike. Have you not noticed his skin colour? And what about his tight curly hair? It's pretty well Afro.'

I am astonished I have got it so wrong, but she is serious. I thought his hair had been styled in that way and it is conceivable that, light skinned as she is, a son of ours could be darker.

'Are you sure? I thought there would be a number of candidates and you couldn't be definite.'

She is certain. Sam finishes her meal while I can't touch what is in front of me. If I had any remaining interest in her, this is the end of it.

She leaves for work saying, 'Keep in touch.'

I get up, and walk out of there in a stupor of grieving. I should be happy that there are no dire problems of incestuous love between my daughter and my newly found son. Yet instead of relief I feel bereaved, because I now understand that I had wanted this son. There had been a chink in the bleakness, through which I could glimpse the future. Nevertheless, it is a resolution of sorts, I suppose.

I ring Mo to arrange to reconcile ourselves to whatever it is he is suffering over.

'It's not you, Petey, it's me. I am being too sensitive. It's an unusual situation, well outside the norm, and you can't help the way you are. You're not to blame'.

I tell him it's okay and that there is no hurry, and then we decide on a day and a time. He is pleased with

175

that and lets me know there will be someone coming with him.

I've had to add a new item to my list, and yes, I've had to begin working to a written list. Carol is turning a spare bedroom into a nursery (she believes it could be needed in the not too distant future). She wants to get curtains in John Lewis and needs some chests of drawers, so she is sending me to IKEA. It is the thing she had thought would be practical enough to occupy my mind. I hate the place.

I'm using my daughter's car because it's a hatch back and I'll be able to squeeze some sets of drawers in there. Driving, especially along this route, isn't my favourite activity. I've taken more pills for the neck and headache. The traffic is bad, with numerous signs for reduced speed limits that there isn't an earthly of ever getting close to. There are big lorries everywhere and each sign I come to is obscured by them, apart from the overhead ones for motorways I don't need. We are going at a snail's pace and I am stuck sitting here, once in a while putting the car in gear and flexing my foot on the clutch, which is giving me cramp. A journey that should take no more than fifteen to twenty minutes has dragged-out to half an hour, now forty-five minutes, and I've lost track.

I think I might have missed the turn. The bridges in front look more like the ones past my exit, near Hanger Lane. I slow down to check, but a young woman hoots and mouths something obscene at me as I drift across lanes.

At last I am in the IKEA car park, or rather in the queue for it. Along one aisle, and down another. I miss one space by seconds, go on to the next and the next, and have to begin over again and re-join the queue, and then race ahead of someone else into a being-vacated spot. It is a wonder the car drawing out doesn't create a suction 'pop,' the space is that tight. My car is in. Off I go, dodging circulating cars and sliding sideways between parked vehicles. I am at the entrance to the blue and yellow super warehouse.

The design of the path in IKEA is intended to bring customers past every section. I have no intention of doing this, so I ignore the arrows. Before long I am lost and can't find one of their maps of the store, which are on columns every so often. I am also bursting for the loo. I see the sign for toilets, go in and ensconce myself in a cubicle. That done I stand to pull up my new Calvin Klein pants, discovering that I still haven't quite got the hang of them yet and they are drenched with my urine. There's nothing I can do. I just do my trousers up and continue my search.

Ah, there is a desk with yellow-shirted personnel, so I get some guidance.

'Ouch!' A trolley catches my Achilles tendon. The yellow shirts want me to go along the conventional track. An IKEA regular is agreeing with her companion that, 'Everything is as cheap as chips, so long as you can find someone to put it together for you.' And me? Well I am defeated; I am following the arrows. Finally I am looking at a display of the chests of drawers I want. I put my glasses on, but still struggle to read near microscopic writing on the guidance sheet. It is supposed to show me where the relevant self-service racks are down stairs. I think I've understood it.

My mobile phone rings. I make out Mo asking, 'Can you hear me?' This is followed by some crackling, and me answering with, 'Can you hear me?' At brief intervals I repeat this three times. I know he is responding in exactly the same way at his end. Eventually we both ring off.

I find the area for my drawers. Loading up on the trolley is hard. I try to put the packs on it, but it keeps wandering off in the opposite direction; a brake

177

would have been useful. I hold the trolley with one foot and try to drag and load with the rest of my body, hands, hips, knees, parts of my rib cage, anywhere not already bruised that I can pressure and nudge it with. The trolley runs over my injured foot. This sends me hopping about and I crash into a shelving rack which re-opens the wound on my forehead. I have also torn my shirt sleeve.

At last I'm done and navigate my way to the checkout, where I join the wrong queue. There is a problem with the till and it will have to wait for a supervisor. It's not really Sod's law again. It's just that failing faculties lead to poor decisions. The older you are, the more it occurs. My tinnitus is sounding off while my heart cranks up to some accompanying arhythm. A torrent is coursing from my underarms and mixing with print on the cardboard packing to stain my shirt. With the weight, the trolley has developed a left lurch. I can only deal with it by standing to the left side, hunching over and pushing as though it's a coal truck. How we got a stacked trolley through the checkouts will be a wonder to future generations on a par with discovering how the pyramids were built.

I've succeeded.

Outside the sun is shining and a worker is going to look after my trolley, while I check for the car. The hard bit is done and my life support systems are back to near normal. I ring Carol to tell her I'll be roughly twenty minutes, and that I love her. She merely responds that she has got the extension lead and my tool box out for when I get back. I try to ring Mo, but the signal disappears once more. I wander forward and look upwards, the sunlight killing off some of my retina.

I can't find the car because I am half blind. My foot has swollen to the extent that I have had to squeeze off the shoe. As I go along my sock is shredding. Then I see the car, but not where I thought I had left it. Wrong. It is the same colour and a similar shape, but no more than that. One or two people are looking at me. I attempt to appear casual and wander back to where my car should be, but it isn't there. I retrace my steps, and work out a different spot where the car should be, but still it isn't there. I find something to stand on to look over the top of the entire parking lot to find my car. I think I've got it, and carefully pick a route, but it is the car I have already tried. I decide I will have to do this systematically; I will go up and down each and every aisle until I spot it. Unbelievably, after a painstaking sweat drenched trek, I don't find it. I am now questioning the basic reality of my day. Did someone give me a lift here? No, that simply doesn't make sense. Did I get a taxi? No, that doesn't make any sense either. I'll do it the other way; I've done east to west, I'll go north to south.

Each time I fail to find the car I feel more of an imbecile. I'm constantly getting that sensation you get in a dream when you step off a pavement and there's nothing there, so you wake with a fright and a jump. And still there's no relief. I've had it. There are bells and sirens going off in my inner ear, there is no recognisable pattern to my pulse, and my clothing is ringing. I go over to the adjoining car park, and do the same cross grid check that I've already done in the car park my memory insists I've used. Pointless. I realise that two explanations alone are possible. I use my mobile, which now has a strong signal, to report a stolen car and am put in a queuing system. Eventually there is an answer. The person at the other end of the phone is not a police officer, and basically doubts what I am saying. They don't get problems of that kind at IKEA, not even vandalism, because security is too good.

'I suggest sir, that to start with you have one more look for it, and if that fails you try Security.'

They call you sir, but treat you like a moron.

179

'I'm not the moron here, you know, pudd'n head,' I say and do the nearest you can get to slamming the phone down with a mobile. My first thought is to let ten minutes go by, then simply ring back and tell him that I have done this, they have checked, and the car is not there, and that, further more, Security doesn't accept that they would necessarily have spotted a theft. Nevertheless, I go through the whole business again. This gets me nowhere, so I find Security and they have a check. The car is not there. Security tell me that they wouldn't necessarily have spotted a theft, which should feel like some sort of vindication, but it doesn't.

Security can see I am in a state and tell me to go to the café while they run more checks. I'm to come back in half an hour. As I sip the coffee I mentally retrace my steps, but I am no longer sure of anything. If someone were to ask my name I would probably be stumped. Security get no result, continue to be pleasant to me and offer to call me a cab, but I decline. It is like that moment when you have been driving in a reverie, until you realise you don't know where you set out for. You don't know whether to brake and pull over, or to look for road names, and then it seeps back to you. You were heading for…wherever, and you are back on track, except I am never going to be back on track.

I have to go and attempt one last look. I think my heart is packing in and it isn't indigestion this time. And then I see it! Thank goodness! What a relief. My hands are shaking a little and it is hard to get my key into the lock. I have to force it in but… Success! However, I can't get into the car, because the key doesn't want to work, it won't turn. In fact the key looked foreign, but I can't have brought the wrong one. That makes no sense; I couldn't have got here. Then the alarm on the car starts incredibly loudly, hooter going, and lights stroboscoping. That is because it is not my car. It has a different number plate. And now the

180

key won't come out. A crowd has gathered and they are critical. In fact some are scathing, and one bastard in particular has laid a hand on me. I am pushing at the door and pulling on the key. My attempts have dented the door.

'That's enough, enough.'

'Take your hand off me.'

'You've damaged the car. You're the sort who won't declare it on the insurance. Just leave it alone and come with me to Security.'

'Is it your car?'

'That's got nothing to do with it. Someone call the police!'

There is a chorus of dialling.

'This is the last time; get your hand off me!'

He starts to say something, 'Look be sensible, you're too old...'

He doesn't finish the sentence because I have wrestled him to the ground and we are rolling all over the place. Two old girls and a young mother pull us apart. One says to me, 'You should know better. It's shameful.'

'You been drinking, sir?'

'What?'

'You heard me.' It's a policeman. While he's saying this, a squad car and a couple more police arrive. 'You have been drinking haven't you, sir?'

'Yes, all my life. Underage when I could. After closing time, moonshine, contraband and knocked off booze as well.'

The arm up my back hurts.

'Look I thought it was my car. I'm not a thief,' I say and pointing with the arm with the torn sleeve which is still free I continue, 'That idiot was assaulting me, not the other way round.'

'What a state he is. He's an old wino,' says one copper looking me up and down. I become aware at

181

this point that I smell of dried urine. I look down at the shredded sock on my foot and can't remember what I have done with the shoe. All three coppers frog march me over to the IKEA Security office where I am expecting some support.

'No.' That is all the guys in there can say. They don't know me, and they've never seen me, apart from my most recent antics on their cameras.

'I was in here. You sat me down, helped me. I told you I couldn't find my car. Come on for Christ's sake.'

But no, they insist they don't know me. It is clear that they would prefer it if the police could relieve them of any responsibility for me.

'Right, sir, driving licence.'

'I never carry one.'

'Wallet, then.' He takes it and looks at the various bits and pieces in it.

'Name?'

'It's on the credit card you're holding.'

'We can do this down at the station if you want.'

I now do something truly stupid. I believe I am angry or panicking or both, and am struggling to get my name out. It is the mental version of a stutter: 'Peter (I'm fine with the p sound) …Piper.'

He starts to write it down, but of course it doesn't accord with what he's just got from my wallet. He stands up, towering over me. I believe he wants to do far more than pick a peck of my pickled pepper. Out come the plastic wrist restrainers.

I am swooningly dizzy. I can't remember where I left my car, people who I am convinced should recognize me claim never to have seen me before and I am struggling with my own name; and now I'm to be cuffed. I feel the inexorable sweeping away my footings. Why didn't they remember me?

'Look, I'm sorry. I'm ill, I have dementia.' I now give

them my full name, and total co-operation.

Eventually after a variety of haughty huffing and puffings and more apologising on my part, and what I take to be a mock caution, the police leave, having handed me over to the Security guys. They are being kind to me, but things they are saying are not going in, and I am silent as the dead.

They have sent for a mini-cab. I shuffle in.

'Where to? Where to?' I panic. I look at him. What is he asking me for? I can't tell him. I don't know, I really don't. 'It's er... It's er... Go straight on, I'll tell you when we get near.'

We stop at lights and I get him to ring Carol's number. The rest of the journey home is mystery and blur because my eyes are wet with self pity. Not even my own house looks familiar as we pull up outside it.

At home, Carol sees the state I'm in and says, 'Nothing can be this bad, can it?' She straightens my hair. 'Chin up, chest out,' she says as she passes me the shoe which the IKEA people had found for me and given to the cabbie. I can't recall anything I've done to make her be this caring with me.

'I've looked, and looked, and I can't find it. For hours, I couldn't find the car. I went up and down every aisle more than once, phoned the police and went to the Security team. I'm going mad.'

'You do know you used Linda's car, don't you?'

She gets yet another cab so she can fetch the car back. She was always kind to my father in his tragic days. She thinks that her words will somehow comfort me, but that I managed to completely forget which car I had used merely underlines my reality.

Carol had no problem finding the car and is home surprisingly quickly.

'You're worrying too much about your illness. You'll be at the hospital in a few days,' she says, trying to take my mind off matters. 'They'll know what to do.'

183

She has obviously been told more than she has let on. 'There's a lot they can do these days,' she assures me. How does she think she'll respond? What does she imagine she'll do? Any fool could see she has no reason to look after me.

'I'll never let myself become a burden, you know,' I tell her.

'You are a burden, you have always been, but then we're all burdens at times. That's life.'

'I would rather die than go in one of those homes. I won't go, no way.'

'Everybody says that.'

Homes. Whoever thought of calling them that? I won't be going to one and I won't be leaving behind a diary with the words, "What is happening to me", inside it. I can't ask Carol to help me kill myself. She'd refuse to talk about anything like that. I can't imagine being in the bath and asking, 'Can you pass me the toaster?' and there is no scope for announcing, 'I am just going outside, and may be some time.' No such luck. What is more, the last thing I want to do is leave any of my family implicated. I have taken steps, alright not the most expert ones, but I've got a contract with the moped men. Unfortunately, I have yet to see anything in return for the money I gave them. I will have to try Jeremy the undertaker once more and see if I can exert some control in all this.

Mo has left a text on my phone. It is in plain English. 'We can't wait. Can you come for a meeting at mine tonight?'

My time is running out, so I ring him back immediately. 'Let's fit it in while we can, but I'm not up to going far, so you'll have to come to mine.'

He agrees.

XVIII

If you discover your wife may be going off with someone close to you, it is more than a little unsettling. When Mo finally came out, it wasn't the final straw, but all I can say is that these two shocks together would have been enough to push any man over the edge.

****

As the car arrives in the Heath car park I can hear Bach's Funeral Cantata. The music is coming from across the road where there is a small orchestra, a jet black carriage with four black horses and dozens of black limousines. The deceased certainly had a lot of money, but who's to say if he was truly loved. It is a short and solitary walk to the hospital.

Carol used to have mood changes, now she is totally unpredictable. She must have been brooding about my behaviour, because when I ask her what Sam had said to her at the restaurant she reacts.

'You know very well!' she shouts.

'I thought you might have got up to much the same in France.'

'Oh, I had the chance, but we've been over that or don't you remember? You can be such an idiot! Look there's no point in talking about this. I'll stick with you until the hospital and that is it.'

Totally justified, I know. I retreat to the bedroom, pick up the phone and dial.

'Jeremy, is that you?'

'You shouldn't be ringing me.'

'I need to know when it's going to happen.'

'That's not the way it works. They won't listen to me anyway.'

'Do you know these people or not?'

'Not really. I met them in a pub and we got

talking. Well, actually I was asking around and was put in touch with them.'

I put the phone down and, strangely enough, fall asleep on the bed. I wake after half an hour and go to the medicine cabinet. I take out a couple of the Valium tablets Carol has abandoned and swallow them dry. They work well, although you get a bit foggy if you take too many. I get some water and take three paracetamol. The Valium packet is there beside them so I take some, only to realise I've had some seconds ago.

I glance out of the window and see Mo arriving. He has someone with him. He has hung around me and Carol for years, so much so I used to think he fancied her. He hasn't had a girlfriend since he was seventeen. I thought it was amazing that three decades later he had finally got one. That, I now understand, is not the actual nature of his liaison. Wrong is my mode of being. I don't know how I'll respond to his mate. Steady, sturdy Mo has always been there for me in the past. It has been everything from getting my car going, to being close to a bodyguard at times. For however long I am around I doubt I'll be his priority any longer, but that's what happens when people fall in love; they make an overriding commitment. The sort I abandoned.

The phone and the door bell go and I freeze in minor indecision. The phone rings longer, so I pick the one beside the bed up.

It's Doc Holiday who strikes up, 'Seen the news about Skye?' I really don't know what he means. 'Marvellous, eh?'

If he says so.

On he goes, 'Reminds me of when I bested the G.M.C.' All I know is he got into trouble over an abortion as a medical student. He carries on, 'Come in for a chat, if you want.' Then he slips in, 'By the way, at the hospital… It's just a thought, but those days can be

so tiring, why don't you take Carol with you?'
The casual way he makes his suggestion is ominous.
It's in direct proportion to the gravity of what I face.

Mo rings the door bell again and Carol lets him in. The Valium has kicked in and is making me vague, but upbeat. I had forgotten in the few minutes of the phone call that he was here. I can't seem to tack one event on to another. There's no sequence to what is happening. I get off the bed Carol's side and see a packed case there once more. I suspect I did not say that the case she packed after the meal with Sam was merely hand-luggage size. This time it's her largest one. The tranquilizers can't quite dull that. After the hospital tomorrow, when she has done her duty, she will leave me.

Mo looks more youthful than I usually think of him. He and the man with him are not quite hand in hand, but whoever it is has Mo's arm in their's. I hope they don't take things any further in front of me; I can't stand it when couples are all over each other. For some reason I had expected a younger bloke than this one, perhaps one of his football team lads. This guy looks... Well, he looks like someone that Mo might call a minger. He doesn't seem to walk properly, either. I shake hands with Mo and hold out my hand to the minger who is introduced with one word, 'Johnno'. His hand is soft and when it shakes mine it is weak, almost lame. Very camp.

A bar is the best spot we all agree. They ask if I know of a good one.

'There aren't any gay bars up here,' I offer.

John rejoins, 'Oh, we'll try to cope with that.'

There are probably dozens. Clearly I am out of touch, because they look at me with forbearance.

On the way to the bar Mo is taking us to, a moped catches his elbow. 'Whoa, that was close,' he says shaking his fist. The bar has got "barristas", and expensive alcohol. Mo, as always, is first up to get the drinks in, with his usual packed wallet. He's too solid to have risked too much with a conman like Nayar. He'll get a mineral water for himself as well as our drinks, so for the moment I'm alone with John. What do you say to your best mate's first (I can't bring myself to say "lover") partner in thirty years?

'He's a decent fellow, Mo.'

'Yes, they all say that at work.' He seems to have a bit of a speech impediment.

'You work with Mo, then?'

'I wouldn't be in a position to say otherwise, would I?'

I don't know about that, and I am wondering if I should be polite to this bloke.

'Mo says you're a decent sort, too.'

I am glad I didn't snap at him.

'He thought you might... could help us.'

'Really?' I'm sure I've not done anything to suggest I'm gay, or know much about that sort of thing.

'Mo says you used to be red hot on terms and conditions, health and safety, the whole lot.'

He left out equal opportunities, but I guess that is what he's after.

'I'll help Mo over with drinks,' I say going to the bar.

'Mo, what's wrong with John's arm?'

'Stroke. I found him lying in the toilets at work.'

Toilets. I hope that's not where they used to meet. 'He's a bit unfortunate looking and he slurs his speech a little, too.'

'Do you think so?' Love is obviously deaf, as well as blind.

On to what's important, 'I'm a little bit out of date you know, with rules and regs on gay rights.'

'What's that got to do with anything?'

'John is gay, isn't he? Isn't he your partner?'

'My partner? You've got eyes in your head, haven't you? He's hardly my sort is he?' he grins.

'I'm glad you can laugh, at least that's different.'

'I've decided that if I am to have it out with you, I will just have to chill. You're a plank, and no Johnno is not my lover, if that's what you're getting at.' He's heading towards the seats as I catch him up

'What's going on? You said to meet. You said you want to discuss your affair, and what's more you said you'd be bringing whoever it was with you.' I'm sure I've got this right. 'Then you turn up with this bloke I've never seen before. If he's not your', I don't know what to say, 'not your bloody boyfriend, then who is he? Why is he here? Why are we here? What's all this for?'

'Petey, you really are a plank. He's here firstly because he's been around the block, seen a lot of things, and got experience of all sorts, especially of the kind you haven't. He's in loads of networks and I wanted some support. I do need to talk to you and up till now I've been finding it very difficult.'

I suppose John could be some sort of experienced mentor or advisor, but it is far from clear to me, so I ask, 'Well what's it got do with him, then?'

'Listen up, I told you minutes or less ago. He knows what's going down, is an understanding guy and will slip into the background once we really get into it. But, as it happens, he needs help. You can see he's not in good shape, which is the second reason for bringing him. And this is right up your street. I spoke to you about him a while back and you said you'd help.'

I don't remember this at all. More to the point I don't know how I could have got it so wrong. If I wasn't so tranquilized I would hardly be able to look his mate in the eye. I finish my pint, and shoot to the sheet metal covered bar for a second round. The only thing I am way ahead of these two on is the speed at which I am consuming alcohol.

189

'So what can I do for you?' I ask.

Mo speaks on John's behalf. 'It's like Doc Holiday used to say (Mo is a patient of his as well), the big boys think of us as drug mules. We're carrying something that's of great value. If we don't give it to them, it'll be wasted or turn to poison inside us.'

This time I know it's not me. It's him, he's talking gibberish. I peer at John to see if there is any hope there, but there's none. He's doing an impression of a vegetable. I really don't know why I am here doing this. There is an altogether other matter ricocheting around inside my skull and taking precedence: I've got an appointment to officially declare me demented tomorrow! What is all this? They can't be expecting help from me.

'We're talking about work,' Mo carries on. 'He used to be able to hack it, but can't anymore. Our firm's been merged and nothing is the same. All the stuff we could do sleep-walking has gone. The routines have been changed, they've introduced shifts...'

And now I get it. Shifts, that's it; shifts explains it, don't you see. No wonder I wasn't recognized by the Security people at IKEA; it was because they were a new shift. They genuinely hadn't seen me. The only question is why didn't I realise that they were not the same people. But then I know the answer to that. I don't think I'm saying this out aloud. Mo's continuing but I am managing to keep up.

'...and the actual office has moved to a different borough. They're trying to get more and more from us.'

'Ah, I understand; it's happening all over,' I tell them. 'It's a given and there's nothing I can offer. What can I, of all people, do for you?'

Mo, continues, 'They're changing our contracts. I didn't think they could do that. I thought that would be illegal.'

'It's a new company in effect, I bet, so it's not.

They can do it even if they're not a new company. They've got the whip hand.' This is the most sense I've talked in months.

'We're an old workforce and people think they'll miss out if they fight,' Mo says.

His sarcastic mate has a real difficulty, but it's nothing compared to mine. The temptation to ask him, 'Ever thought about what it would be like going down with Alzheimer's?' clatters around in my head.

'And you know what, the pension scheme looks done for. They're ripping us off,' Mo tells me.

Poor sods. I am in familiar territory. Modern advances have simply meant people live longer and so have to work longer. And now I understand why a drug mule: for as long as we have the energy in us, for as long as we have something to give, they want it. They want to unburden us of our vitality. I am truly sorry for them all. 'And you Mo,' I ask, 'surely you're desperate as well.' Half as desperate as me? I'm going to be declared witless in twenty four hours!

'No, you know me. I've got PEPS, TESSAs, AVCs, even though some are not doing so hot. And my flat is paid for; that takes the pressure off. Besides, I'll just carry on. They can throw what they want at me and if I can't do it, it won't get done. Some of the managers are scared of me. I can butt-out any time I like.'

'I thought you were over the limit on your cards.'

'No. What made you think that?"

'You said it.'

'You must be thinking of someone else, Bro" '

"Thinking" – he's flattering me there. 'Look, you've got my total sympathy, but really, what can I do for you?'

'You bailed out early on a sickie, but you're fit as a fiddle,' Mo carries on. 'You nailed it. You're legend, because you found a way to quit while you're ahead.'

Ahead? A head? Mine's decomposing. I've got

raving Alzheimer's! They must be in a bad way to think I can help. 'Look Mo, nobody gets sick retirement for stress these days. They can't give in on that basis because everybody would qualify. Have you considered M.E? They can't disprove it.' I don't know how that thought got permission for take-off.

There is a long pause where they think my mind has gone completely. They think I have spelt "me", and can't come up with a response. It's embarrassing. They stare. I've lost them, and now I mislay me. There are no bookmarks for my thoughts. I don't know where I was, where I was going or what I was about to say. Then John works it out.

'It's Yuppie flu, a post viral thing. Scarcely meant for the likes of us.'

I must be missing something here. I come up with a decent suggestion, and John starts talking as though we're proletarians.

'It leaves you completely exhausted,' I justify myself. 'Too exhausted for work. It can drag on for years.'

'What would Johnno have to do?'

'He'll have to act as though he's a virtual invalid for a couple of years, and possibly use a wheelchair.'

There's a long silence. John is crushed. Nil response from him could mean "No". So as far as I am concerned that is it. I don't like the bloke and I've got bigger things to perplex me.

I can't believe that I agreed to help someone like him. I glance at Mo and he looks very down. He sometimes picks up needy people, and brings them to me, and usually he's a fair judge. Somewhere in all this, John could be a decent man. Just because I can't see it, doesn't mean it isn't so; then again he doesn't even have to be. I've been through this loads of times before, representing people I can't stand.

I relent. 'Let's get another drink in and see what

we can do.' I am the only one with an empty glass.

John slowly starts to rise to go to the bar and he really is quite unsteady. Mo stands as you might do for a woman and puts a hand under his arm to help him up. It's so caring it borders on the affectionate. If it's not sex, I can't understand what he sees in this bloke. Are they sure they're not lovers?

I say to Mo, 'I thought we were going to discuss you getting your end away. When is that going to happen?'

'I never said anything like that.'

I'm sure I didn't get that wrong; it was him who raised it, not me.

'Let's put this one to bed first, and then we'll see if you can handle talk of my sex life.'

'Is it unconventional?'

'Very, I suppose.'

I am lost. I thought we'd dispensed with the homosexuality thing. Perhaps he is gay, but is with a younger man, one of the football team, as I first thought.

'One question,' I ask, 'Is it anything to do with football?'

'In a way, yes, but let's get back to dealing with Johnno's situation first. It should be the easiest, so we should get it out of the way.'

We drink, and from somewhere it comes to me. It's alcohol inspired, but… 'Forget the M.E,' I say. 'I've got the perfect one, but he's got to go for it, he's got to stick with it, and be consistent.' I am going to talk about Alzheimer's, faking it, as a way out, but as I am about to start Mo gets up to help John bring the drinks from the bar. I tell him I'll do it. When I get there I ask John the second most pressing thing on my mind, 'Why does Mo need your support to discuss his sex life? What is the difficulty?'

'You haven't exactly been Brain of Britain over this. You're going to have to ask him. All I can tell you is anybody would find it difficult to talk to someone like you about it.'

'Just listen to me for a minute, will you.' I am going to row with him when suddenly it hits me. I know why it is so difficult. From the pit of murk and mire in my head it rises and it is sharp and clear. There's always been a little something going on, a little bit of spice in there, a frisson between them. This is not a difficulty involving a covert homosexual relationship, far from it. 'It's Carol, isn't it?'

He heads for Mo, saying, 'Got to get the drinks back.' He's just avoiding the subject.

'Hold up. It's Carol isn't it?' I've stopped him by getting hold of his dodgy arm.

'I don't know the name,' he says and scoots to the stools we're uncomfortably seated on. I've put him in a difficult spot and he's lying.

This just doesn't make sense. If Carol had an affair it was in France, wasn't it? But she says she didn't and I've never known her not to tell the truth. And on the other hand, it is the only thing that makes sense. Carol and Mo? No, they're more like sister and younger brother. Titillation at the thought of a bit of a sexual romp in France doesn't apply to something involving Mo. No wonder she is going to leave me; she has somewhere to go, and has had it for some while. After all, she will have realised a point is coming where living together is going to be far from pleasant. Mo is now next in line of accession to my bedroom: the heir apparent. I can make head nor tail of the rest either: a guy wants my help in return for sarcasm; a partial invalid wanting to be declared a complete invalid; a gay coming out, then going back in; and me making light of Alzheimer's, actually suggesting it as an easy exit. There's a fire crackling away in my head, with bits spitting out all over.

I look at Mo and softly ask, 'Carol?' He raises

his eyebrows, rolls his eyes, looks at the ceiling and frowns. It's a delaying tactic and I don't know where to go with it. I'll come back to it because I won't be able to stay away.

Where was I? 'Alzheimer's!' I say it to them, again. I was turning my head quickly both ways to check over my shoulders as it came out - it's not the sort of thing you want the general public to overhear - and I yelped because I'd ricked my wounded neck.

They are stumped, or perhaps they didn't catch it. They look at each other and clearly don't know what to think. I'm putting on a weird performance, I guess. In my own head it sounded as though it was the answer, but that could be the Valium.

'It's the answer to John's prayers. All you've got to do is act like me.'

'We thought you'd go directly for Johnno's illness,' says Mo.

Now it's me who is lost once more. 'What did I just say?' I ask.

'You said 'Carol'.'

'Carol?'

'You know the woman who makes your world tick over, the one you'd be lost without,' Mo informs me.

'Ever since you first met her, Mo, you've liked her, haven't you?'

'No, mate, I love her. She might as well be family. She is family.' This doesn't sound sexual at all. He continues, 'She's the best thing that ever happened to you and I'd do anything for her.' Anything? 'If someone was to hurt her, I'd mullah them. You should do whatever it takes and stick with her mate, never let her go.'

I never get anything right. I obviously didn't take a single word John said in the right way. I look over at him, but all he does is shake his head.

I am pleased it's not Carol. I jolt back to the job

195

in hand; the subject has come back to me. 'Look super stud,' I suddenly say and the big lump nearly falls off his seat. 'Alzheimer's! That's what I said. And I know the perfect coach.'

'That's not a good idea. You forget I saw it when your dad had it. You start messing with stuff like that and before you know it, you'll cease to be normal, you'll lose your faculties because you'll have thrown them away, and then you will be demented for real. You act it, then you feel it, and then you'll be trapped in it. You shouldn't mess with it.'

'That's just you; you're too honest, too straightforward. The question is how desperate is your mate?' I turn to John. 'What do you think of Alzheimer's? It's one of those they can't disprove. I saw an autopsy report done on my father by the Maudsley Hospital. They are working on ways of diagnosing Alzheimer's, but the single means of getting a definite result at the moment is by slicing up your brain for microscope slides, that is once you're dead.'

John doesn't feel the same as Mo. 'Give the man a coconut,' he says.

'You sure? There must be some tests they do,' Mo asks, gulping down his mineral water. He's a big stallion of a man. I'm no longer sure of anything, but if I was, I'd be confident that if he is heterosexual, a sexually receptive woman would be bound to want to couple with him.

'They're working on some tests right now, but there's no end result yet.'

'That can't be all there is to it,' says Mo.

His mate is not saying a word, clearly trying to follow closely what is being said.

'No, of course not. This is a day in, day out thing, going on for a long, possibly very long, period.' I tell them John has got to get lost, and I enjoy the irony. 'Generally you've got to act forgetful and deranged, and your wife is going to have to help you in this. Are you married?'

'His wife left him,' says Mo.

'Well, you'll need someone who can support you, corroborate what you say and what you can't say.'

John looks at Mo.

'Alright, that'll be me I suppose,' he says with a glum shrug.

'You'll be the one who has to ring the doctor and tell him how bad things are getting, and to apologise for John's conduct. This isn't easy,' I tell Mo, 'but you'll have to see it through. It's horrendous, the ugliest illness you could think of.' I reel off an inventory of what is facing me, topped with a description of a 'dribbling ghoul.'

Mo looks unhappy.

'You've got to convince your bosses they don't want to keep you on; that it is in the firm's interest to let you go, even if it costs them. Do a turd on the floor, that should do it.'

'That's disgusting,' says Mo.

'Mohammed,' I call him by his full name, 'I couldn't agree more. It is the vilest thing and yet I have actually got it.'

'Getaway, that's gross bringing it up now. That sucks, Petey. I'd know already, and you'd have said it earlier.'

'I did.'

'No you didn't.'

'Yes I did, but you two completely ignored it. I shouted it out, and said it again when I ricked my neck.'

'No you didn't!' they both say again.

The conversation hasn't been that tortuous. I said it, I'm sure, or did I only think it?

'You're the only one in my family..,' I do include him in that, he's been with us for so long, '...who doesn't know I'm going down with it. That's the diagnosis they

197

are going to unveil at the Royal Free.'

'It's just your obsession, Petey. It can't be true.'

Whether it's the beer or the shock of my announcement, I don't know, John hasn't drunk much and Mo's drunk only mineral water, but all they can do is look at each other. This is not the conversation they came here for and what's more they don't believe me. It comes as no surprise that I am not to be taken seriously. Alternatively, it could be that it's so horrible they don't want to know; I've seen that reaction before.

'Can you get me in with Doc Holiday? Mo says it would be good to have him on side whatever I go in for.' John has decided to return to what interests him.

'Would he back us?' Mo asks. Clearly they don't want to discuss my problem and once more I am lost.

'I don't know what you are on about,' I tell the pair of them.

'You know, say Johnno has got Alzheimer's or M.E. or the stroke or whatever.'

'Oh. Doc Holiday thinks of himself as a rebel, but I don't know. The trouble is once it's in the open, you've been exposed. No, do yourself a favour, go and see a consultant privately. If you're paying, they'll be on your side, and if they're not, don't put up with it. Go and see someone who'll do as you say.' That's rich coming from me, but these two should have the capacity to be masters of the situation.

'Whoa, now I see it. Do you know what? Zowie is illiterate, she can't read anything, except tea leaves that is', I say. 'I don't know why I didn't spot it earlier.'

'Who's Zowie? Oh, never mind. Try and stick to the subject for once. Alzheimer's is incurable, isn't it? What happens afterwards? You can't simply get better, take the money and run. Your Dad got worse and worse, and then died.'

I can remember that much, unfortunately. John has the cheek to look scathingly at me. There's a lot in it for him; if he does it and gets it right, he'll be free. There's no reason I should help him. I've had it with this game, but Mo looks pleadingly at me. Being resolute never was one of my qualities, so I'll give it a last try. After all it is my best subject.

'True, but there are precedents. You don't have to have actually had it to start with. It can turn out to have been something else. Do you remember the director of a big brewers, I think it was...,' I can't for the life of me remember. I look at the dark pint I am drinking, and say, '...Guinness. Who was the director? You know, he was supposed to have it, got let out of gaol as a result, and then, lo and behold, he recovered.'

'Ernest Saunders.' There is no problem with John's memory.

'That's right,' I say.

'That's disgusting,' Mo says again.

'It's only an idea, but think on it. How many escape plans actually have any chance at all?'

'But what about Johnno's disability? Isn't he in with a chance there?'

'Why didn't you raise this earlier?'

'We did!'

'No you didn't.' Then I hold my hands up. I'm not going along with that routine again, or someone will bring on the pantomime horse. They probably did say it. It turns out that they'd got advice. John's on medication that means he shouldn't suffer any more strokes and his disability does not prevent him from doing his office job. There was no point in asking me, then. Do they truly believe I'll have anything more to offer? John's desperate, I suppose, and I well know that can explain a lot. 'That means there's not much scope. I don't know any better than what you've already been told. You're left with Alzheimer's. You can take it or leave it, unlike me.'

John looks inclined to consider it as his only

option. Mo looks neutral, which is a step forward.

In the space I've created I decide to move on to a happier subject. Valium and a third pint are compounding in me. I think I've understood that Mo isn't gay, so some ribaldry is allowed.

'How's it going with your love-life, you well oiled sex machine? Got your oats recently? What's the most times you've done it in one session?' I can see he wants to interrupt me, but I don't let him. I burp and carry on, 'Is she drawing a pension? What does she look like? Blonde, brunette, raven black, mousey, red head, bald? Is she a screamer?' I can tell by looking at them that I am hugely wide of the mark, but I don't care.

'Just cut it out,' says Mo.

John seems to want to go. I thought heterosexual blokes were wild for this sort of thing. Mo is signalling John to stay. I would have thought he would be desperate to brag, unless he is in fact gay and I've simply misjudged what I've been told and am being inappropriate. Perhaps I should just stop, give it up, but this could provide me with the one light moment, so I don't.

'Look, we have known each other a long time...'

Mo interrupts. 'Yes, that's what makes it so difficult and why I brought Johnno here...'

'So you've got some moral support, but I've heard all this already. Come on, tell me something to cheer me up. It's a mad world in here,' I say tapping my temple.

'I know how it feels, Petey. You want to shut down, and re-boot the whole thing.'

More gibberish, which leaves me not knowing which way to go. I lurch elsewhere. 'Get it into your head. The problem you have is small compared to mine. Once you understand this, revealing whatever it is won't seem much at all. Do you remember when we talked about dementia? We promised to help whoever got it to do themselves in. Well I've got it.' I can see he doesn't believe it. 'Look, nothing makes sense, so give up doubting. What I am telling you is not a fantasy. You've got some sort of difficulty you're finding it hard to deal with. Well mine's impossible. You need help and understanding, so give me some too. I need tons of it. Some of us are desperately looking for a way through, and some for a way out. You help me and I'll help you.'

'Get real, Petey. Ever since your dad went down with it it's been a worry of yours twenty-four seven. That and the booze are making you talk as though you're off your head. I've seen it before.'

'Look, I've been desperate to hear all the sordid details of your sex life, legends of rogering some succulent woman. It is the only potential bright spot for me, but it doesn't look like it's going to happen does it? You can't or won't oblige me. Well I want something from you two. I asked you weeks ago. You work in pharmaceuticals, and said you might be able to get hold of botulism. How about it?'

'That's the other reason Johnno is here; he knows all about botulism.'

John obliges with stupendous technical detail, finally telling me, 'It's highly toxic; dangerous enough to kill you.'

'Oh really? Why do you think I want it?'

My words set off alarms in John who demands, 'What could you possibly want it for?'

Mo seems dumbfounded

'To state the obvious: kill myself. I can't carry on.'

John shakes his head. 'Mo must have told you we can't get that sort of thing; we're in admin. I don't know what your problem is, but this isn't the way. Suicide is giving in, giving up. Ask Mo, he helped me to get over it.'

'Suicide? Suicide! You never said anything

about suicide. You're bang out of order. What are you talking about? Nothing can be that bad. It's what you said, you know, we've all got problems, but that's no way to go, Petey.'

'I've told you, but you're not listening. It's that ugly, hideous thing you two are so reluctant to fake; well, I've actually got it. The hospital appointment I've got is to give me the final verdict, after all the head scans they've been doing. Look at how I gave you the wrong day for the funeral Mo. That's not me, not how I used to be. I forgot my way home from IKEA. Ask Carol, she knows all about it. Doc Holiday is in on it too. I've got to have someone with me when I go to the Royal Free, because of what they'll tell me and because I am no longer capable.'

'You sometimes talk this way. It's rewind and replay with you.'

'It needs erasing, if you ask me,' says John.

'Ignore him. You've just got a bad memory, Petey. I'm sure it's the booze, and you've always got too many things going on in your head at once.'

'Look this is real, it's true. We made promises on this once, Mo.'

There is a big tear the size of a pumpkin seed on his cheek. This is one of the least lachrymose characters that ever lumbered across the face of the Earth. He has begun to believe me and shakes his head. There is a long silence.

'Alright,' says John with no sarcasm for once, 'we'll see what we can do.'

He's a cold fish. It's difficult to tell if he is being sincere. I think he's trying to bring this discussion to an end because Mo can't take it.

'I need a little bit of help from a friend before all that's left is the care of strangers. You are the only person I can turn to for help.' I won't let this one drop; I'll keep on and on until they come up with the goods.

202

John has got his working arm around Mo; around Mo, mind you, not me.

'Do you want me to tell him now?' he asks Mo.

'I don't think now is the time,' he replies.

I've got an undertaking from them, so I am only too pleased to move on to a happier subject.

'Now is the only time!' I tell them. 'I am no longer expecting tales of wanton exploits and new found capacities for rampant shagging. I've told you something terrible. What you have to say can't compare. If you're into blokes you're into blokes, and if, instead, you're sleeping with some figure of a woman who is horrendous in an inconceivable way, I will neither despise you nor her. Out with it for Christ's sake!'

'But… I need you to listen to me, Petey, without going mad.'

'In practical terms I am going mad.'

'I need you to think on what I've got to tell you. When I tell you, perhaps you'll just have to walk away, go back to Carol, talk it over, sleep on it, let it settle, and then we can talk again.'

Why does he have to keep bringing Carol into it? I thought that one had been seen off. 'Carol probably won't be there, we're splitting up.'

'I can't believe that, Petey. You're making a big mistake there.'

'I know, but leave that out of it and get on with your story. It's my only hope for the day.'

'Alright, it's like this, Petey. We're on a bit of a break at the moment.'

Who does he think he is, a teenager?

'It doesn't mean we don't love each other, but we're just trying to get our heads round it.'

'That's the stuff I wanted to hear. Getting your heads around what, eh?' I really must be desperate for a diversion to be this pathetic. He ignores me and continues.

203

'Key people know and don't think it's too bad.'

Naturally, everybody else but me knows. The one thing I know is that I know nothing. Is he having a torrid affair or not?

'Is she a monster, someone we'd both be hysterical over? Look I promise not to laugh. It's later in life than for most, but you've come into the rutting season. Come on, open up. Boast!'

'Shut up.' It's John.

'I've had it with you. You should have come here, got my help and been grateful. Now you can just piss off.'

Mo doesn't attempt to stop him. He looks one way and then the other. He clasps his mouth in his big mitt, sighs, breathes in slowly and looks in the direction John has taken. Then he lowers his hand and comes out - with it. He tells me who his lover is. If I cringed at the word before it was nothing. I am overwhelmed by his revelation, folded under and washed away by polluted waters. Mo's mouth is moving. It's an explanation, a plea for understanding, but I'm not listening to a word and he can see it is hopeless.

At the end I do catch him say, 'We'll talk again, Petey.' He puts that big hand on my shoulder to say goodbye, but I shrug it off and he goes.

'I don't think so!' I shout after him.

Mo being gay would have been something we could have worked around. It would have been better if he was actually having an affair with Carol. We could have worked around that too, eventually. I'd had sex with Carol's old friend and she had done the same to me. That could have been how I came to see it. But oh no, nothing so easy. He has stabbed me in the soul. I go back to the pub and try to dash what is left of my addled brains out with one more pint, but half way through it I feel sick.

I am trying not to fall over as I totter my way

home. Carol isn't there. Perhaps she has left me permanently already. The fastest hangover I have ever known attacks me. I take four paracetamol then lie on the settee and attempt to sleep through the ferment. I doze for only a few minutes then lay there, lurid images clambering all over me.

That filthy, conniving, treacherous, bestial bastard has been my life long friend, has had my help no matter what, has been welcomed into my family home, spent virtually every holiday with us, has been trusted around all those I love most ; I've even asked him to do the most precious thing one man can do for another: to help me die decently. And this is how he repays me.

It is him. He is the one who has been seeing my youngest daughter. He is the one who got the vulnerable young thing pregnant. He's a paedophile, and it's virtually incestuous. I can never meet him again without revulsion. In fact, I refuse to ever meet him again. It'll be so hard facing my daughter, and her sister too. She's bound to know. It's almost as though I've been cuckolded while everyone else knew. It can't all be me, can it? A weak mind, yes, but in a warped world. This cannot be acceptable. Surely this wouldn't fit into any norm of behaviour these days. A man should be able to rely on his friend and have some faith in his daughter's judgement, shouldn't he? Where is there a measure to gauge this by? I have to talk with Carol first; she's always been able to plot her way through emotional calamities. She'll know what light to put it in.

Carol still isn't back – if she's coming back at all. So what is a condemned man with an ounce of will left to do? I plonk myself in front of the computer, summon up the internet and browse through entries for poisons. There are thousands of them. That doesn't actually feel like it is a useful thing, particularly when, as usual, E bay has got the first entry. Once again they are doing it at a

205

better rate than anyone else, apparently. My stiff neck and the headache are really revving up, tempting me to take more paracetamol. I'm not up to this. I pack it in with the web. I'm having nothing more to do with Mo; pistols aboard mopeds may be my only option.

As I get off the computer stool, Linda comes in. I do not know where to begin. She scrutinizes me. Obviously she, among others, knew Mo was going to confess.

'You're not alright are you, Dad? Mum will be in any minute. I've asked her specially to be here. I'll make tea, and we can all sit down and work it out. I've just got to pop out first.'

I know why and I know where, or rather who, she's popping to.

As I slump into the settee, Carol breezes in. I take one look at her and I know she knows.

'Why didn't you tell me, at least give me a clue?'

'It was obvious. If you couldn't work it out, you weren't ready to deal with it.'

'I'll never be ready for it. The treacherous bastard. I don't get it. What is wrong with her?'

'That kind of talk doesn't help. First of all, the baby is no longer an issue. Secondly, there is no way of telling whether this is going to last. Both the girls have had fairly earnest relationships come and go. But face it, you are not going to stop loving her, and you will either put up with whoever she settles with, or work your way round it. Think of some of the problem blokes she's been out with in the past. Mo is solid, with something behind him.'

'True, but so what? There are lots of them out there. Why pair up with someone on the way to being geriatric? I can't believe she's actually attracted to this man.'

'Sylvia and I talked it all through with her. She is sensible, and she does love him. Now the baby has

206

gone they're taking a few days away from each other to think about it.'

'It sounds as though it is finished.'

'Not really. If they still decide they love each other, they'll move in together. You'll be the one missing out if you turn your back on them, so you have no choice really.'

Carol seems quietly adjusted to the situation. I don't get it. He's old enough to be her dad's best mate. How can Mo and my daughter be in love?

'They're both concerned about you. Mo felt terrible.'

'Really! That makes it all so much better. And that's it? You don't feel betrayed? You don't blame him, see him as a predator?' It can't be me alone who is experiencing it this way.

'Predator? Come on, this is Mo we're talking about. You've got it all wrong. It was her who set out to get him. She used to pretend to be a fan of football and go and watch him play, and then hang around him after the game. He thought she was just being relaxed with her uncle. He's that naïve.'

'You sure he's the bloody naïve one, not you?'

'Old Mo is more than naïve, he's gullible. Don't forget all those years ago when he introduced me to you, he thought I was his girlfriend. You do realise that the baby might not have been his, do you? Their relationship isn't necessarily how I would have wanted it, but it is how things are. There's no tragedy involved.'

What a strong woman she is. I am limbless, swimming against the tide. When the person whose opinion you trust most accepts what you find appalling, what do you do, what can you think? You are wandering on a demolition site of your old neighbourhood. Everything you knew has changed. All you can do is turn to someone who knows their way around and take their word for it. 'It doesn't sound like

207

there's any talk of marriage.'

'Not at the moment; that is for the future, if at all.'

So that's it: you have sex, get pregnant and prepare to have a family, ponder moving in together and need time to consider marriage and its appropriateness. Not exactly Brief Encounter is it? I am simply not qualified to judge here. It could only resemble conduct I am familiar with if I looked at it in a broken mirror standing on my head. Even if I had any intellect left, I couldn't make sense of this. If Carol accepts it, I will.

My daughter re-enters, as though by specific stage direction, and smiles at me. I give her some sort of look, half friendly, half neutral, half bemused. (I'm aware that doesn't add up, but that's how it is).

She goes into what is becoming the nursery, and tells me it will come in handy one day. Then she puts her arms around me and gives me a long hug. There is a subject lodged in both of our minds like something stuck in a blocked soil pipe. She hands me a bunch of papers. Apparently she is thinking of volunteering for Medicine Sans Frontières. This must have been what she was talking to Oliver about. I suppose there is a new kind of family unit. The kids yo-yo back and forth from far and wide, while the parents-cum-grandparents keep open house for them, new offspring and all. There's some fission in the nuclear family, and the extended family only survives in some communities. What we've got now is the distended family. I don't see where Mo fits into all this, but that is his problem. I tell them I'm going out for some air.

On the street I hear the sound of a moped slowly following me. I stand still. Out of the corner of my eye I can see the rider is holding something in his outstretched hand. I fear the best and stand rigid, gazing up at the infinite dark beyond the stars. As he goes by me he tilts his head to swig the coke in his hand. He is delivering a pizza.

XIX

End of journey. I am here. This is not so much the pivotal point of the story, as the moment the rut in which it has travelled becomes the chasm down which it drains. I am here at the entrance to the hospital grounds. The Valium had vanished from the cabinet this morning. I'll be in a condition to take the full impact.

I must have been lying badly last night because I have a terrific neck ache. When I'd put my clothes on this morning, I'd found myself brushing my teeth for the second time, having already brushed them before I dressed. I am moving from the now where am I stage? to the who am I stage?

I don't think it is hysteria, but I picked up the phone last night and a complete stranger asked me to confirm my name, and I was so angry I couldn't get it out; my name simply wouldn't come. They seemed to know my name, my date of birth and indeed my address, but wouldn't tell me, so I put the phone down.

I couldn't sleep alongside Carol because she went out and never came home. Her largest case is still by the side of the bed, however, so she hasn't definitively left me yet.

It is clear Carol has not told our daughters about my misconduct and we have agreed that we would not tell them how serious my health is at the moment. I never thought I would make this journey alone. I cannot understand it; just desserts or not, Carol is too kind to have left me on my own for this.

The solidity of the pavement as I get out of the car, the grey sky covered by one single monotone cloud seem special to me. The metallic hardness of the door as it closes and the steam ascending from the car bonnet all take on a preciousness. Any cliché would seem wonderful. I am beholding some irreplaceable world. Every single phenomenon I can take in - and

209

there are far too many as I trundle along - is beautiful and, in some form, touching. Walking by the last of the Heath leaves me in awe. My maximum ambition would be to consciously experience this every day.

If there is any thing positive to the occasion, it is that I am aware of being glad it is this particular hospital I am going to. It is a teaching hospital and these are clearly better places to be. It is real luck if you are sent to one.

A cut above other hospitals it may be, but I'm standing outside, delaying. I don't know how I will react when I get in there. I don't associate cures with hospitals. Alongside a feeling of powerlessness, I think of them largely as places of pain. To doctors your pain is more essential than what you actually think. That's why they prod and poke you until they hit the bulls-eye. If you question them, you're hostile. I am to see a consultant and the one certain thing is that there will be no consultation. The best politely nod as you're talking. If what you're saying doesn't fit in with the notes they attempted to read as you came through the door, forget it. They don't trust you to know anything significant regarding yourself. Except, that is, if it hurts.

I am shown to a spot, past the crowded waiting areas, which is pretty exclusive. In fact, I am the only one waiting. In the room I am to go in I know someone else is getting bad news, and I know there will be a small high-powered team two, three at most, breaking the news as comfortingly as possible.

Mo also rang me last night. I put the phone down half a dozen times and then finally relented, intending to have a blazing row.

'Don't say anything. Listen for a moment because you'll want to hear this. Johnno put in stacks of time. He's not just a random I picked up. I know he's a pain, but he's got a lot to put up with.'

I couldn't say I cared.

'He's sure he's found something that can't be detected, but he says it's all crazy and I should talk to you.'

Then he pleaded with me to think again, not to rush into anything. His call sent me back to the computer to use the blessed internet. Search and ye shall find. What a wonderful thing technology is in the right hands. I searched, typing in what he told me. Ignoring the usual E Bay entry there were a dozen or more pages, most of which were irrelevant. There were, however, a fair number of useful entries.

I was looking at entries for a mushroom Mo had just told me about. It has a minor drawback: once you eat it you feel ill and vomit, but then you feel fine until, more or less a week later, your liver packs in and you drop dead. Not everybody's dream, I know, but it works for my circumstances. The Death Cap mushroom, Amanita Phalloides, is found all over the world, including in English woodlands, around the base of oak trees. It is easily mistaken for other non-poisonous mushrooms. On the web there is an account of a woman in Australia who died after making soup from it, believing it was a honey mushroom, so it can't taste bad. There are lots of reports of them being confused with straw mushrooms in the States. One commentator sets out to calm the worries of wild mushroom pickers by assuring them that the practice is, "no more dangerous than driving a car."

It could all be an understandable accident that can't be disproved. Death on a plate, literally. No insurance company will be able to turn a claim down, because even if they were able to detect the substance involved they couldn't prove I didn't eat it innocently.

I texted Mo back. There were no niceties. It said, 'I've found it on the internet. You and your mate will have to get it for me.'

He rang back, but I refused to speak to him.

211

I quite like mushrooms. Death isn't my first choice, but it will be a cake walk compared to dementia.

Sitting here, waiting to be summoned, I am imagining Carol being with me. She has her arm around my shoulder. I ask, 'It is very bad news, isn't it?' really wanting to be told otherwise.

'Yes, darling, but there is a lot they can do these days', she replies in her usual honesty.

Then my miserable reverie is ended. I hear my name. It is repeated and my turn has come. As I stand up the person who has come to get me looks and looks once more, obviously expecting someone to be with me. They take me by the hand, and this time it is me following just like a little boy.

As I go in I am dazzled. It should be sombrely swish. There should be dark wood panelling and a red carpet, dark enough to hide deep blood stains. There should be a figure who would look best cloaked in black, shortly to be topped by a black cap, but it isn't like that at all. There is a small table. On it is what appears at first to be a set of pens, but they are too shiny for that. They are glistening metal instruments that I am going to have no truck with. On one side of the table are two empty bare wooden seats for me and whoever, and on the other are two more empty bare wooden seats for the head man and his young assistant. Towards the back of the inappropriately big room is a sort of audience. Some must be students, perhaps one or two are the underlings who are intended to deal with me subsequently. One has a large pack of what look like oversize nappies. Of course, they are incontinence pads and I will need tutoring. I think I am asked if I mind them all being there.

'No,' I find myself saying. It's deliberate, a fait accompli. I wonder if any of the suffering and vulnerable who have sat here in thrall have ever felt able to refuse their presence. There are few things that

212

should be more intimate. The audience is an irrelevance, no, an impertinence. On another day I might have said the time to ask me was before they all got there, but today I couldn't care less. Let them gawp. The single medical person I'd welcome right now is Dr Guillotine. I look over at them, intently, but nobody's eyes will meet mine. Instead they deliberately focus on the table and its instruments, or their leader's empty seat. It's a bare scene like an Absurdist stage set.

The head man and his assistant enter. I have the advantage. There is immediate consternation. The doctor who is in charge of my demise attempts a joke, 'Where is your wife? You haven't lost her have you?'

I reply, 'I think so.'

They have heard nonsense before, so they prepare to move on. They introduce themselves and some others. It's almost a sales pitch where they give you their first name and use yours to implicate you in the transaction. As if their names are of interest to me. The consultant is being warm and friendly, but his own body is working against the affect he is trying to achieve. It is so striking it might be a condition: he is gaunt and has overlong, spidery fingers. His eyes have big dark rings under them; his facial features are all huge, and his voice is deep. He has an uncanny resemblance to the drunken undertaker at my aunt's funeral. A trick of the mind? Maybe, but it is the most appropriate part of the scene. I am finding it hard to take it all in.

The door fairly bursts open and Carol is escorted in. She sits down and squeezes my hand. 'You were supposed to pick me up on the Broadway, silly. I told Mo to tell you.'

I recall no such conversation, but, as I said before, she doesn't lie.

Everyone is delighted she is there. The consultant goes through a question and answer session

213

with me, while his underling makes notes. The further we get, the more he looks concerned. It is another sort of cognitive test and he is demonstrating to the audience just how far gone I am.

The consultant then asks me if I have heard of the Epstein Barr virus. I have and know it is implicated in any number of dire conditions. He does not wait for my answer, moving on to talking about head scan results, drug therapy and even radiotherapy. Two of those assembled at the back indicate they will be the ones in charge of this.

I look at Carol and she seems perfectly calm. I manage to ask what name they have got on the papers they have in front of them. It is definitely mine they say, and decline to check it further. Carol squeezes my hand again.

The consultant actually takes hold of my head and scrutinizes it like a phrenologist. He pokes my neck wound, and then exclaims, 'What's that?' pressing the partially healed scar on my forehead. Carol explains and he loses interest in it and begins to blether on and on. There was just something about a head and neck tumour. They're all looking at me now, plenty of eye contact if I want it, because they want to see my reaction. Tough! I am inscrutable even to myself.

I have entered a trance. This is of no concern to me. They've either read the wrong notes and got the wrong man, or I am in a dementia induced delusion.

Then the consultant is poking something metal and hard up my nose, and down my throat. He is a doctor, but I don't think he is looking for the site of pain this time; it's some other thing he's after. Yet this procedure smarts, a lot. Every entrance and exit to my body is narrow. I swear when the last breath escapes me it will have to fight its way out. I believe I groan. He apologises. This is no dream, but my will power is fixed in a daze, it's still there, somewhere, but it can't move. I do not see the point in the procedure, let alone the pain, but I have no control of my situation.

Did he really say "tumour"? I try to turn to Carol, but he has a grip on my skull.

He apologises again for the discomfort caused, having prolonged it by ensuring his students take a look.

'Discomfort?' I try to say and fail because of the instruments. It's the sort of term the rest of us use when there's not enough leg-room, or if the fans are not working properly. Doctors share the occasion, but not the experience. And the cancer? Experts can be so wide of the mark.

Carol is squeezing my hand again as the consultant and others give me all the bad news there is. It must be policy to be frank bordering on the brutal on these occasions. My facial hair will go permanently. The radiotherapy doctor actually uses the word, 'blast' in her delivery. This is shaping up as a fantasy. It is possible I will lose my voice. Definitely a point will be reached where I will have to be fed through a 'PEG'. They do say what the letters stand for, but I miss it. This will pass some nutrient gunge directly into my gut when my throat packs up. I actually caught this bit fully, remembering a friend's account of a dementia case they fed in this way. It may, or may not need to become permanent. Carol's hand goes limp at this moment and falls away.

Oh yes, there are appointments, clinics, departments, and, depending on how I respond, there may be a need for me to be an in-patient at some unspecified point. The term, 'residential' may have crept in there somewhere. I hope Carol is following all this because hardly a single detail is any longer going in, and I cannot begin to fathom what is happening. They move on from the clinical realism to a lighter note because they are nearing the end of the presentation.

I cannot cope with this any more and emerge

215

from trance to blurt out, 'What about dementia? What is happening to my brain?'

I grab the papers the consultant is handling to check the name on them. It is definitely mine. They all look at each other. The head man whispers to some of the others and is clearly demanding the relevant reports. Carol takes the papers and returns them. A brief chat, a double take on some charts and more discussion, then the consultant turns and appoints a student to reveal the medical wisdom to me.

'Oh no, the tumour is a safe distance from there. That is not a concern. Such head and neck tumours are not related to dementia.'

Is he trying to say I haven't got Alzheimer's? I am told that while there are no guarantees, the areas will be so targeted that there should be no danger of damaging my brain.

I ask Carol, 'Cancer?'

She nods.

There are some more details, but I am not even bothering to listen and Carol has now become incapable herself. It goes on for a little while longer and culminates in them asking, 'Do you have any questions, anything you might like to ask?'

Carol and I look at each other, not so much to see if our partner has a question, but to see if the face opposite shows a sign of any longer having a clue as to what is going on. She looks shocked and I am sure I look deranged.

The head man and the radio/chemotherapy doctors make encouraging noises concerning the array of what is going to be brought to bear and how effective the treatment can be. It is all going to begin imminently. I know I should be impressed. Carol and I slowly turn back to face them, clearly stumped.

They, to be fair, see this and ask again if we have any questions. At moments such as these the average person doesn't, outside of, 'Could you go over all that again, slowly?' It isn't that that much information is too complicated, it is just that it is like asking if you've understood a conversation in the midst of a massive blast. Of course you didn't; you didn't catch it at all. All you are aware of is there has been an explosion. They should allot an appointment for a day or two later for these questions, which certainly will come.

It is time to go. We rise automatically, probably smiling and seem to be moving off. Someone comes rushing over and grabs my arm. It is a Macmillan nurse who wants to take us into her adjoining office to talk. I hear they are good, but my brain is with me, and I know it, and so is the me who can suit myself.

'We'll come back to you, but we have to go somewhere. Sorry, won't be long.'

She has probably seen this reaction before and I have to wrest my arm away from her. She is a trifle unhappy with this, obviously feeling she is failing us.

'We'll be back!' I emphasise. 'We're okay. Time off for bad behaviour.' It's not appreciated, and I don't care one jot.

I may be okay, but as we get out on the causeway, Carol is shaking, and then the tears come. Me? I am elated. I hold her, part sympathy and support, and part celebratory hug, while she vents her misery. It goes on for some time.

I say, 'It's alright; I'm alright. Come on, there is a pub twenty yards this way, and don't worry I've got it right this time.' I lead her there, but before we enter I step back and have to let it go. I punch the air and punch it again, and then do a jig shouting, 'Yes, yes, yes!' I'd appreciate a band striking up 'Glory, Glory Hallelujah' at this point. I go to a grand old mahogany bar with the jolliest bar tender beaming away from behind it and order a bottle of champagne. 'My good man,' I call him. I rush back to the now seated Carol

217

who is not looking too good.

'So I don't have Alzheimer's after all.'

'What made you think you did?'

I am not going into that and she hasn't got the emotional wherewithal to pursue it.

'You knew about all this didn't you? Why did you get upset at the end?'

'I knew it was very serious,' she says and starts sobbing. Then she is trembling, and shaking. Is there anything more distressing than to see your dearest deeply upset, when you don't have a clue what is wrong? You cannot begin therefore to console them.

The cork pops and we toast the future.

'It was obvious: the biopsy on the lump in your neck, the aches, all the scans. I thought you knew it was cancer.'

'No, that was a welcome surprise, but if you knew, what upset you so much?'

'It was that gastric PEG thing, alongside the crazy outburst.'

'The Alzheimer's one?'

'Yes!'

'You know how I feel about that! You know I need my head examining.'

She laughs and then weeps again. She cannot bear the idea of a tube in my stomach, but not because she is squeamish.

'It's more tubes in and out of you. It just seems a spitefulness too far.'

I don't see it; it's the least of my problems.

'You've got to learn how to work it at home,' she tells me.

'I'll be on my own, will I?'

'Sometimes.'

'I was hoping you still loved me.'

'You are hoping you will have a helper, and you will.'

'I'll get the hang of it,' I assure her. The machine is a benign device and it will be good for me in all senses.

'This is cancer, you know, the treatment isn't going to be very nice.' To everything of that ilk that she comes up with there is an obvious answer.

'Darling, you must see it: while I've still got me I can fight anything. Cancer isn't usually a cause for high spirits, but I would choose it over dementia any day.' I believe she is beginning to grasp my mood, if not my point. While I'm on a winning streak I am going to press home my advantage. 'So you will stick around, and you do still love me, and maybe you still want me?'

'I don't know about want you, but I do know I don't want to lose you. If, on the other hand, you are talking about sex, we'll have to see. If we both feel we want to, there is no harm.'

'I think I might need help, something like Viagra, I mean.' It is alright wanting sex, but being able to perform, well, I sometimes kid myself.

Carol looks at me, and I think there is going to be a sudden mood change and she will rebuff me.

'You take too many pills as it is. You don't need to use condoms anymore, you know.'

I had wondered and now I wonder further, 'Shall we go home and not make babies?'

XX

I had my first sessions of chemo and radiotherapy the very next day after my appointment, which is impressive. The sessions are fairly sensation-less, although I feel tired and nauseous the next day.

I still intend to occasionally dip into in my father's diary. It keeps me focused on all that's good in living sanely. I noticed recently that I have drawn cartoons on the top right hand corner of every page. As the corners are flicked in quick succession the character slowly loses its head.

Carol was late to the meeting in the hospital not just due to Mo's message failing to get through, but because she and Sylvia had rushed down to see my uncle, whose condition has deteriorated. This home, the one he had been moved to, had rung because of an enquiry from my uncle's M.P. – one I had insisted he make. The home then felt obliged to inform us about uncle's condition. In response, Sylvia and Carol had dashed to Ramsgate at six a.m. that morning. Apparently he looks terrible.

What must come first is the rescue of my uncle. Less than forty-eight hours to celebrate my diagnosis, the phone summoned me.

'It's Uncle Bob,' is what the voice said, but I knew it was Sylvia, although not quite in her usual clipped tones. 'You have to do something. You have to go and see him.'

'I'm on my way,' I said replacing the phone.

Now I am leaping down the stairs, having had no difficulty finding my keys for once. I am sure Carol would have come with me, but she is out somewhere. I do not know where; she's even firmer in refusing to publish her timetable these days.

As I get in the car, I recall the last occasion like

this and the memory accompanies me throughout the drive: 'You will never forgive yourself,' is what Sylvia said to me. I am not repeating it out of forgetfulness. Six to nine months prior to that, my father had walked around to my house. It was miles from his place and I don't know how he made it. He was deeply agitated. He insisted my mother was not his wife and implied she was in some sort of conspiracy against him. 'I don't want to go into one of those homes.' That is where he thought this strange woman would put him, and it was a plea not to let it happen. I assured him that the woman he was talking about was genuinely, truly his wife. I went through every family member, repeatedly telling him they all absolutely knew for certain that this woman was his wife of five decades plus. It was a solid cast iron fact. What was more, it was in her very nature, her core, to look after him, never to put him in a home. She wouldn't do it. He didn't argue further, but I could tell he simply did not accept it.

Hopelessly adrift, he somehow maintained an amazing focus on why he had come to find me, his favourite son. He took my hands in his. I will always remember looking at the back of his hands and seeing the darkness of the veins, and thinking there was an awful poison moving through him. Sylvia was there with me. She came and sat on his lap and put her cheek on his. He clearly recognized her, and how he loved her warmth. He looked at me with piercing clarity and begged that I make a promise. I had seen my grandfather in his later days. I had seen him forsaken by his own humanity. I had seen him cast down below the level of a beast. I knew the course the disease took and the utter dependency it brought with it. I also knew the life of misery that befell carers. Nevertheless, and with all my heart, I promised, 'Dad, trust me, you will never go into one of those places. I promise. I guarantee it as Sylvia is my witness.'

221

He was happy when we took him back to his house. I was working full time, but I knew my mother would devote all her energy to caring for him and I was more than prepared to put my shoulder to the wheel in support. The assurances to my father eased his temper and made life easier for my mother, for a while at least.

When I arrive at the new institution in which my uncle has been interred, it doesn't have the same pretensions as his previous home. This is an asylum for the impossibly ailing, with a security man in the grounds. The people at the desk look as though they feel threatened when I ask them about my uncle. They send for someone. A beaming lady comes. Short of curtseying she couldn't be more deferential. She leads me through a set of dark, heavy doors that look as though they are locked of a night time.

We traverse a lounge, which I have pictured all too often. It is almost exclusively female with the odd, stubbly old boy. In the air, the odours of the kitchens and the toilets are intermixing. No one is standing, apart from one professional helper. The inmates are in old, and in some instances, poorly cleaned and regularly soiled armchairs; they and the armchairs are sagging. None of those seated can bring one knee within a yard of the other. Many of the eyes don't look up, instead gazing downward or aimlessly anywhere, with odd pairs occasionally drawn to the strongest light source. The glasses most are wearing are pointless. There's a degree of shaking, nodding and rocking, some of which is rhythmic, some spasmodic. Worst of all is the lucidity of the occasional one who is able to grasp the hideousness of where they have been abandoned.

My guide whisks me through the lounge, pretending to have jolly exchanges with various inmates, some of whom smile but whose acknowledgements are clueless. This place is neither bright nor swish. There are dark and darker shades of brittle green gloss everywhere on the walls. We pass an old lady sitting on a toilet with the door wide open. The woman leading me explains that they can have heart attacks in the cubicles, so having no locks on the doors is a precaution.

When we reach my uncle's room, the woman firmly moves a tall wiry looking resident out of the doorway. 'He likes to dip into the biscuits in here,' she says, expecting me to be impressed that such things are provided.

My uncle does not stir. He is lying flat in the bed and his breathing rasps and rattles. He is hardly recognizable. His eyes have receded way back into what is scarcely more than a skull.

I look at the woman with me and stare at a point on her jacket where the rest of the staff is wearing badges, and she isn't.

'He won't eat,' she says and turns to my uncle, calling to him as a primary school teacher might, 'Robert, Robert. Come on, Robert, you've got a guest.'

I believe he hears, but is not interested. She bends over, puts her arm around his back and forces him upright. I am hoping she is trained to do this.

My uncle's jaw drops and I see a largely toothless mouth with a dark tongue. His eyes open at some unseeable horror and he looks as though he is in agony, even though his breathing eases.

'He shouldn't get out of bed,' she says, but declines to say why. She props him up, checks the pads around his backside and leaves us to 'chat'.

I talk to my uncle at length, giving him all the family news I can, inventing a sympathetic tale to explain why his one daughter is not here, when in fact she has turned her convalescence in to an extended holiday. I tell him everyone is thinking of him and how much he is loved. I don't believe he hears a single word

223

and I can see he wants out; out, at the very least, of the slightest hint of consciousness. I stroke his head, but still with no response. Finally I lay him down as gently as possible, and watch as he instantly closes his eyes, hearing him resume his difficult breathing.

In London I cannot contact Carol and cannot bring myself to contact Linda. I phone Sylvia, and she answers her mobile almost before it rings.

'We did it before. Alright this will be more difficult, but what have we got to lose? What has he got to lose? It has to be better,' she insists and she is right.

At four a.m. we are on our way to rescue my uncle. Sylvia is wearing a white coat. My cousin has had him sectioned and somehow managed to get his care paid for on medical grounds. Getting him out of there by conventional means will not be possible, not if we are to be in time to save him at least. There is little traffic and a few flashes of speed cameras. We get there in an hour and forty minutes.

'I'm not clear how we're going to do this,' I tell Sylvia.

'We take him to Accident and Emergency and when he's discharged we get him to Junction Road, arrange a social services package, and you and me take it in turns to visit him every day, the way we did with aunt.'

We saw it through to the end with her right there. I don't know about home births but there's a lot to be said for a home death. At the time I thought it would mend matters with Sylvia, but we did it in different spells to make sure aunt was never alone for long and hardly saw each other.

'No, I know what we did with aunt, but I mean how are we going to get him out? The doors won't be unlocked yet and what's more they are bound to resist us, and he can't walk.'

'There will be side doors. You know how

useless those places are, not all of them will be locked, and they don't like to let the oldies walk so there will be loads of wheelchairs.'

We've driven around the side where there are a number of doors. There is an alarm by one which looks armed. We try a door, but several coats of paint have formed a join between the frame and door. It hasn't been opened in years and is jammed tight. Above it, it says, "Fire Door." We go back to the car, and think frantically of a possible Plan B. Within minutes one of the night staff comes from a door we had not spotted, and it is ajar. Sylvia is already in, and although it squeaks badly there are no alarm noises. Apart from one old girl roaming like a geriatric ghost there is nobody to be seen.

We cannot find a wheelchair anywhere and will have to go through the lounge area. A dozing woman on reception stirs and spots us. We wave gaily, and then appear to be engrossed in chat with each other. I think Sylvia's white coat has done the trick. I approach the desk and say, 'We've come for Robert, but some idiot has taken the wheelchair from the ambulance.' With one hand she covers a yawn and with the other she indicates the stairwell. We are on our way with a wheelchair. As we go, except for snoring, it is virtually silent, although there might be the faint sound of dialling on a telephone.

My uncle lies dead to the world; his breathing is worse than ever. It sounds as though a rusty axe-saw is cleaving his breast plate. Sylvia pauses and I know why. The question is, how are we going to get him into the wheelchair?

'He won't weigh much more than six stone,' I tell her. I don't want to disturb him, but I have to. I place my arm around his back, where each vertebrae stands out like a small clenched fist. He expels some air, but doesn't open his eyes and I can see he is even worse

225

than when I saw him yesterday. This move could kill him, but that would be the least of his problems. His pyjamas, like prison issue, are huge on him.

Sylvia takes the wheelchair to the far end of the bed. We are going to have to get his legs over the side of the bed, turn him to face the headboard, bring the wheelchair to the rear of his knee joints, spring its sides open and ease him into it.

'We'll need a blanket,' I tell Sylvia. As I do, every light in the home comes on. It is blinding in my uncle's bedroom. Through the glare enters the woman I met yesterday, who turns out to be one of the owners of the establishment. There is a mixture of apprehension and aggression on her face. And there is something else: another white coat has entered the room.

Reception phoned the owner and she has reinforced herself with a figure from officialdom. He is a doctor; one in her service no doubt. Sylvia goes to the other side of the bed to support my uncle's back. He has now begun to moan horrendously.

'We are going to take him out for some air,' says Sylvia.

'It's a little early for that, isn't it? Besides, he will need to have breakfast first,' snarls the owner.

'You're not trying to tell us he eats it, are you?' Sylvia snaps. The woman turns to the doctor who is looking earnestly at my uncle.

'He is suffering, you know. His hip is broken.' While saying this, the doctor is stroking my uncle's hair, taking care to adjust it into some form.

'And how did that happen? That happened in your care,' Sylvia all but screams.

'I'm not here that often,' the doctor says, 'but you wouldn't want to see your uncle permanently in a restraint. Short of that, this was always possible.'

'You mean with staffing levels of the sort they've got here, don't you?' she responds angrily.

226

His look could not be clearer; there is no answer to this.

Sylvia turns to the owner. 'You must have beds with rails that can be pulled up around them. This could have been avoided.'

The doctor looks at the owner, turns back, applies the stethoscope to the rasping chest, looks grim and expertly lays my uncle down again. 'Could you fetch two more chairs, please,' he tells rather than asks the owner.

There are only seats for three: the doctor, Sylvia and me. We are down by the outside wall where there is a small window about twelve feet up, while the owner is left stranded at the other end of the room. It is only a few feet, but it might as well be a mile.

'He has pneumonia and is in pain. We tried to contact his daughter, because the only thing keeping him alive is antibiotics. We can carry on giving them to him, if you say so. We have delayed and they are overdue.'

I look at Sylvia, but she is incapable of words. Nonetheless, I can still hear her from that other time.

"We have to help him. You can't let him go. You will never forgive yourself.'

Sylvia actually came with me on that day to the meeting of my father's doctors and the administrators. She was probably too young, but she had desperately wanted to come and I had stupidly relented. My father had become threatening to my mother and I thought there was only one solution. It was the meeting where my father's future was decided and it was there that Sylvia was aghast. She didn't think I would do it; she thought she would be able to stop me. On the bleakest day of my life I agreed to the unacceptable.

Within a week I had taken my ailing, bewildered father and put him in one of those homes. The next

227

time I saw him he didn't recognize me, and was not capable of blaming me, because what was left of him had finally disintegrated. His granddaughter could blame me though. I should have known so much better. Some things you learn and others you should just know.

'We'll leave you for a while,' the doctor tells us and I am impaled on the present. He ushers the owner from the room. Half an hour later, tea and doughnuts arrive. The tea is drunk to the broken noise of my uncle's breathing.

Sylvia weeps a little and from what she says it is clear she is at a loss. I will have to take the decision.

'We cannot leave him in here like this; it would be the cruellest thing,' I tell her.

'I know. I know,' she says.

The doctor reappears and asks, 'Is there anything I can do?' He has a Gladstone bag with him and doubtless the antibiotics are in there.

'Yes,' I say and then search Sylvia's face. She returns my gaze in full. 'Yes. We...' I pause to look at Sylvia again and she simply nods. 'We don't think he should have any more antibiotics.'

There is more tea and even a burger the doctor sends in at some stage. The owner comes back in to tell us that she would be perfectly happy to carry on looking after my uncle if we decide to continue with the antibiotics. I tell her that we are sticking with our decision and as I do, Sylvia puts her arm around my shoulder.

It gets dark again and becomes light again before the lengthening space between my uncle's breaths becomes total. He has escaped this place.

Shortly after my uncle's death, Sylvia and I went on an anti-war demonstration together, joining it on the last mile to Hyde Park. There were some unusual banners, among which was one with the letters W.A.W. Underneath it read, Winchester against War. I never used to be able to read things at that distance.

I am taking care of myself with vitamins and herbs, etc. Loads are doing it, so I am in a sort of co-operative really. I checked out three health clubs, but refused to join. They kept ringing me and lowering their bids, so I went with the cheapest in the end.

I kind of feel privileged; Doc Holiday did a home visit for me the other day. There should have been a cavalcade and a fanfare for that one. There was no straightforward medical reason for him to come. He went through the formalities, and then asked, 'Do you have any outstanding matters in your life to take care of?'

Charming, but I understood. He wasn't saying my departure is imminent; he was simply letting me know that I am at greater risk than most. So I opened up to him.

'My best friend Mo ...'

'The big Turkish chap you often moan about?'

'That's him. He's the one who went and got Linda pregnant.' This didn't appear to be news to him. 'It all feels wrong to me. Dignified celibate, that was his vocation, and then the dirty so and so does that.'

'Look, Mo was vulnerable. He has not had daughters and he's younger than you, too.'

'A few years.'

'What happened is against the odds and that's something we're both keen on, isn't it?'

'I'm not so sure about that. He was my best mate and one of the world's leading virgins. She'd turned adolescence into a trajectory heading for her thirties. The next thing I know they are having sex together.'

229

'Mo and your daughter is not a bad thing. It's a triumph of life.'

'Really? Well, I just wish he'd triumphed with somebody else's daughter,' I sighed. 'You can do one thing for all of us, Doc.' He'd irritated me.

'Just one thing? Name it.'

'Give up the fags! Your clothes make the surgery smell.'

He rolled up his sleeve and there was what I took to be a nicotine patch. The yellow on his fingers had become no more than a hint of vanilla.

'I'm on my way!' he'd said.

'How come?'

'I was on a short holiday in Fez, took a drag on something local in a hookah, thought of the tobacco companies and decided, stuff 'em!'

Carol continues to come and go without notifying me these days. We still sleep in the same bed when she is here, and we are never less than civil to each other.

The chemo' suite is good, relatively luxurious, and the workers there seem to regard you more as a member than a patient. It's my fifth session; it's all quite relaxed. I've got a big cold sore. It isn't stress: I get them when I am run down. I am due another round of radiotherapy tomorrow.

I had a narrow escape with a moped the other day - it nearly ran me over. I had been taking the contract on me less and less seriously, believing I had been conned. Sooner or later I would address it and the money owed to me. The brush with the moped made me realize that I really had to get hold of Jeremy. I rang him at the Funeral Director's immediately afterwards, but he refused to come to the phone – twice. I heard

230

him in the background calling me a "loser". I rang under a guise and got hold of him.

'Look, you're finished, mate,' he said as soon as he knew it was me. 'We're done. You're on your own. I can't have anything more to do with this, it's too dangerous.'

'Hold on just a second. There could still be something in this for you. I am prepared to pay for you to arrange a cancellation. I don't need the hired gun.'

'We can't talk about this now.'

'What time do you finish there?' He told me and I insisted, 'Get your mate and we won't meet in that café-football-club-gambling-den hole. We'll meet in the Salisbury.'

I'm in the Salisbury Pub, sipping a beer. Jeremy comes in. With him is not the Albanian guy, but a monster of a Somali. He has a huge shinning ebony forehead and several gold teeth, which can be seen through the beaming grin he directs at me. It's a grin of homicidal menace. This guy would torture you wearing the same grin. He is the tank moving forwards; two troopers are tucked in behind him: one short and muscular and the other tall, slim and pure malevolence. They refuse to drink or to shake hands. They're probably Muslim and abhor alcohol and public houses, and maybe they despise the people who use them.

The smile disappears and the tank asks, 'What do you want?'

I guess that he feels he could be earning serious money bumping someone off somewhere else, rather than wasting time in this pub.

'To be left to myself,' I say.

He turns to Jeremy who looks scared and trips over his words as he tries to explain I want a cancellation.

'We could kill you now,' the tall streak of

malevolence stands and tells me. He would happily do it this instant. The tank rises and puts a hand firmly on his shoulder and compresses him back into his seat in a way that suggests he'll let him spring forward when needed.

'There is a price; it will cost,' he says.

Jeremy chips in, 'You're okay for money, so it shouldn't be a problem. There are plenty of banks around here and yours is bound to be one of them.' He is obviously on to a percentage.

I don't say anything, because I am flummoxed: a drink for Jeremy maybe, but another fee!

'Fifty per cent to cancel, and the money must come now!' The words jet from between golden teeth.

'They've spent too much time on this already,' adds Jeremy. 'It's not good business.'

The words, 'Fuck you,' almost breach my voice box.

'A thousand pounds in cash at a moment's notice is not easy. It's twice as much as I can get from a cash machine. I have to have a passport and an explanation for that. Let me make a call.'

The shorter stocky Somali looks at his watch and sighs; the tank nods and says, 'But fucking quick.'

'They'll have to wait,' I tell Jeremy who really does not want to hear this.

Some other black guys come in, one of whom is of bouncer proportions. They take one look in our direction and go to the point furthest away from us. I get out my phone, fumble it, and the flash goes off. It lights up most of the sombre cavernous old pub.

The streak of malevolence is furious and his hand moves momentarily for his breast pocket where there is a bulge big enough to hold a hatchet.

'I'm sorry. Just a second, I'm not very good with new technology. This Blueberry is new,' I say holding up the Blackberry I've bought (I may have mentioned it before.)

'Blackberry!' snaps the tank.

I use the phone key pad, press more buttons and tell the Somalis, 'There is no answer. I'll ring someone else. I've got to do this if I'm going to get cash that quickly. Give me a minute, please. I'm all fingers and thumbs. Bear with me.' I turn in different directions and the flash goes off several times more. They won't be constrained much longer. Nevertheless I do the same thing a few more times.

Jeremy is looking at the exit, and their patience is shredded; they are ready for the kill.

'That's it, it's done,' I tell them. There is a big golden toothed smile from the opposite side of the table, and it is genuine.

Several minutes later we are all still sitting here. I am sipping my beer and saying nothing, and they are becoming concerned. The squat muscular one, after some golden-toothed words in his ear, stands behind me. As he moves, the light of a lamp reveals something: his skin is paler than his two comrades and on it at regular intervals are much darker spots, almost like a leopard's. No wonder the poor sod has turned bad.

The tank holds out his hand for the money he is demanding, even though he must realise I haven't got it. I take his hand firmly, shake it vigorously and say, 'Thank you very much and that will be all now. You may go. Oh, but just before you do, could you take a snap of me on this?'

The tank takes the Blackberry I hand to him, pauses and chucks it straight back at me. They all, Jeremy included, look as though they think they've lost something in translation.

'I'm finished here,' I tell them. 'Your services are no longer required, because I've had a better offer.'

Jeremy is terrified.

233

'Do you know what's going to happen, right now? You'll get me killed too. Have you gone mad?'

'No, although I was working on it for sometime.' I turn to the chief assassin. 'Don't you know what I've done? No, obviously not then. I've just taken your photographs and sent them to half a dozen different places and I've emailed them to the police. The station is only up the road.' This last is a lie but the rest is fairly accurate. They, however, are not looking deterred. 'I don't think Jeremy has told you, has he?'

I am about to do something pretty evil, but I feel the bloke deserves it. There is complete consternation. Of course, Jeremy can't tell them what he doesn't know.

'Cancelling was meant to be a favour to you. I don't need you because I have terminal cancer. Can you see the scarlet on my neck and the side of my head? That's radiotherapy. See the scar here, that's where they did the biopsy.' They are beginning to look dismayed. 'Cancer can be a heck of a lot more painful, so if you still want to do the job go ahead and be my guest. It'll get it done one way or the other. The one thing that is for certain is that there is no more money.'

Some of it is going over their heads, so I put two fingers to my temple with a cocked thumb, say, 'Bang, bang,' grin and add, 'Waste a bullet if you want.'

'If you're so brave, why the meeting here, eh?' asks the evil streak in perfect English.

'I've got a few things that need a little time to sort out, but they're not worth paying for. The important thing is my family will get an insurance payout either way. I am tired, I am not bothered and I am going. Do what you want.'

They believe me, have turned their attention to Jeremy and are staring imminent murder at him. I get up, grin and inappropriately say, 'Cheers one and all,' swallow what is left of my pint and leave.

Their attention is still on Jeremy. The best he

can hope for is to keep his ear out for the sound of a moped for the rest of his days, and be prepared to run.

My throat is becoming difficult. It hasn't prevented me talking to Linda, though. I was at home and Carol was wherever it is she goes, when Linda arrived. She wanted to know if hostilities were over and I said they were - between me and her. Then she made me cringe by referring to Mo. Apparently he'd got something for me, something very important. Unless it was news of his departure it would have to be very special to interest me.

'Do you know what it is?' I asked her.

She didn't and he wanted to meet me alone. It was something I truly wanted she said, and it was urgent.

He asked to come round to my house, but I wasn't having that, so we're meeting in a coffee bar. He arrives and irks me by bringing his minging mate, John. He wants to shake hands, but I decline. They put down a package in front of me and I ask how much they want for it.

'There's no way I'll take money for it,' Mo protests. There is a big gelatinous tear perched on his lower eyelid. Torrents of them might soften the biscotti but it does nothing for me.

John got the package from a friend of a friend whose hobby is spotting and collecting all varieties of mushrooms. What they have brought is a crop of Death Cap. We're done, and I stand up. They stand up too and John puts one hand on my shoulder and the other on Mo's. I don't resist. We go, but within seconds, Mo is tapping me on the back. The gelatinous tear has now formed a wide sticky film on his cheek. He passes me the package, which I had left by the empty cups. I don't let my eyes meet his. The only time our eyes may meet will be the day he passes me a different package, one to baby-sit.

From now, and for whenever I might need it, they have provided me with a licence to fly, albeit with the divine wind.

People are just a surprise, aren't they? You think you've got them taped and then they do it, reveal a part of themselves that you couldn't have guessed existed. Even though it makes me shudder, I know that life can never have felt greater for Mo, to whom the idea of suicide must seem like insanity. And look at that John: a man festooned with his own problems, a mickey-taker, and yet he's gone out of his way for me.

I've had quite a few sessions of radiotherapy now, but they cut the chemo because I wasn't coping well with it. The consultant has been having a joke with me. He knew he was winning me round, and tried to get me to agree to having tissue taken from the lumps in my hand. I refused. He'll try again, and I'll refuse. They are going to put the PEG in earlier than I thought, because they want it in situ before my throat packs in. It's important that I don't lose too much weight. They do not know about my secret weapon, Adnam's ale. I reckon its mellow calories will still flow down my ravaged gullet. The hospital is fitting me in for the day after tomorrow for an outpatients op' to insert the PEG. It's pretty relentless. Thankfully Carol is around a bit more because she wants to see me through the next stages. I suspect she still loves me, just not in the old way and possibly not exclusively.

The inflammation on my head and neck is so deep and dark it is verging on the black. I am on a variety of opiates, which sometimes make me a bit foggy. They've had to put me on much stronger laxatives. I am currently sitting down with both my daughters and we are actually talking about the future, and my condition. On the table is a leaflet about green burials which, naturally, upsets them.

'It was there with the holiday mags!' I croak.

I should admit, however, that when I finally go at some point in the future, I wouldn't mind a burial with a tree to remember me by. That would sort of be planting me in the future.

Sylvia passes me a tissue because the gastric PEG is leaking through my shirt a little. They both look grief stricken.

'Cut it out the pair of you,' I manage. 'It's alright, I am not losing the greatest brain the world has ever known me to have. I've got my long lost self back.'

They are not convinced, but it does the trick. Linda feeds me some news from Mo. He and John don't feel comfortable about feigning Alzheimer's. They are going with back injury, which John has anyway. Good for them; it's a bad idea trying to mimic those whose social position is so high it places them above the law.

I have had the last of the treatment and have to come back in a month for a check up, but the opiates will continue for some time. My throat is murder if I am late with them. Carol is with me for the moment and she has taken me to a restaurant, which is truly big of her because I am a mess.

We are alone at the table. We've eaten, (I had soup) but we're staying because there is going to be some live jazz. She smiles. She is coping well with the menopause, what is left of it. I have been hopeless with it, so I guess on this and any other issue, it's a matter of trying harder. I can't hope to have the benefit of loving her and being loved in return, if I don't show a little tenderness, even if it is belated.

As I sit opposite Carol, I try to make intelligible conversation, but end up gazing soporifically at her.

237

There she intensely is, a fully formed, alluring woman. She has become very different, and I too am different. I am not pleased with what I have done, but it would not have been good to continue as we were.

I am more gone than ever. The level of opiates I am on would give dementia a good run for its money. Why on earth Carol is sticking it out with me I don't know.

Sam rang my mobile. Her hearing and my frazzled, constantly cutting out voice would have been a scream. She had been able to give Oliver a forwarding address for his father. It hadn't been that long since the guy had stayed at her place. I take my hat off to her for that, but I won't be seeing any more of her. I had thought that people with their feet that far off the ground didn't leave shadows behind them, but I was wrong.

Six months ago the hospital gave me the all clear. I am due my next review tomorrow. Carol went away on a Francophone jaunt to the island of Reunion and has come back from her travels to be with me. We didn't tell Sylvia about the appointment and its importance, so she is the one who has gone now on her own travels. I could think of good reasons for her not to go, but I didn't bother her with them. I am shifting one way, while she is shifting the other, so it is not possible that we see everything in the same shade. We drove her to Heathrow where sub-machine guns and car-bomb-proof concrete barriers did not enhance a fond farewell.

The world seems a threatening place when I think of her travelling and where she will go. I understand why it is dangerous; I know we've treated a lot of the planet badly, but I am terrified it could be my daughter who pays the price. I can't help it; it just seems our children have become a threatened species.

The day is here and I hope there will be many more of these six monthly visits. My saliva glands have finally packed in. The good news is my facial hair has gone, so I will never have to shave again. I struggled for a while to get the hang of the 'kangaroo' pump which feeds the nutrients into my gut, but Carol helped me master it. This morning I shot some diamorphine straight through the port into my stomach, knowing what is to come at the hospital.

Carol comes in with me. She has been sleeping poorly, worrying there will be bad news. It doesn't seem any less alien than before, in spite of the familiar faces. The MacMillan nurse is there. I went back to see her and assure her that if there is a role for her I won't resist it. That may have been a lie, but it made her happy. I guessed right, those shiny implements are there on that little table. The diamorphine was a good precaution.

It is all very friendly. They are evidently pleased with themselves and with me. Up and round go the steel implements with two students observing. They ask me something and I give an answer which I know is barking silly, because Carol has to interrupt with a response to whatever it is they were asking. I have, in the meantime, noticed that one of the students is wearing a very short skirt and has a fine pair of legs. I hope I am not leering. Amazing, long after the testosterone flood has receded there is still this aching awe at beauty. And I know what this means; although I've had the equivalent of a red hot poker down my throat repeatedly, I am not ready to let them zip up the body bag for a while yet.

It is done. A haze of general smiles and I am pronounced in the clear once more. There are no promises and I've got to keep coming back for metal up my nose. I think I might refuse that bit.

Carol is completely with it and asks about the PEG. There is a discussion, they check charts. Next they stun me by asking what I think. I straighten, pause and then lean way to the left in the hope the opiates swilling around my brain will drain to one side. I try to make sure my tongue is not dangling out of my mouth, squirt in some of the artificial saliva I have been prescribed, and struggle to be sane. I am hallucinating a bit, with two images alternating in my head. The first is of a train thundering towards me with its driver leaning out of the cab singing, 'Can't you hear the steel rails humming.' I go with the second image: 'The red star on Che's beret burns bright.' I want away with the PEG and to make a trip to Cuba.

Not a flutter of one eyelash hair occurs. They must have seen this kind of performance often enough before. I've had sufficient debates with the consultant and he knows my wishes. He knows I want my digestive system back to as normal as it can get, and where I want to go. 'Ah, you want to be unchained. We'll see what we can do for you.'

'It's not being used that much. We've dropped the feed right down and he can swallow most things cut up small and soaked in gravy. I am sure we can manage it.' Bless you Carol.

The medics discuss matters further and, ignoring me, reply to Carol that there is a slot in a couple of days when they can remove it.

I ask, 'Why so long?' but do not get an answer.

Carol is away again. She is back in France where she has a lot of friends, one of whom I think is rather special to her. She's entitled, I suppose. I can't pretend, however, that it doesn't agitate me, but…but, well just but. There is, of course, a chance she won't come back.

I won a raffle with The Alzheimer's Research Trust. Among other things it paid for Carol to go back for that cooking course. I feel able to go for my check-up on my own. I am off the opiates and have recovered most of my spirits. Linda is popping round a lot while Carol is away. The usual crowd is there for my examination and I allow those instruments access to some narrow passages. The doctors don't seem worried, but some papers have been mislaid so they will have to write to me shortly.

I am out coffeeing. The days are too much of a routine for me right now and I am missing Carol. Linda rings my mobile. There is an important looking letter at home for me. She doesn't say so, but she believes it is from the hospital and I know she fears the worst. 'I think you should come straight away,' she tells me.

When I get in, Linda kisses me, hands me a cup of tea and leads me to a chair. She is disguising her anxiety perfectly and wears just enough of a smile to make it seem unremarkable. She has opened the letter, which was something she, Sylvia and Carol were doing all the time at the height of my morphine intake.

Once I'm seated she flourishes a photograph. I take it. It is of a young man with his aging mum and dad. As always, they look familiar, which usually means nothing, but this lad is definitely, strikingly so. He is in the middle and they have their arms around his shoulders. Initially I struggle and then I recognize him. I take the letter to read, but first look at the postmark on the envelope. It is from Eastbourne.

NOT THE END

BY AIRMAIL

Just to let you know.......................................

You will want to hear that everything fell into place between Carol and me; we adapted and moved on. It happens in real life after all. You'd like to hear we fell in love all over again and that we embraced under the icon of Che in Revolution Square. You hope to hear that Mo and I are reconciled. You'd also like to read that my cancer is a distant thing of the past, forever vanquished and my memory is sound.

For the most part I can't help you I am afraid, because it didn't happen. For a start off, this message is by airmail because my memory failed when it came to a new email password. (I'd spent some time just getting the opportunity to email, as well).

What I can tell you is that when Carol and I returned from the first hospital appointment to make love it was different. At its best in the past we did it in the manner of visiting old friends who have moved some miles away. You don't feel enthusiastic about setting off, but you are glad when you finally get there. This time it was different; it wasn't like routine sex at all. Do we love each other? Of course. Will we grow older together? I am prepared to and Carol is prepared to see me through my illness, which will never quite go away, so who knows. But we won't be constantly in each other's company. She comes and goes as she sees fit. Where she stays the rest of the time she still doesn't say. I believe she is doing a degree course among other things. I am trying to show an interest, but she won't let me anywhere near what she calls "her business". I am lucky any part of our affection survived. If anything worthwhile emerges from the wreck of our relationship it will be because of Carol. I had abandoned it, so to her go the rights of salvage and she will call the tune.

As for Mo, I did in fact go to his wedding to my

242

daughter, Linda (who now raises funds for M.S.F in this country). I didn't forget to mention it, I just couldn't bring myself to do so any earlier. It was a brief civic service, thank goodness. Giving Linda away to him would not have been possible for me. Thus he is my son-in-law. Any friendship isn't going to happen, not for some time.

And valuing Linda more? I'm sorry I thought I'd made it perfectly clear I am doing that.

You will not only want to hear that Sylvia is back from her travels, but has settled down with a nice man. Probably that's just me. Anyway, she has extended her travels. Perhaps most importantly, I can tell you that when Sylvia and I went on the peace demonstration she held my hand throughout. So at least I can report some success where my daughters are concerned.

Did I make it to Havana and partake of the embargoed rum and Cohibas? I can't touch spirits, let alone tobacco. However, I am in Cuba, although without Carol. This airmail is from Varadero. I could complain that the bastards charged more for the insurance than the holiday, but the important thing is that the Cuban capital is but a short guided tour away.

And my health? You are concerned about my heart? No? You are right, it's not worth discussion. Regarding the tumour, I am still in the clear, although I have a persistent slough in my throat, which I don't think will ever disappear. Cancers are sneaky things though. They can quickly and quietly metastasize. The dementia? I regard that as bordering on the guaranteed, it gets so many of the old. Check the figures. Meanwhile, I gladly recognise I've got a decent quality of life.

What is more, if things take a turn for the worse, I have securely kept the package of Amanita Phalloides. I will know when the time has come.

STILL NOT THE END

243

Paul Lefley

Educated in Australia, Tottenham and at Sussex University.

National Schools Boxing Champion 1966

Taught at an inner city comprehensive school for the best part of twenty years. At the same time he held a series of labour and trade union movement posts ranging from the purely local on up to the national level. His only previous publications were in this field.

Having been on the executive committee of the Communist Party of Britain in the 1980s he has been a property developer for the last decade and a half. He still holds an officer post in his local trade union branch.

Lightning Source UK Ltd.
Milton Keynes UK
12 November 2010

162736UK00001B/2/P